Express
Daily MAIL
Ke

EX LIB

LUNCH
COLD
SOUP.
OR
SANDWICH
(BOTH)

VINTAGE CLASSICS

Radio
Times

CW00336670

# LIARS IN LOVE

Richard Yates was born in 1926 in Yonkers, New York. After serving in the US Army during the Second World War, he worked as a publicity writer for the Remington Rand Corporation, and for a brief period in the sixties as a speech-writer for Senator Robert Kennedy. His prize-winning stories first appeared in 1953 and his first novel, *Revolutionary Road*, was nominated for the National Book Award in 1962. He is the author of eight other works, including the novels *A Good School*, *The Easter Parade* and *Disturbing the Peace*, and two collections of short stories, *Eleven Kinds of Loneliness* and *Liars in Love*. Richard Yates was twice divorced and the father of three daughters. He died in 1992.

RICHARD YATES

# Liars in Love

**VINTAGE BOOKS**
London

Published by Vintage 2007

2 4 6 8 10 9 7 5 3 1

Copyright © Richard Yates 1978, 1980, 1981

Richard Yates has asserted his right under the Copyright, Designs
and Patents Act 1988 to be identified as the author of this work

'Oh, Joseph, I'm So Tired' and 'Regards at Home' first appeared in
the *Atlantic Monthly*; 'A Compassionate Leave' in *Ploughshares*.

First published in the United States by Delacorte Press/Seymour
Lawrence in 1981

First published in Great Britain in 2008 by Vintage

Vintage
Random House, 20 Vauxhall Bridge Road,
London SW1V 2SA

www.vintage-classics.info

Addresses for companies within The Random House Group Limited
can be found at: www.randomhouse.co.uk/offices.htm

The Random House Group Limited Reg. No. 954009

A CIP catalogue record for this book
is available from the British Library

ISBN 9780099518594

The Random House Group Limited supports The Forest Stewardship
Council (FSC), the leading international forest certification
organisation. All our titles that are printed on Greenpeace approved
FSC certified paper carry the FSC logo. Our paper procurement
policy can be found at: www.rbooks.co.uk/environment

**Mixed Sources**
Product group from well-managed
forests and other controlled sources
www.fsc.org  Cert no. TT-COC-2139
© 1996 Forest Stewardship Council
FSC

Printed in the UK by CPI Bookmarque, Croydon, CR0 4TD

# CONTENTS _____

# LIARS
# IN LOVE

# OH, JOSEPH,⎯
# I'M SO TIRED

WHEN Franklin D. Roosevelt was President-elect there must have been sculptors all over America who wanted a chance to model his head from life, but my mother had connections. One of her closest friends and neighbors, in the Greenwich Village courtyard where we lived, was an amiable man named Howard Whitman who had recently lost his job as a reporter on the *New York Post*. And one of Howard's former colleagues from the *Post* was now employed in the press office of Roosevelt's New York headquarters. That would make it easy for her to get in—or, as she said, to get an entrée—and she was confident she could take it from there. She was confident about everything she did in those days, but it never quite disguised a terrible need for support and approval on every side.

She wasn't a very good sculptor. She had been working at it for only three years, since breaking up her marriage to my father, and there was still something stiff and amateurish about her pieces. Before the Roosevelt project her specialty had been "garden figures"—a life-size little boy whose legs turned into the legs of a goat at the knees and another who knelt among ferns to play the pipes of Pan; little girls who trailed chains of daisies from their upraised arms or walked beside a spread-winged goose. These fanciful children, in plaster painted green to simulate weathered bronze, were arranged on homemade wooden pedestals to loom around her studio and to leave a cleared space in the middle for the modeling stand that held whatever she was working on in clay.

Her idea was that any number of rich people, all of them gracious and aristocratic, would soon discover her: they would want her sculpture to decorate their landscaped gardens, and they would want to make her their friend for life. In the meantime, a little nationwide publicity as the first woman sculptor to "do" the President-elect certainly wouldn't hurt her career.

And, if nothing else, she had a good studio. It was, in fact, the best of all the studios she would have in the rest of her life. There were six or eight old houses facing our side of the courtyard, with their backs to Bedford Street, and ours was probably the showplace of the row because the front room on its ground floor was two stories high. You went down a broad set of brick steps to the tall front windows and the front door; then you were in the high, wide, light-flooded studio. It was big enough to serve as a living room too, and so along with the green garden children it contained all the living-room furniture from the house we'd lived in with my father in the suburban town of Hastings-on-Hudson, where I was born. A second-floor balcony ran along the far end of the studio, with two small bedrooms and a tiny bathroom tucked away upstairs; beneath that, where the ground floor continued through to the Bedford Street side, lay the only part of the apartment that might let you know we didn't have much money. The ceiling was very low and it was always dark in there; the small windows looked out underneath an iron sidewalk grating, and the bottom of that street cavity was thick with strewn garbage. Our roach-infested kitchen was barely big enough for a stove and sink that were never clean, and for a brown wooden icebox with its dark, ever-melting block of ice; the rest of that area was our dining room, and not even the amplitude of the old Hastings dining-room table could brighten it. But our Majestic radio was in there too, and that made it a cozy place for my sister Edith and me: we liked the children's programs that came on in the late afternoons.

We had just turned off the radio one day when we went out into the studio and found our mother discussing the Roosevelt project with Howard Whitman. It was the first we'd heard of it, and we must have interrupted her with too many questions because she said "Edith? Billy? That's enough, now. I'll tell you all about this later. Run out in the garden and play."

She always called the courtyard "the garden," though nothing grew there except a few stunted city trees and a patch of grass that never had a chance to spread. Mostly it was bald earth, interrupted here and there by brick paving, lightly powdered with soot and scattered with the droppings of dogs and cats. It may have been six or eight houses long, but it was only two houses wide, which gave it a hemmed-in, cheerless look; its only point of interest was a dilapidated marble fountain, not much bigger than a birdbath, which stood near our house. The original idea of the fountain was that water would drip evenly from around the rim of its upper tier and tinkle into its lower basin, but age had unsettled it; the water spilled in a single ropy stream from the only inch of the upper tier's rim that stayed clean. The lower basin was deep enough to soak your feet in on a hot day, but there wasn't much pleasure in that because the underwater part of the marble was coated with brown scum.

My sister and I found things to do in the courtyard every day, for all of the two years we lived there, but that was only because Edith was an imaginative child. She was eleven at the time of the Roosevelt project, and I was seven.

"Daddy?" she asked in our father's office uptown one

afternoon. "Have you heard Mommy's doing a head of President Roosevelt?"

"Oh?" He was rummaging in his desk, looking for something he'd said we might like.

"She's going to take his measurements and stuff here in New York," Edith said, "and then after the Inauguration, when the sculpture's done, she's going to take it to Washington and present it to him in the White House." Edith often told one of our parents about the other's more virtuous activities; it was part of her long, hopeless effort to bring them back together. Many years later she told me she thought she had never recovered, and never would, from the shock of their breakup: she said Hastings-on-Hudson remained the happiest time of her life, and that made me envious because I could scarcely remember it at all.

"Well," my father said. "That's really something, isn't it." Then he found what he'd been looking for in the desk and said, "Here we go; what do you think of these?" They were two fragile perforated sheets of what looked like postage stamps, each stamp bearing the insignia of an electric light bulb in vivid white against a yellow background, and the words "More light."

My father's office was one of many small cubicles on the twenty-third floor of the General Electric building. He was an assistant regional sales manager in what was then called the Mazda Lamp Division—a modest job, but good enough to have allowed him to rent into a town like Hastings-on-Hudson in better times—and these "More light" stamps were souvenirs of a recent sales convention. We told him the stamps were neat—and they were —but expressed some doubt as to what we might do with them.

"Oh, they're just for decoration," he said. "I thought

you could paste them into your schoolbooks, or—you know—whatever you want. Ready to go?" And he carefully folded the sheets of stamps and put them in his inside pocket for safekeeping on the way home.

Between the subway exit and the courtyard, somewhere in the West Village, we always walked past a vacant lot where men stood huddled around weak fires built of broken fruit crates and trash, some of them warming tin cans of food held by coat-hanger wire over the flames. "Don't stare," my father had said the first time. "All those men are out of work, and they're hungry."

"Daddy?" Edith inquired. "Do you think Roosevelt's good?"

"Sure I do."

"Do you think all the Democrats are good?"

"Well, most of 'em, sure."

Much later I would learn that my father had participated in local Democratic Party politics for years. He had served some of his political friends—men my mother described as dreadful little Irish people from Tammany Hall—by helping them to establish Mazda Lamp distributorships in various parts of the city. And he loved their social gatherings, at which he was always asked to sing.

"Well, of course, you're too young to remember Daddy's singing," Edith said to me once after his death in 1942.

"No, I'm not; I remember."

"But I mean really remember," she said. "He had the most beautiful tenor voice I've ever heard. Remember 'Danny Boy'?"

"Sure."

"Ah, God, that was something," she said, closing her eyes. "That was really—that was really something."

7

When we got back to the courtyard that afternoon, and back into the studio, Edith and I watched our parents say hello to each other. We always watched that closely, hoping they might drift into conversation and sit down together and find things to laugh about, but they never did. And it was even less likely than usual that day because my mother had a guest—a woman named Sloane Cabot who was her best friend in the courtyard, and who greeted my father with a little rush of false, flirtatious enthusiasm.

"How've you been, Sloane?" he said. Then he turned back to his former wife and said "Helen? I hear you're planning to make a bust of Roosevelt."

"Well, not a bust," she said. "A head. I think it'll be more effective if I cut it off at the neck."

"Well, good. That's fine. Good luck with it. Okay, then." He gave his whole attention to Edith and me. "Okay. See you soon. How about a hug?"

And those hugs of his, the climax of his visitation rights, were unforgettable. One at a time we would be swept up and pressed hard into the smells of linen and whiskey and tobacco; the warm rasp of his jaw would graze one cheek and there would be a quick moist kiss near the ear; then he'd let us go.

He was almost all the way out of the courtyard, almost out in the street, when Edith and I went racing after him.

"Daddy! Daddy! You forgot the stamps!"

He stopped and turned around, and that was when we saw he was crying. He tried to hide it—he put his face nearly into his armpit as if that might help him search his inside pocket—but there is no way to disguise the awful bloat and pucker of a face in tears.

"Here," he said. "Here you go." And he gave us the least convincing smile I had ever seen. It would be good to report that we stayed and talked to him—that we hugged him again—but we were too embarrassed for that. We took the stamps and ran home without looking back.

"Oh, aren't you excited, Helen?" Sloane Cabot was saying. "To be meeting him, and talking to him and everything, in front of all those reporters?"

"Well, of course," my mother said, "but the important thing is to get the measurements right. I hope there won't be a lot of photographers and silly interruptions."

Sloane Cabot was some years younger than my mother, and strikingly pretty in a style often portrayed in what I think are called Art Deco illustrations of that period: straight dark bangs, big eyes, and a big mouth. She too was a divorced mother, though her former husband had vanished long ago and was referred to only as "that bastard" or "that cowardly son of a bitch." Her only child was a boy of Edith's age named John, whom Edith and I liked enormously.

The two women had met within days of our moving into the courtyard, and their friendship was sealed when my mother solved the problem of John's schooling. She knew a Hastings-on-Hudson family who would appreciate the money earned from taking in a boarder, so John went up there to live and go to school, and came home only on weekends. The arrangement cost more than Sloane could comfortably afford, but she managed to make ends meet and was forever grateful.

Sloane worked in the Wall Street district as a private secretary. She talked a lot about how she hated her job and her boss, but the good part was that her boss was often out of town for extended periods: that gave her time to use the office typewriter in pursuit of her life's ambition, which was to write scripts for the radio.

She once confided to my mother that she'd made up

both of her names: "Sloane" because it sounded masculine, the kind of name a woman alone might need for making her way in the world, and "Cabot" because—well, because it had a touch of class. Was there anything wrong with that?

"Oh, Helen," she said. "This is going to be wonderful for you. If you get the publicity—if the papers pick it up, and the newsreels—you'll be one of the most interesting personalities in America."

Five or six people were gathered in the studio on the day my mother came home from her first visit with the President-elect.

"Will somebody get me a drink?" she asked, looking around in mock helplessness. "Then I'll tell you all about it."

And with the drink in her hand, with her eyes as wide as a child's, she told us how a door had opened and two big men had brought him in.

"Big men," she insisted. "Young, strong men, holding him up under the arms, and you could see how they were straining. Then you saw this *foot* come out, with these awful metal braces on the shoe, and then the *other* foot. And he was sweating, and he was panting for breath, and his face was—I don't know—all bright and tense and horrible." She shuddered.

"Well," Howard Whitman said, looking uneasy, "he can't help being crippled, Helen."

"Howard," she said impatiently, "I'm only trying to tell you how *ugly* it was." And that seemed to carry a certain weight. If she was an authority on beauty—on how a little boy might kneel among ferns to play the pipes of Pan, for example—then surely she had earned her credentials as an authority on ugliness.

"*Any*way," she went on, "they got him into a chair, and

he wiped most of the sweat off his face with a handker-chief—he was still out of breath—and after a while he started talking to some of the other men there; I couldn't follow that part of it. Then finally he turned to me with this smile of his. Honestly, I don't know if I can describe that smile. It isn't something you can see in the news-reels; you have to be there. His eyes don't change at all, but the corners of his mouth go up as if they're being pulled by puppet strings. It's a frightening smile. It makes you think: This could be a dangerous man. This could be an evil man. Well anyway, we started talking, and I spoke right up to him. I said 'I didn't vote for you, Mr. President.' I said 'I'm a good Republican and I voted for President Hoover.' He said 'Why are you here, then?' or something like that, and I said 'Because you have a very interesting head.' So he gave me the smile again and he said 'What's interesting about it?' And I said 'I like the bumps on it.' "

By then she must have assumed that every reporter in the room was writing in his notebook, while the photog-raphers got their flashbulbs ready; tomorrow's papers might easily read:

GAL SCULPTOR TWITS FDR
ABOUT "BUMPS" ON HEAD

At the end of her preliminary chat with him she got down to business, which was to measure different parts of his head with her calipers. I knew how that felt: the cold, trembling points of those clay-encrusted calipers had tickled and poked me all over during the times I'd served as model for her fey little woodland boys.

But not a single flashbulb went off while she took and recorded the measurements, and nobody asked her any

questions; after a few nervous words of thanks and goodbye she was out in the corridor again among all the
hopeless, craning people who couldn't get in. It must
have been a bad disappointment, and I imagine she tried
to make up for it by planning the triumphant way she'd
tell us about it when she got home.

"Helen?" Howard Whitman inquired, after most of
the other visitors had gone. "Why'd you tell him you
didn't vote for him?"

"Well, because it's true. I *am* a good Republican; you
know that."

She was a storekeeper's daughter from a small town in
Ohio; she had probably grown up hearing the phrase
"good Republican" as an index of respectability and
clean clothes. And maybe she had come to relax her
standards of respectability, maybe she didn't even care
much about clean clothes anymore, but "good Republican" was worth clinging to. It would be helpful when she
met the customers for her garden figures, the people
whose low, courteous voices would welcome her into
their lives and who would almost certainly turn out to be
Republicans too.

"I believe in the aristocracy!" she often cried, trying to
make herself heard above the rumble of voices when her
guests were discussing communism, and they seldom
paid her any attention. They liked her well enough: she
gave parties with plenty of liquor, and she was an agreeable hostess if only because of her touching eagerness to
please; but in any talk of politics she was like a shrill,
exasperating child. She believed in the aristocracy.

She believed in God, too, or at least in the ceremony
of St. Luke's Episcopal Church, which she attended once
or twice a year. And she believed in Eric Nicholson, the
handsome middle-aged Englishman who was her lover.

He had something to do with the American end of a British chain of foundries: his company cast ornamental objects into bronze and lead. The cupolas of college and high-school buildings all over the East, the lead-casement windows for Tudor-style homes in places like Scarsdale and Bronxville—these were some of the things Eric Nicholson's firm had accomplished. He was always self-deprecating about his business, but ruddy and glowing with its success.

My mother had met him the year before, when she'd sought help in having one of her garden figures cast into bronze, to be "placed on consignment" with some garden-sculpture gallery from which it would never be sold. Eric Nicholson had persuaded her that lead would be almost as nice as bronze and much cheaper; then he'd asked her out to dinner, and that evening changed our lives.

Mr. Nicholson rarely spoke to my sister or me, and I think we were both frightened of him, but he overwhelmed us with gifts. At first they were mostly books—a volume of cartoons from *Punch,* a partial set of Dickens, a book called *England in Tudor Times* containing tissue-covered color plates that Edith liked. But in the summer of 1933, when our father arranged for us to spend two weeks with our mother at a small lake in New Jersey, Mr. Nicholson's gifts became a cornucopia of sporting goods. He gave Edith a steel fishing rod with a reel so intricate that none of us could have figured it out even if we'd known how to fish, a wicker creel for carrying the fish she would never catch, and a sheathed hunting knife to be worn at her waist. He gave me a short axe whose head was encased in a leather holster and strapped to my belt—I guess this was for cutting firewood to cook the fish—and a cumbersome net with a handle that hung from an elastic shoulder strap, in case I should be called upon to wade in and help Edith land a tricky one. There was nothing to do in that New Jersey village except take walks, or what my mother called good hikes; and every day, as we plodded out through the insect-humming weeds in the sun, we wore our full regalia of useless equipment.

That same summer Mr. Nicholson gave me a three-year subscription to *Field and Stream,* and I think that impenetrable magazine was the least appropriate of all his gifts because it kept coming in the mail for such a long, long time after everything else had changed for us: after we'd moved out of New York to Scarsdale, where Mr. Nicholson had found a house with a low rent, and after he had abandoned my mother in that house—with no warning—to return to England and to the wife from whom he'd never really been divorced.

But all that came later; I want to go back to the time between Franklin D. Roosevelt's election and his Inauguration, when his head was slowly taking shape on my mother's modeling stand.

Her original plan had been to make it life-size, or larger than life-size, but Mr. Nicholson urged her to scale it down for economy in the casting, and so she made it only six or seven inches high. He persuaded her too, for the second time since he'd known her, that lead would be almost as nice as bronze.

She had always said she didn't mind at all if Edith and I watched her work, but we had never much wanted to; now it was a little more interesting because we could watch her sift through many photographs of Roosevelt cut from newspapers until she found one that would help her execute a subtle plane of cheek or brow.

But most of our day was taken up with school. John

Cabot might go to school in Hastings-on-Hudson, for which Edith would always yearn, but we had what even Edith admitted was the next best thing: we went to school in our bedroom.

During the previous year my mother had enrolled us in the public school down the street, but she'd begun to regret it when we came home with lice in our hair. Then one day Edith came home accused of having stolen a boy's coat, and that was too much. She withdrew us both, in defiance of the city truant officer, and pleaded with my father to help her meet the cost of a private school. He refused. The rent she paid and the bills she ran up were already taxing him far beyond the terms of the divorce agreement; he was in debt; surely she must realize he was lucky even to have a job. Would she ever learn to be reasonable?

It was Howard Whitman who broke the deadlock. He knew of an inexpensive, fully accredited mail-order service called The Calvert School, intended mainly for the homes of children who were invalids. The Calvert School furnished weekly supplies of books and materials and study plans; all she would need was someone in the house to administer the program and to serve as a tutor. And someone like Bart Kampen would be ideal for the job.

"The skinny fellow?" she asked. "The Jewish boy from Holland or wherever it is?"

"He's very well educated, Helen," Howard told her. "And he speaks fluent English, and he'd be very conscientious. And he could certainly use the money."

We were delighted to learn that Bart Kampen would be our tutor. With the exception of Howard himself, Bart was probably our favorite among the adults around the courtyard. He was twenty-eight or so, young enough so that his ears could still turn red when he was teased by children; we had found that out in teasing him once or twice about such matters as that his socks didn't match. He was tall and very thin and seemed always to look startled except when he was comforted enough to smile. He was a violinist, a Dutch Jew who had emigrated the year before in the hope of joining a symphony orchestra, and eventually of launching a concert career. But the symphonies weren't hiring then, nor were lesser orchestras, so Bart had gone without work for a long time. He lived alone in a room on Seventh Avenue, not far from the courtyard, and people who liked him used to worry that he might not have enough to eat. He owned two suits, both cut in a way that must have been stylish in the Netherlands at the time: stiff, heavily padded shoulders and a nipped-in waist; they would probably have looked better on someone with a little more meat on his bones. In shirtsleeves, with the cuffs rolled back, his hairy wrists and forearms looked even more fragile than you might have expected, but his long hands were shapely and strong enough to suggest authority on the violin.

"I'll leave it entirely up to you, Bart," my mother said when he asked if she had any instructions for our tutoring. "I know you'll do wonders with them."

A small table was moved into our bedroom, under the window, and three chairs placed around it. Bart sat in the middle so that he could divide his time equally between Edith and me. Big, clean, heavy brown envelopes arrived in the mail from The Calvert School once a week, and when Bart slid their fascinating contents onto the table it was like settling down to begin a game.

Edith was in the fifth grade that year—her part of the table was given over to incomprehensible talk about English and History and Social Studies—and I was in the first. I spent my mornings asking Bart to help me puzzle out the very opening moves of an education.

"Take your time, Billy," he would say. "Don't get impatient with this. Once you have it you'll see how easy it is, and then you'll be ready for the next thing."

At eleven each morning we would take a break. We'd go downstairs and out to the part of the courtyard that had a little grass. Bart would carefully lay his folded coat on the sidelines, turn back his shirt cuffs, and present himself as ready to give what he called airplane rides. Taking us one at a time, he would grasp one wrist and one ankle; then he'd whirl us off our feet and around and around, with himself as the pivot, until the courtyard and the buildings and the city and the world were lost in the dizzying blur of our flight.

After the airplane rides we would hurry down the steps into the studio, where we'd usually find that my mother had set out a tray bearing three tall glasses of cold Ovaltine, sometimes with cookies on the side and sometimes not. I once overheard her telling Sloane Cabot she thought the Ovaltine must be Bart's first nourishment of the day—and I think she was probably right, if only because of the way his hand would tremble in reaching for his glass. Sometimes she'd forget to prepare the tray and we'd crowd into the kitchen and fix it ourselves; I can never see a jar of Ovaltine on a grocery shelf without remembering those times. Then it was back upstairs to school again. And during that year, by coaxing and prodding and telling me not to get impatient, Bart Kampen taught me to read.

It was an excellent opportunity for showing off. I would pull books down from my mother's shelves—mostly books that were the gifts of Mr. Nicholson—and try to impress her by reading mangled sentences aloud.

"That's wonderful, dear," she would say. "You've really learned to read, haven't you."

Soon a white and yellow "More light" stamp was affixed to every page of my Calvert First Grade Reader, proving I had mastered it, and others were accumulating at a slower rate in my arithmetic workbook. Still other stamps were fastened to the wall beside my place at the school table, arranged in a proud little white and yellow thumb-smudged column that rose as high as I could reach.

"You shouldn't have put your stamps on the wall," Edith said.

"Why?"

"Well, because they'll be hard to take off."

"Who's going to take them off?"

That small room of ours, with its double function of sleep and learning, stands more clearly in my memory than any other part of our home. Someone should probably have told my mother that a girl and boy of our ages ought to have separate rooms, but that never occurred to me until much later. Our cots were set foot-to-foot against the wall, leaving just enough space to pass alongside them to the school table, and we had some good conversations as we lay waiting for sleep at night. The one I remember best was the time Edith told me about the sound of the city.

"I don't mean just the loud noises," she said, "like the siren going by just now, or those car doors slamming, or all the laughing and shouting down the street; that's just close-up stuff. I'm talking about something else. Because you see there are millions and millions of people in New York—more people than you can possibly imagine, ever —and most of them are doing something that makes a sound. Maybe talking, or playing the radio, maybe closing doors, maybe putting their forks down on their plates if they're having dinner, or dropping their shoes if they're going to bed—and because there are so many of them, all those little sounds add up and come together in a kind of hum. But it's so faint—so very, very faint—that you can't hear it unless you listen very carefully for a long time."

"Can you hear it?" I asked her.

"Sometimes. I listen every night, but I can only hear it sometimes. Other times I fall asleep. Let's be quiet now, and just listen. See if you can hear it, Billy."

And I tried hard, closing my eyes as if that would help, opening my mouth to minimize the sound of my breathing, but in the end I had to tell her I'd failed. "How about you?" I asked.

"Oh, I heard it," she said. "Just for a few seconds, but I heard it. You'll hear it too, if you keep trying. And it's worth waiting for. When you hear it, you're hearing the whole city of New York."

The high point of our week was Friday afternoon, when John Cabot came home from Hastings. He exuded health and normality; he brought fresh suburban air into our bohemian lives. He even transformed his mother's small apartment, while he was there, into an enviable place of rest between vigorous encounters with the world. He subscribed to both *Boys' Life* and *Open Road for Boys,* and these seemed to me to be wonderful things to have in your house, if only for the illustrations. John dressed in the same heroic way as the boys shown in those magazines, corduroy knickers with ribbed stockings pulled taut over his muscular calves. He talked a lot about the Hastings high-school football team, for which he planned to try out as soon as he was old enough, and about Hastings friends whose names and personalities grew almost as familiar to us as if they were friends of our own. He taught us invigorating new ways to speak, like saying "What's the diff?" instead of "What's the difference?" And he was better even than Edith at finding new things to do in the courtyard.

You could buy goldfish for ten or fifteen cents apiece in Woolworth's then, and one day we brought home three of them to keep in the fountain. We sprinkled the water with more Woolworth's granulated fish food than they could possibly need, and we named them after ourselves: "John," "Edith," and "Billy." For a week or two Edith and I would run to the fountain every morning, before Bart came for school, to make sure they were still alive and to see if they had enough food, and to watch them.

"Have you noticed how much bigger Billy's getting?" Edith asked me. "He's huge. He's almost as big as John and Edith now. He'll probably be bigger than both of them."

Then one weekend when John was home he called our attention to how quickly the fish could turn and move. "They have better reflexes than humans," he explained. "When they see a shadow in the water, or anything that looks like danger, they get away faster than you can blink. Watch." And he sank one hand into the water to make a grab for the fish named Edith, but she evaded him and fled. "See that?" he asked. "How's that for speed? Know something? I bet you could shoot an arrow in there, and they'd get away in time. Wait." To prove his point he ran to his mother's apartment and came back with the handsome bow and arrow he had made at summer camp (going to camp every summer was another admirable thing about John); then he knelt at the rim of the fountain like the picture of an archer, his bow steady in one strong hand and the feathered end of his arrow tight against the bowstring in the other. He was taking aim at the fish named Billy. "Now, the velocity of this arrow," he said in a voice weakened by his effort, "is probably more than a car going eighty miles an hour. It's probably more like an airplane, or maybe even more than that. Okay; watch."

The fish named Billy was suddenly floating dead on the surface, on his side, impaled a quarter of the way up the arrow with parts of his pink guts dribbled along the shaft.

I was too old to cry, but something had to be done about the shock and rage and grief that filled me as I ran from the fountain, heading blindly for home, and half-way there I came upon my mother. She stood looking very clean, wearing a new coat and dress I'd never seen before and fastened to the arm of Mr. Nicholson. They were either just going out or just coming in—I didn't care which—and Mr. Nicholson frowned at me (he had told me more than once that boys of my age went to boarding school in England), but I didn't care about that either. I bent my head into her waist and didn't stop crying until long after I'd felt her hands stroking my back, until after she had assured me that goldfish didn't cost much and I'd have another one soon, and that John was sorry for the thoughtless thing he'd done. I had discovered, or rediscovered, that crying is a pleasure—that it can be a pleasure beyond all reckoning if your head is pressed in your mother's waist and her hands are on your back, and if she happens to be wearing clean clothes.

There were other pleasures. We had a good Christmas Eve in our house that year, or at least it was good at first. My father was there, which obliged Mr. Nicholson to stay away, and it was nice to see how relaxed he was among my mother's friends. He was shy, but they seemed to like him. He got along especially well with Bart Kampen.

Howard Whitman's daughter Molly, a sweet-natured girl of about my age, had come in from Tarrytown to spend the holidays with him, and there were several other children whom we knew but rarely saw. John looked very mature that night in a dark coat and tie, plainly aware of his social responsibilities as the oldest boy.

After a while, with no plan, the party drifted back into the dining-room area and staged an impromptu vaude-ville. Howard started it: he brought the tall stool from my mother's modeling stand and sat his daughter on it, fac-ing the audience. He folded back the opening of a brown paper bag two or three times and fitted it onto her head; then he took off his suit coat and draped it around her backwards, up to the chin; he went behind her, crouched out of sight, and worked his hands through the coat-sleeves so that when they emerged they appeared to be hers. And the sight of a smiling little girl in a paper-bag hat, waving and gesturing with huge, expressive hands, was enough to make everyone laugh. The big hands wiped her eyes and stroked her chin and pushed her hair behind her ears; then they elaborately thumbed her nose at us.

Next came Sloane Cabot. She sat very straight on the stool with her heels hooked over the rungs in such a way as to show her good legs to their best advantage, but her first act didn't go over.

"Well," she began, "I was at work today—you know my office is on the fortieth floor—when I happened to glance up from my typewriter and saw this big old man sort of crouched on the ledge outside the window, with a white beard and a funny red suit. So I ran to the window and opened it and said 'Are you all right?' Well, it was Santa Claus, and he said 'Of course I'm all right; I'm used to high places. But listen, miss: can you direct me to number seventy-five Bedford Street?' "

There was more, but our embarrassed looks must have told her we knew we were being condescended to; as soon as she'd found a way to finish it she did so quickly. Then, after a thoughtful pause, she tried something else that turned out to be much better.

"Have you children ever heard the story of the first Christmas?" she asked. "When Jesus was born?" And she began to tell it in the kind of hushed, dramatic voice she must have hoped might be used by the narrators of her more serious radio plays.

". . . And there were still many miles to go before they reached Bethlehem," she said, "and it was a cold night. Now, Mary knew she would very soon have a baby. She even knew, because an angel had told her, that her baby might one day be the saviour of all mankind. But she was only a young girl"—here Sloane's eyes glistened, as if they might be filling with tears—"and the traveling had exhausted her. She was bruised by the jolting gait of the donkey and she ached all over, and she thought they'd never, ever get there, and all she could say was 'Oh, Joseph, I'm so tired.' "

The story went on through the rejection at the inn, and the birth in the stable, and the manger, and the animals, and the arrival of the three kings; when it was over we clapped a long time because Sloane had told it so well.

"Daddy?" Edith asked. "Will you sing for us?"

"Oh, well, thanks, honey," he said, "but no; I really need a piano for that. Thanks anyway."

The final performer of the evening was Bart Kampen,

persuaded by popular demand to go home and get his violin. There was no surprise in discovering that he played like a professional, like something you might easily hear on the radio; the enjoyment came from watching how his thin face frowned over the chin rest, empty of all emotion except concern that the sound be right. We were proud of him.

Some time after my father left a good many other adults began to arrive, most of them strangers to me, looking as though they'd already been to several other parties that night. It was very late, or rather very early Christmas morning, when I looked into the kitchen and saw Sloane standing close to a bald man I didn't know. He held a trembling drink in one hand and slowly massaged her shoulder with the other; she seemed to be shrinking back against the old wooden icebox. Sloane had a way of smiling that allowed little wisps of cigarette smoke to escape from between her almost-closed lips while she looked you up and down, and she was doing that. Then the man put his drink on top of the icebox and took her in his arms, and I couldn't see her face anymore.

Another man, in a rumpled brown suit, lay unconscious on the dining-room floor. I walked around him and went into the studio, where a good-looking young woman stood weeping wretchedly and three men kept getting in each other's way as they tried to comfort her. Then I saw that one of the men was Bart, and I watched while he outlasted the other two and turned the girl away toward the door. He put his arm around her and she nestled her head in his shoulder; that was how they left the house.

Edith looked jaded in her wrinkled party dress. She was reclining in our old Hastings-on-Hudson easy chair with her head tipped back and her legs flung out over both the chair's arms, and John sat cross-legged on the floor near one of her dangling feet. They seemed to have been talking about something that didn't interest either of them much, and the talk petered out altogether when I sat on the floor to join them.

"Billy," she said, "do you realize what time it is?"

"What's the diff?" I said.

"You should've been in bed hours ago. Come on. Let's go up."

"I don't feel like it."

"Well," she said, "I'm going up, anyway," and she got laboriously out of the chair and walked away into the crowd.

John turned to me and narrowed his eyes unpleasantly. "Know something?" he said. "When she was in the chair that way I could see everything."

"Huh?"

"I could see everything. I could see the crack, and the hair. She's beginning to get hair."

I had observed these features of my sister many times —in the bathtub, or when she was changing her clothes —and hadn't found them especially remarkable; even so, I understood at once how remarkable they must have been for him. If only he had smiled in a bashful way we might have laughed together like a couple of regular fellows out of *Open Road for Boys*, but his face was still set in that disdainful look.

"I kept looking and looking," he said, "and I had to keep her talking so she wouldn't catch on, but I was doing fine until you had to come over and ruin it."

Was I supposed to apologize? That didn't seem right, but nothing else seemed right either. All I did was look at the floor.

When I finally got to bed there was scarcely time for

trying to hear the elusive sound of the city—I had found that a good way to keep from thinking of anything else —when my mother came blundering in. She'd had too much to drink and wanted to lie down, but instead of going to her own room she got into bed with me. "Oh," she said. "Oh, my boy. Oh, my boy." It was a narrow cot and there was no way to make room for her; then suddenly she retched, bolted to her feet, and ran for the bathroom, where I heard her vomiting. And when I moved over into the part of the bed she had occupied my face recoiled quickly, but not quite in time, from the slick mouthful of puke she had left on her side of the pillow.

For a month or so that winter we didn't see much of Sloane because she said she was "working on something big. Something really big." When it was finished she brought it to the studio, looking tired but prettier than ever, and shyly asked if she could read it aloud.

"Wonderful," my mother said. "What's it about?"

"That's the best part. It's about us. All of us. Listen."

Bart had gone for the day and Edith was out in the courtyard by herself—she often played by herself—so there was nobody for an audience but my mother and me. We sat on the sofa and Sloane arranged herself on the tall stool, just as she'd done for telling the Bethlehem story.

"There is an enchanted courtyard in Greenwich Village," she read. "It's only a narrow patch of brick and green among the irregular shapes of very old houses, but what makes it enchanted is that the people who live in it, or near it, have come to form an enchanted circle of friends.

"None of them have enough money and some are quite poor, but they believe in the future; they believe in each other, and in themselves.

"There is Howard, once a top reporter on a metropolitan daily newspaper. Everyone knows Howard will soon scale the journalistic heights again, and in the meantime he serves as the wise and humorous sage of the courtyard.

"There is Bart, a young violinist clearly destined for virtuosity on the concert stage, who just for the present must graciously accept all lunch and dinner invitations in order to survive.

"And there is Helen, a sculptor whose charming works will someday grace the finest gardens in America, and whose studio is the favorite gathering place for members of the circle."

There was more like that, introducing other characters, and toward the end she got around to the children. She described my sister as "a lanky, dreamy tomboy," which was odd—I had never thought of Edith that way —and she called me "a sad-eyed, seven-year-old philosopher," which was wholly baffling. When the introduction was over she paused a few seconds for dramatic effect and then went into the opening episode of the series, or what I suppose would be called the "pilot."

I couldn't follow the story very well—it seemed to be mostly an excuse for bringing each character up to the microphone for a few lines apiece—and before long I was listening only to see if there would be any lines for the character based on me. And there were, in a way. She announced my name—"Billy"—but then instead of speaking she put her mouth through a terrible series of contortions, accompanied by funny little bursts of sound, and by the time the words came out I didn't care what they were. It was true that I stuttered badly—I wouldn't get over it for five or six more years—but I hadn't expected anyone to put it on the radio.

"Oh, Sloane, that's marvelous," my mother said when the reading was over. "That's really exciting."

And Sloane was carefully stacking her typed pages in the way she'd probably been taught to do in secretarial school, blushing and smiling with pride. "Well," she said, "it probably needs work, but I do think it's got a lot of potential."

"It's perfect," my mother said. "Just the way it is."

Sloane mailed the script to a radio producer and he mailed it back with a letter typed by some radio secretary, explaining that her material had too limited an appeal to be commercial. The radio public was not yet ready, he said, for a story of Greenwich Village life.

Then it was March. The new President promised that the only thing we had to fear was fear itself, and soon after that his head came packed in wood and excelsior from Mr. Nicholson's foundry.

It was a fairly good likeness. She had caught the famous lift of the chin—it might not have looked like him at all if she hadn't—and everyone told her it was fine. What nobody said was that her original plan had been right, and Mr. Nicholson shouldn't have interfered: it was too small. It didn't look heroic. If you could have hollowed it out and put a slot in the top, it might have made a serviceable bank for loose change.

The foundry had burnished the lead until it shone almost silver in the highlights, and they'd mounted it on a sturdy little base of heavy black plastic. They had sent back three copies: one for the White House presentation, one to keep for exhibition purposes, and an extra one. But the extra one soon toppled to the floor and was badly damaged—the nose mashed almost into the chin—and my mother might have burst into tears if Howard

Whitman hadn't made everyone laugh by saying it was now a good portrait of Vice President Garner.

Charlie Hines, Howard's old friend from the *Post* who was now a minor member of the White House staff, made an appointment for my mother with the President late on a weekday morning. She arranged for Sloane to spend the night with Edith and me; then she took an evening train down to Washington, carrying the sculpture in a cardboard box, and stayed at one of the less expensive Washington hotels. In the morning she met Charlie Hines in some crowded White House anteroom, where I guess they disposed of the cardboard box, and he took her to the waiting room outside the Oval Office. He sat with her as she held the naked head in her lap, and when their turn came he escorted her in to the President's desk for the presentation. It didn't take long. There were no reporters and no photographers.

Afterwards Charlie Hines took her out to lunch, prob- ably because he'd promised Howard Whitman to do so. I imagine it wasn't a first-class restaurant, more likely some bustling, no-nonsense place favored by the work- ing press, and I imagine they had trouble making conver- sation until they settled on Howard, and on what a shame it was that he was still out of work.

"No, but do you know Howard's friend Bart Kampen?" Charlie asked. "The young Dutchman? The violinist?"

"Yes, certainly," she said. "I know Bart."

"Well, Jesus, there's *one* story with a happy ending, right? Have you heard about that? Last time I saw Bart he said 'Charlie, the Depression's over for me,' and he told me he'd found some rich, dumb, crazy woman who's paying him to tutor her kids."

I can picture how she looked riding the long, slow train back to New York that afternoon. She must have sat staring straight ahead or out the dirty window, seeing nothing, her eyes round and her face held in a soft shape of hurt. Her adventure with Franklin D. Roosevelt had come to nothing. There would be no photographs or interviews or feature articles, no thrilling moments of newsreel coverage; strangers would never know of how she'd come from a small Ohio town, or of how she'd nurtured her talent through the brave, difficult, one-woman journey that had brought her to the attention of the world. It wasn't fair.

All she had to look forward to now was her romance with Eric Nicholson, and I think she may have known even then that it was faltering—his final desertion came the next fall.

She was forty-one, an age when even romantics must admit that youth is gone, and she had nothing to show for the years but a studio crowded with green plaster statues that nobody would buy. She believed in the aristocracy, but there was no reason to suppose the aristocracy would ever believe in her.

And every time she thought of what Charlie Hines had said about Bart Kampen—oh, how hateful; oh, how hateful—the humiliation came back in wave on wave, in merciless rhythm to the clatter of the train.

She made a brave show of her homecoming, though nobody was there to greet her but Sloane and Edith and me. Sloane had fed us, and she said "There's a plate for you in the oven, Helen," but my mother said she'd rather just have a drink instead. She was then at the onset of a long battle with alcohol that she would ultimately lose; it must have seemed bracing that night to decide on a drink instead of dinner. Then she told us "all about" her trip to Washington, managing to make it sound like a success. She talked of how thrilling it was to be actually inside the White House; she repeated whatever small, courteous thing it was that President Roosevelt had said to her on receiving the head. And she had brought back souvenirs: a handful of note-size White House stationery for Edith, and a well-used briar pipe for me. She explained that she'd seen a very distinguished-looking man smoking the pipe in the waiting room outside the Oval Office; when his name was called he had knocked it out quickly into an ashtray and left it there as he hurried inside. She had waited until she was sure no one was looking; then she'd taken the pipe from the ashtray and put it in her purse. "Because I knew he must have been somebody important," she said. "He could easily have been a member of the Cabinet, or something like that. Anyway, I thought you'd have a lot of fun with it." But I didn't. It was too heavy to hold in my teeth and it tasted terrible when I sucked on it; besides, I kept wondering what the man must have thought when he came out of the President's office and found it gone.

Sloane went home after a while, and my mother sat drinking alone at the dining-room table. I think she hoped Howard Whitman or some of her other friends might drop in, but nobody did. It was almost our bedtime when she looked up and said "Edith? Run out in the garden and see if you can find Bart."

He had recently bought a pair of bright tan shoes with crepe soles. I saw those shoes trip rapidly down the dark brick steps beyond the windows—he seemed scarcely to touch each step in his buoyancy—and then I saw him come smiling into the studio, with Edith closing the door behind him. "Helen!" he said. "You're back!"

She acknowledged that she was back. Then she got up

from the table and slowly advanced on him, and Edith and I began to realize we were in for something bad.

"Bart," she said, "I had lunch with Charlie Hines in Washington today."

"Oh?"

"And we had a very interesting talk. He seems to know you very well."

"Oh, not really; we've met a few times at Howard's, but we're not really—"

"And he said you'd told him the Depression was over for you because you'd found some rich, dumb, crazy woman who was paying you to tutor her kids. Don't interrupt me."

But Bart clearly had no intention of interrupting her. He was backing away from her in his soundless shoes, retreating past one stiff green garden child after another. His face looked startled and pink.

"I'm not a rich woman, Bart," she said, bearing down on him. "And I'm not dumb. And I'm not crazy. And I can recognize ingratitude and disloyalty and sheer, rotten viciousness and *lies* when they're thrown in my face."

My sister and I were halfway up the stairs, jostling each other in our need to hide before the worst part came. The worst part of these things always came at the end, after she'd lost all control and gone on shouting anyway.

"I want you to get out of my house, Bart," she said. "And I don't ever want to see you again. And I want to tell you something. All my life I've hated people who say 'Some of my best friends are Jews.' Because *none* of my friends are Jews, or ever will be. Do you understand me? *None* of my friends are Jews, or ever will be."

The studio was quiet after that. Without speaking, avoiding each other's eyes, Edith and I got into our pajamas and into bed. But it wasn't more than a few minutes before the house began to ring with our mother's raging voice all over again, as if Bart had somehow been brought back and made to take his punishment twice.

". . . And I said *'None* of my friends are Jews, or ever will be . . .' "

She was on the telephone, giving Sloane Cabot the highlights of the scene, and it was clear that Sloane would take her side and comfort her. Sloane might know how the Virgin Mary felt on the way to Bethlehem, but she also knew how to play my stutter for laughs. In a case like this she would quickly see where her allegiance lay, and it wouldn't cost her much to drop Bart Kampen from her enchanted circle.

When the telephone call came to an end at last there was silence downstairs until we heard her working with the ice pick in the icebox: she was making herself another drink.

There would be no more school in our room. We would probably never see Bart again—or if we ever did, he would probably not want to see us. But our mother was ours; we were hers; and we lived with that knowledge as we lay listening for the faint, faint sound of millions.

# A
# NATURAL
# GIRL

In the spring of her sophomore year, when she was twenty, Susan Andrews told her father very calmly that she didn't love him anymore. She regretted it, or at least the tone of it, almost at once, but it was too late: he sat looking stunned for a few seconds and then began to cry, all hunched over to hide his face from her, trying with one unsteady hand to get a handkerchief out of his dark suit. He was one of the five or six most respected hematologists in the United States, and nothing like this had happened to him for a great many years.

They were alone in Susan's dormitory room at a small, celebrated liberal arts college called Turnbull, in Wisconsin. She had worn a demure yellow dress that day because it seemed appropriate for his visit, but now she felt constricted by the primness of it and the way it obliged her to keep her narrow, pretty knees pressed together. She would much rather have been wearing faded jeans and a man's shirt with the top two buttons unfastened, as she did on most other days. Her brown eyes were big and sorrowful and her long hair was almost black. She had recently been told many times, in ardor and with justice, that she was a lovely girl.

She knew that if she'd made her declaration in anger or in tears there might now be some way to take it back, but she wasn't really sorry to have that option closed. She had come to learn the value and the price of honesty in all things: if you dealt cleanly with the world there was never any taking of anything back. Still, this was the first time she had ever seen her father cry, and it brought a heaviness of blood to her own throat.

"All right," Dr. Andrews said in a broken voice, still

hanging his head. "All right, you don't love me. But tell me this much, dear. Tell me why."

"There *is* no why," Susan said, grateful that her voice came out in a normal way. "There's no more why to not loving than there is to loving. I think most intelligent people understand that."

And he got slowly to his feet, looking ten years older than he'd looked a few minutes before. He had to get home to St. Louis, and the drive would be an agony of distance. "Well," he said, "I'm sorry I cried. Guess I'm turning into some kind of maudlin old man or something. Anyway, I'd better be getting started. I'm sorry. I'm sorry about everything."

"I wish you wouldn't apologize; I'm sorry too. Wait, I'll walk you out to the car."

And all the way back to the sun-dazzled parking lot, past very old, neat college buildings and clusters of boisterously laughing kids—had anybody ever dreamed there would be this many *kids* in the world?—Edward Andrews tried to plan his parting words. He didn't want to say he was sorry again, but couldn't think of anything else. At last he said "I know your mother'd like to hear from you, Susan, and so would your sisters. Why don't you call home tonight, if you're not too busy."

"Okay, sure," she said. "I'm glad you reminded me. Well. Drive carefully." Then she was gone, and he was on the road.

Edward Andrews had seven daughters, and he liked being known as a family man. It often pleased him to consider that all his girls were nice-looking and most of them smart: the oldest was long married to a deep-thinking professor of philosophy who might have been intimidating if he hadn't continued over the years to be a shy and vulnerable boy; the second was rarely seen because her husband was an admirably steady lawyer in Baltimore who didn't like to travel, and the third was in evidence perhaps a little too much—a sweetly dopey girl, knocked-up in high school and quickly married to a nice, bumbling kid for whom jobs had frequently to be found. And there were the three little girls still living at home, all of them solemn about hair styling and menstrual cycles, and all an exasperating joy to have around the house.

But there was only one Susan. She was the middle child, born soon after he'd come back from the war, and he would always associate her birth with the first high hopes of world peace. Framed photographs on the walls at home showed her reverently kneeling as a six-year-old Christmas angel, with gauze-and-wire wings, or seated with far more decorum than anyone else at a birthday-party table. And he couldn't even flip through the family snapshot albums without having his heart stopped, every time, by those big, sorrowful eyes. I know who I am, she seemed to be saying in each picture; do you know who you are?

"I don't like *Alice in Wonderland*," she had told him once when she was eight.

"You don't? Why?"

"Because it's like a fever dream."

And he had never again been able to read a page of either of those books, or to look at the famous Tenniel illustrations, without seeing what she meant and agreeing with her.

Making Susan laugh had never been easy unless you had something really funny to say, but it was always well worth the effort if you did. He could remember staying late in the office, when she was ten or twelve—or, hell, right on up through her high-school years, for that matter—in order to sort out all the funny things that came into his head and to save only one, the best, for trying out on Susan when he got home.

Oh, she had been a marvelous child. And although it had seemed to surprise her, it was no surprise at all to him when she was accepted into one of the finest colleges in the country. *They* knew an exceptional person when they found one.

But how could anyone have guessed she would fall in love with her history teacher, a divorced man of twice her age, and that she would then insist on going with the man to his new job at a state university, even though it meant forfeiting the Turnbull tuition that had been paid in full?

"Dear, look," he had said in the dormitory this afternoon, trying to reason with her, "I want you to understand this: It isn't the money. That's not important, apart from its being a little on the irresponsible side. The point is simply that your mother and I feel you're not old enough to make a decision like this."

"Why bring Mother into it?" she said. "Why do you always need Mother to support whatever it is you want?"

"I don't," he said. "I'm not doing that. But we're both deeply concerned—or I'll put it this way, if you like: *I'm* deeply concerned."

"Why?"

"Because I love you. Do you love me?"

And so he had walked right into it, like a comedian walking into a thrown custard pie.

He knew she might not really have meant it, even if she'd thought she did. Girls of that age were so busy being overwhelmed by romance and sex that they didn't even know what they were saying half the time. Still, there it was—the last thing he had ever expected to hear from his favorite child.

And he was ready to crumple up and cry all over again as he held the car down to the speed limit on the Interstate, but he fought back the tears because he had to keep his eyes clear, and because his wife and the younger girls were waiting at home, and because everything else that made sense in his life would be waiting there too; and besides, no civilized man would go to pieces twice in the same day.

As soon as she was alone, Susan hurried to David Clark's apartment and into his arms, where she cried for a long time—surprising herself, because she hadn't meant to cry at all.

"Oh, baby," he said, stroking her shuddering back. "Oh, now, baby, it can't have been all that bad. Come and have a drink and we'll talk it over."

David Clark was neither strong nor handsome, but the bewildered look that had blighted his boyhood was long submerged now in a face that suggested intelligence and humor. For years he had made it a point of honor not to mess around with the girls in the classes he taught. "There isn't any sport in it," he would explain to other teachers. "It's taking unfair advantage. It's shooting fish in a barrel." It was shyness, too, and a terrible fear of rejection, though he didn't usually mention those aspects of the matter.

But the whole of that argument had vanished some months ago when he found he could get through a lecture only by letting his gaze go back time and again, like that of a man seeking nourishment, to Miss Andrews in the front row.

"Oh, Jesus Christ Almighty," he told her during their first night together. "Oh, baby, you're like nothing else

I've ever known. You're like—you're like—oh, Jesus God, you're extraordinary."

And she told him, in whispers, that he had opened a whole new world for her. She told him he had brought her to life.

Within a very few days she moved in with him, leaving only enough of her belongings in the dormitory room to make it "presentable," and so began the happiest time in David Clark's memory. There was never an awkward or a disappointing moment. He couldn't stop marveling at how young she was, because she was never silly and often wise. He loved to watch her walk around his place, naked or dressed, because the look on her sweet, grave face made clear that she felt at home.

"Oh, don't go away . . ." That was the cry, or the plea, that had broken from David Clark's mouth as if wholly beyond his control with almost all the women he'd known since his divorce. Several girls had seemed to find it endearing, others had been baffled by it, and one sharp-tongued woman had called it "an unmanly thing to say."

But after the first few nights with Susan he rarely fell back on that line. This magnificently young, long-legged girl, whose flesh held the very pulse and rhythm of love, was here to stay.

"Hey, Susan?" he said once. "Know what?"

"What?"

"You make me feel calm. That may not sound like a very big deal, but the point is I've wanted to be calm all my life, and nobody else has ever made me feel that way."

"Well, that's certainly a nice compliment, David," she said, "but I think I can top it."

"How?"

"You make me feel I know who I am."

On the afternoon of her father's visit, when she tried to explain how she'd felt on seeing her father cry, David did his best to soothe and comfort her. But before long she withdrew from him to grieve in solitude, in another room, and the silence went on a little too long for his liking.

"Look," he told her. "Why don't you write him a letter. Take three or four days over it, if you want, to make it nice. Then you'll be able to put the whole thing behind you. That's what people do, haven't you noticed? People learn to put things behind them."

They were married a year and a half later, in a Presbyterian church near the vast university campus where David was then employed. They had a spacious old apartment that visitors frequently found "interesting," and for a while they felt little need of anything to do except take pleasure in each other.

But soon David began to worry long and hard about the outrage of the war in Vietnam. He lectured angrily about it in the classroom; he helped to circulate petitions and to organize campus rallies; and he got quietly drunk over it a few times, alone, stumbling to bed at two or three in the morning and muttering incomprehensibly until he passed out in the warmth of Susan's sleep.

"You know something?" he asked her one evening in the kitchen, when he was helping her wash the dishes. "I think Eugene McCarthy is going to emerge as the greatest political hero of the second half of this century. He makes the Kennedy brothers look sick."

And later that night he began to complain that he'd never liked academic life in the first place. "Teachers simply aren't plugged *in* to the world," he told her as he

43

walked dramatically around the living room with a drink in his hand. She was curled up on the sofa with her sewing basket, mending a torn seam in a pair of his pants.

"Christ's sake," he said, "we read about the world and we talk about it, but we're never a part of it. We're locked safe away somewhere else, off on the sidelines or up in the clouds. We don't *act*. We don't even know *how* to act."

"It's always seemed to me that you do," Susan said. "You apply professional skills to sharing your knowledge with others, and so you help to broaden and enrich people's minds. Isn't that acting?"

"Ah, I don't know," he said, and he was almost ready to pull back from the whole discussion. Disparaging his work might only undermine the very foundation of her respect for him. And this was an even more chilling thought: There might have been a hint, when she'd said "Isn't that acting?" that she meant "acting" in the theatrical sense, as if all those lectures back at Turnbull, when he'd paced the head of the classroom to the music of his own voice, pausing again and again to turn and look at her—as if all that had been nothing more than what an actor is expected to do.

He sat quietly for a while, until it occurred to him that this too might be considered an act: a man with a drink in the lamplight, brooding. Then he was on his feet and in motion again.

"Okay," he said, "but look. I'm forty-three. In ten more years I'll be wearing carpet slippers. I'll be watching *The Merv Griffin Show* and getting peevish from wishing you'd hurry up with the popcorn—do you see what I'm trying to say? And the point is, this whole McCarthy thing is enormously attractive to me. I'd really like to be mixed up in something like that—if not with McCarthy himself, then at least with *some*body who's on our side, *some*body who knows the world's going to fall apart unless we can wake people up and make them—help them to see their—oh, shit, baby, I want to get into politics."

Many carefully worded letters went out over the next few weeks, and many nervous phone calls. Old acquaintances were revived, some of them leading to new acquaintances; there were interviews and lunches, in various cities, with men who could either help him or not and who often kept their secret until the moment of the parting handshake.

In the end, when it was too late to do any useful work for the McCarthy campaign anyway, David was hired to write speeches for a handsome, vigorous Democrat named Frank Brady, who was then running for Governor of a heavily industrial Middle Western state and had been acclaimed in several national magazines for his "charisma." And when Frank Brady won the election, David was retained in the State House as a member of the Governor's inner circle.

"Oh, it isn't just writing speeches," he explained to his wife when they were settled with their belongings in the drab suburban metropolis of the state's capital city. "The speeches are only the gravy. A lot more of my time is spent in things like—well, like getting up position papers and keeping them fresh."

"What are position papers?" Susan asked.

"Well, Frank has to be ready with well-reasoned opinions on all the issues—issues like Vietnam and civil rights, of course, but a lot of other stuff too: farm prices, labor-management relations, the environment and all that. So I do some research—oh, and there's a really good staff of research people in the office to make it easy

for me—and I put together four or five typewritten
pages, something Frank can read and digest in a few
minutes, and that's his—that's his position paper. It
becomes the position he'll take on whatever issue it is,
whenever it's being discussed."

"Oh," Susan said. While listening to him talk she had
decided that their sofa and coffee table didn't look right
where they were, against the far wall of this unfamiliar,
oddly proportioned room. By moving them over here,
and by putting these chairs over there, it might be possible to restore the pleasing order of their old "interesting" place. But she didn't have much hope for her plan:
the new arrangement probably wouldn't look right either. "Well," she said, "I see. Or at least I think I see.
It means that apart from writing every word that comes
out of the man's mouth—except of course for the television talk-shows, when all he does is mumble and grin at
movie stars—apart from that, you do his thinking for him
too. Right?"

"Oh, now, come on," he said, and he gestured widely
to show how foolish and how wrong she was. He wished
they weren't in chairs, because if they'd been on the sofa
he would have taken her in his arms. "Baby, come on.
Look. Frank Brady is a man who came up out of nowhere,
who made his own way without owing anybody anything,
who then waged a strong and inspiring campaign, and
who's been freely elected Governor. Millions of people
trust him, and believe in him, and look to him for leader-
ship. On the other hand, all I am is an employee—one
of his aides, or what I guess is called a 'special counsel.'
Is it really so terrible that I feed him words?"

"I don't know; I guess not. And I mean that's good,
that's fine, everything you've said; only, listen: I'm really
tired out. Could we sort of go to bed now?"

* * *

When she became pregnant, Susan was pleased to discover that she liked it. She had heard any number of women talk of pregnancy as a slow ordeal to be endured, but now from month to month she felt only a peaceful ripening. Her appetite was good, she slept well, she was hardly ever nervous, and toward the end she was willing to acknowledge that she enjoyed the deference of strangers in public places.

"I almost wish this could go on forever," she said to David. "It does slow you down a little, but it makes you feel—it really makes your body feel good."

"Good," he said. "I knew it would. You're a natural girl. Everything you do is so—so natural. I think that's what I've always liked best about you."

Their daughter, who they named Candace, caused substantial changes in their lives. They had suddenly relinquished their privacy; they were jittery all day; everything looked fragile and smelled sour. But they both knew better than to complain, and so by finding ways to encourage and console each other they got through the early, most difficult months without making any mistakes.

Several times a year David traveled to a distant Eastern town to visit the children of his first marriage, and those were never happy occasions.

The boy was sixteen now and failing all his courses in high school—failing too, it seemed, in all attempts at making friends. He was mostly silent and evasive around the house, cringing away from his mother's tactful suggestions about "professional counseling" and "getting help," rousing himself only to laugh at the silliest jokes on television. It seemed clear that he would soon leave home to join the floating world of hippies, where brains didn't count for much and friendship was held to be as universal as love.

The girl was twelve and much more promising, though her sweet face was blotched with bad skin and seemed set forever in a melancholy look, as if she couldn't stop contemplating the nature of loss.

And their mother, once a girl on whom David Clark had believed his very life depended ("But it's true; I mean it; I can't live without you, Leslie. . . ."), had become a harried, absent-minded, stout, and pathetically pleasant creature of middle age.

He always felt he had blundered into a house of strangers. Who are these people? he kept asking himself, looking around. Are these people supposed to have something to do with me? Or I with them? Who's this wretched boy, and what's the matter with this sad little girl? Who's this clumsy woman, and why doesn't she do something about her clothes and her hair?

When he smiled at them he could feel the small muscles around his mouth and eyes performing the courteous ritual of each smile. When he had dinner with them he might as well have been eating in some old and honorable cafeteria where tables were shared for convenience, but where all customers, hunched over their plates, respected one another's need to be alone.

"Well, I wouldn't be alarmed about it, David," his former wife said once, when he'd taken her aside to discuss their son. "It's an on-going problem, and we'll simply have to deal with it on those terms."

Toward the end of that visit he began counting the hours. Three hours; two hours; oh, Jesus, one hour more —until finally, gulping fresh air on the street, he was free. All the way back on the plane that night, riding over half of America as he munched dry-roasted peanuts and drank bourbon, he did his best to empty his mind of everything and to keep it that way.

And at last, trembling with fatigue at three in the morning, he carried his suitcase up the steps of his own house and into the living room, where he felt along the wall for the light switch. He meant to tiptoe quickly through the rooms and go to bed, but found instead that he had to stand a long time in the brightness, looking around, stunned by a sense of having never seen this place before.

Who lived here? And he started down the shadowed hall to find out. The door of the baby's room was only partly open and there wasn't much light, but he could see the tall white crib. And between the slender bars of it, deep in the scents of talcum powder and sweet piss, he could see a lump that occupied hardly any space but seemed to give off energy in its very stillness. Someone alive was in there. Someone was in there who would grow up soon, and who might turn out to be anybody at all.

He hurried to the other dark bedroom, where he allowed himself just enough light from the hall for guidance.

"David?" Susan said, half asleep, turning heavily in the bedclothes. "Oh, I'm so glad you're home."

"Yeah," he told her. "Oh, Jesus, baby, so am I."

And in her arms he discovered that his life wasn't over yet, after all.

Susan found little to like in the capital city: it went on for miles, everywhere you looked, without ever really becoming a city at all. There were many trees—that was nice—but the rest of it seemed to be all shopping malls and gas stations and gleaming fast-food franchises. When the baby was old enough to ride in a stroller she hoped she might explore new parts of town and find better things, but that turned out to be as futile as wishing David hadn't gone to work for Frank Brady in the first place.

One warm afternoon, having ventured too far from home for comfort, she was on her way back, pushing the stroller, when it began to seem that she might not make it. There were only about three blocks to go, but in the shimmering haze of the day they looked like five or six, or more. She stopped to rest, breathing hard, and became very much aware of her heart—the approximate size and shape and weight of it, the feel of it, as well as its beating and its terrible mortality. The baby turned in the plastic seat to look up and to ask, with round eyes, why they had stopped, and Susan did her best to answer that look with a reassuring smile.

"We're okay, Candace," she said, as if Candace could understand. "We're okay. We'll be home in just a minute."

And she made the distance. She even made the stairs, which were the worst part. She got Candace bedded down, got the contraption of the stroller folded flat and put away; then she lay on the living-room sofa until her heart came back to normal—until the big thumping threat of it receded and was absorbed once again into the body that had been made to feel so good in pregnancy.

She was still on the sofa, wondering whether or not to take a nap, when David came home from work.

"Wow," he said, sinking into one of the chairs across the room from her. "Jesus. Talk about a hard day at the office. I want to tell you, baby, this one was a bitch. . . ."

As she listened, or rather as she tried to listen while watching him talk, it occurred to Susan that he looked older than his age. He had taken to wearing a short beard, at her suggestion—it was she who trimmed it for him every three weeks or so—but she wasn't sure she would have suggested it if she'd known it would be white. And she didn't know if she would ever get used to his new hair, which had been entirely his own idea. As long as she'd known him his straight brown hair had been heavily streaked with gray, and she'd always found that attractive, but some months ago he had decided to let it grow because he didn't want to be the only man in the State House with a nineteen-fifties haircut, and now in luxuriance it was far more gray than brown. It was long enough in back to hide the collars of his shirt and his coat, long and heavy enough on the sides to cover his ears and to swing against his cheeks when he leaned forward, and it hung cropped in carefully irregular bangs across his forehead in the manner of the actress Jane Fonda.

That wasn't all: His legs, which she would have described as "lean" only a few years ago, looked so thin now in their neat gray flannel trousers as to suggest that he wouldn't be able to ride a bicycle without wobbling and veering slowly all over the street.

". . . And there are times," he was saying, delicately rubbing his closed eyelids with thumb and forefinger, "there are times when I wish Frank Brady would just go away and get lost. You can't imagine what the pressure's like in that sweatshop. Well. Get you a drink?"

"Sure," she said. "Thanks." And she watched him walk out of the room to the kitchen. She heard the soft slam of the big refrigerator door and the breaking open of an ice tray, and then came something unexpected and

frightening: a burst of high, wild laughter that didn't
sound like David at all. It went on and on, rising into
falsetto and falling only part of the way down as he
gasped for breath, and he was still in the grip of its
convulsions when he came weakly back into the room
with a very dark bourbon and water rocking and clinking
in his hand.

"Baby, listen," he said as soon as he was able to speak.
"I've just thought of the perfect revenge to take on Frank
Brady. Listen. Staple—" But he got no further than that
before the laughter hit him again. When he'd recovered
he took a deep breath, made a sober face, and said "Staple his lower lip to his desk."

She achieved a smile, but it wasn't enough to please
him.

"Oh, shit," he said, looking hurt. "You don't think
that's funny."

"Sure I do. It's pretty funny, when you picture it."

Then they were sitting close together on the sofa, and
he was taking greedy swigs of his drink as if this rich,
good whiskey was the main thing he had waited for all
day.

"Could I have one too?" she asked.

"Have one what?"

"You know; a drink."

"Oh, Jesus, I'm sorry," he said as he got up to lunge
for the kitchen again. "I'm sorry, dear. I meant to fix you
one and I just forgot, that's all. I'm getting absent-
minded in my old age, that's all."

And she waited, still smiling, hoping he wouldn't want
to talk about his old age anymore. He wasn't yet forty-
seven.

Another time, late one night when they were alone and
cleaning up after having several people in for dinner,

David remarked sourly of one guest that he was a pompous, humorless young twerp.

"Oh, I wouldn't say that," Susan said. "I think he's nice."

"Oh, yeah, 'nice.' That word covers just about everything for you, doesn't it. Well, fuck it. Fuck 'nice.' " And he slammed out of the room and down the hall as if he meant to go straight to bed. There was a good deal of thumping and banging in the bedroom for a minute or two; then he came back and faced her again, trembling. " 'Nice,' " he said. " 'Nice.' Is that what you want? You want the world to be 'nice'? Because listen, baby. Listen, sweetheart. The world is about as nice as shit. The world is struggle and rape and humiliation and death. The world is no fucking place for dreamy little rich girls from St. Louis, do you understand me? Go *home,* for Christ's sake. Get outa here and go home to your fucking *father* if you want to find 'nice.' "

While he stood shouting at her, with all that gray and white hair shaking around his almost eclipsed, almost forgotten face, it was like watching a child's tantrum enacted in the person of a crazy old man.

But it didn't last long. It was over quickly when he sat down in shame and silence to hold his elaborate head in his hands. Then, soon enough, came his choked-out, abject apology. "Oh, Jesus, Susan, I'm sorry," he said. "I don't know what gets into me when I'm like that."

"It's all right," she told him. "Let's just—let's just sort of go easy on each other for a while."

And going easy on each other turned out to be almost a pleasure. The gentleness and quiet of it, the temperance of it, permitted them both to shy away from the heat of each other's concerns without ever seeming to flinch, yet it permitted them the old intimacy too, when they both felt like it, and so they got along.

Through the difficulties of two more years there were times of peace, times of exultant companionship and other times of exasperation and bickering, or of silence; it all seemed to settle out into what David called a good marriage.

"Hey, Susan?" he would ask now and then, affecting a boyish bashfulness. "Think we'll make it?"

"Sure," she would say.

Not long after his nation's withdrawal from the war that had impelled him to change his life, David Clark made arrangements to go back to his teaching job. He then wrote a letter of resignation to Governor Brady, an act that made him feel "wonderful," and he urged his wife not to worry about the future. These years away from the classroom, he explained, had simply been a mistake—not a bad or a costly mistake, perhaps even one he could ultimately find profit in—but a mistake nonetheless. He was a school man. He had always been a school man, and would probably always be.

"Unless," he said, looking suddenly shy, "unless you think of all this as kind of—going backwards, or something."

"Why would I think that?"

"I don't know. Sometimes it's hard to tell what you're thinking. It always has been."

"Well," she said, "I suppose that's something I can't help, isn't it."

And they both fell silent. It was a warm afternoon at the end of summer. They were sitting with iced-tea glasses in which the ice had melted and the watery tea was almost gone.

"Oh, baby, listen—" he began, and he reached over to clasp her thigh for emphasis but hesitated and drew his hand back. "Listen," he said again. "Let me tell you something: We'll be all right."

After a long pause, examining her warm glass, she said "No we won't."

"Huh?"

"I said no we won't. We haven't been all right for a long time and we aren't all right now and it isn't going to get any better. I'm sorry if this comes as a surprise but it really shouldn't, and it wouldn't if you'd ever known me as well as you think you do. It's over, that's all. I'm leaving. I'll be taking Candace to California as soon as I can get our stuff packed, probably in a day or two. I'll call my parents tonight and tell them, and then my whole family will know. Once everybody knows, I imagine it'll be easier for you to accept."

All the blood seemed to have gone out of David's face, and all the moisture out of his mouth. "I don't believe this," he said. "I don't believe I'm sitting in this chair."

"Well, you'll believe it soon enough. And nothing you can say is going to stop me."

He set his empty glass on the floor and got quickly to his feet, as he always did for shouting, but he didn't shout. Instead he peered very closely at her face, as if trying to penetrate the surface of it, and said "My God, you really mean this, don't you. I've really lost you, haven't I. You don't—love me anymore."

"That's right," she said. "Exactly. I don't love you anymore."

"Well, but for Christ's sake, Susan, why? Can you tell me why?"

"There *is* no why," she said. "There's no more why to

not loving than there is to loving. Isn't that something most intelligent people understand?"

In an excellent residential suburb of St. Louis, a place of broad lawns and of deep, cool houses set back among shade trees, Edward Andrews sat alone in his study, trying to finish an article he'd been asked to write for a medical journal. He thought he had most of it right, but he couldn't find a way to work up the final paragraphs into a real conclusion, and every time he tried something different it seemed to get worse. The thing kept coming to a stop, rather than to an end.

"Ed?" his wife called from the hallway. "That was Susan on the phone. She's on the Interstate, and she'll be here with Candace in half an hour. You want to get dressed or anything?"

He certainly did. He wanted to take a quick hot shower too, and to stand at the mirror solemnly combing and recombing his hair until he got it parted just the right way. A clean shirt then, with the cuffs folded back two turns, and a fresh pair of lightweight flannels—all this to prove that at sixty-three he could still be spruce and vigorous for Susan.

When she arrived there were huggings and kissings in the front hall—Dr. Andrews's lips brushed the cool lobe of an ear—and there were happy exclamations at how much Candace had grown, how different she looked, since the last time her grandparents had seen her.

Alone in the kitchen, preparing drinks and coming to an abrupt, nervous decision that he'd better have a quick one now, here, before taking the tray into the living room, Dr. Andrews wondered once again what it was that could make him tremble in the presence of this dearest child, this particular girl. She was always so calm and so competent, for one thing. She had probably never done an incompetent or irresponsible thing in her life, except for wasting her Turnbull College tuition that time—and that, now that he thought of it, was nothing at all compared to the way millions of other children had behaved in those years, with their flowers and their love beads, their fuzzy-headed Eastern religions and their mindless pursuit of drug-induced derangement. Maybe David Clark could be thanked, after all, for having steered her away from all that; but no, that wasn't right. The credit couldn't go to Clark because it belonged to Susan herself. She was too intelligent ever to have been a vagabond, just as she was too honest to go on living with a man she no longer loved.

"So what are your plans, Susan?" he asked as he brought the bright tinkling tray of drinks into the room. "California's kind of a big place. Kind of a scary place too."

"Scary? How do you mean?"

"Oh, well, I don't know," he said, and he was ready to back down on anything now if it meant avoiding an argument. "All I meant was—you know—judging from some of the stuff you read in magazines, and so forth. I don't really have any first-hand information at all."

Susan explained, then, that she had a few friends in Marin County—"that's up north of San Francisco"—so she wouldn't be starting out among strangers. She would find a place to live, and then she'd look for some kind of work.

"What kind?" he asked. "I mean, is there anything in particular you'd like to do?"

"I don't really know yet," she said. "I'm pretty good with children; I might work in a nursery school or a day-care center; otherwise I'll look for something else."

She crossed her narrow, pretty knees under the hem of an attractive tweed skirt, and he wondered if she had changed into fresh clothes in some motel room on the road in order to look nice for this homecoming.

"Well, dear," he said. "I hope you know I'll be happy to help out in any way I can if you're—"

"No, no, Daddy, that's okay. We can get along easily on what David sends us. We'll be all right."

And it was such a fine thing to hear her say "Daddy" that he allowed himself to sit back, silent and almost relaxed. He didn't even ask the one question foremost in his mind: How *is* David, Susan? How's he taking all this?

He had met and talked with David Clark only a few times—first at the wedding, and on four or five occasions since then—and he'd been surprised each time to discover that he liked the man. Once, tentatively, they had begun to discuss politics, until David said "Well, Doctor, I guess I've always been a bleeding-heart liberal," and Edward Andrews found that appealing—the humor and the self-deprecation of it, if not the way it might apply to current issues. He had even decided not to mind David's being twenty years older than Susan, or his having another, earlier family far away, because all that seemed to suggest he wasn't likely to make any more mistakes; he would devote the prime of his middle age to his second marriage. And the best part, the thing that seemed to make nothing else matter, was that this shy, courteous, sometimes bewildered-looking stranger could never take his eyes away from Susan in any gathering. Couldn't everybody see he was in love with her? And wasn't that the first thing to look for in a son-in-law? Well, sure it was. Of course it was. And so, therefore, what now? What was the poor son of a bitch going to do with the rest of his life?

Susan and her mother were talking of family matters. All three of the younger girls were living away from home now, two of them married, and there were other bits of news to be exchanged about the older girls. Then after a while—inevitably, it seemed—they took up the subject of childbearing.

Agnes Andrews would be sixty before very long, and for many years she had been obliged to wear spectacles with lenses so thick that it wasn't easy to see the expression in her eyes: you had to rely on the smile or the frown or the patient, neutral look of her mouth. And her husband had to acknowledge that the rest of her was rapidly aging too. There wasn't much left of her once-lustrous hair except what the hairdresser could salvage and primp; her body sagged in some places and was bloated in others. She looked like what she was: a woman who'd been called "Mother" in shrill, hungering voices for most of her life.

Long ago, almost beyond memory, she had been a neat, crisp, surprisingly passionate young nurse whose flesh he had been wholly unable to resist. The only minor deterrent, easily ignored from their first night right on up through the night he'd proposed to her ("I love you, Agnes; oh, I love you, and I need you. I need you. . . ."), the only qualifying aspect of his love had been his knowledge that some people—his mother, for one—might think it strange of him to marry a girl of the working class.

". . . Well, Judy was my easiest," she was saying. "I never knew a thing. I went into the hospital and they put me under, and when I woke up it was all over. She was born, I was full of painkillers so I felt all right, and somebody gave me a bowl of Rice Krispies. No, but some of the others were a lot harder—you, for instance. Yours was a difficult birth. Still, I think my worst times were with the younger girls, probably because I was getting older. . . ."

Agnes rarely talked at such length—whole days could pass without her saying a word—but this had come to be her favorite topic. She sat leaning forward, her forearms on her knees and her clasped hands rolling this way and that to emphasize the points she was making.

". . . And you see Dr. Palmer thought I was unconscious—they all did—but the anesthetic wasn't working. I could feel everything, and I could hear every word they said. I heard Dr. Palmer say 'Watch out for that uterus: it's thin as paper.' "

"God," Susan said. "Weren't you frightened?"

And Agnes gave a tired little laugh that made her glasses gleam in the fading afternoon light. "Well," she said, "when you've been through it as many times as I have, I guess you don't really think much about being frightened anymore."

Candace, who had been given a glass of ginger ale with a cherry in it, went over to stand and stare out of the big windows that faced west, almost as if she were trying to gauge the distance to California. "Mommy?" she called, turning back. "Are we staying here tonight, or what?"

"Oh, no, honey," Susan told her. "We can only stay a little while. We've got a long drive ahead."

Out in the kitchen again, Edward Andrews broke open a tray of ice cubes with more force and noise than necessary, hoping it might stifle his mounting rage, but it didn't. He had to turn away and press his forehead hard against the heel of one trembling hand, like a God damned actor in a tragedy.

Girls. Would they always drive you crazy? Would their smiles of rejection always drop you into despair and their smiles of welcome lead only into new, worse, more terrible ways of breaking your heart? Were you expected to listen forever to one of them bragging about how paper-thin her womb was, or to another saying "We can only stay a little while"? Oh, dear Christ, how in the whole of a lifetime could anybody understand girls?

After a minute or two he achieved a semblance of composure. He carried the fresh drinks back into the living room with an almost stately bearing, determined that for this next, last little while he would keep everything down and quiet inside him so that neither of these girls, these women, would sense his anguish.

Half an hour later, in the early dusk, they were all out in the driveway. Candace was seated and belted in on the passenger side of the car, and Susan, with the car keys out and ready in her hand, was embracing her mother. Then she stepped over to give her father a hug, but it wasn't really much of a hug at all; it was more like an agreeable gesture of dismissal.

"Drive carefully, dear," he said into the softness of her dark, fragrant hair. "And listen—"

She drew away from him with a pleasant, attentive look, but he had swallowed whatever it was or might have been that he wanted her to know, and all he said instead was "Listen: Keep in touch, okay?"

# TRYING OUT____
# FOR THE RACE

Elizabeth Hogan Baker, who liked to have it known that both her parents were illiterate Irish immigrants, wrote feature stories for a chain of Westchester County newspapers through all the years of the Depression. Her home office was in New Rochelle but she was on the road every day in a rusty, quivering Model A Ford that she drove fast and carelessly, often squinting in the smoke of a cigarette held in one corner of her lips. She was a handsome woman, blond, sturdy, and still young, with a full-throated laugh for anything she found absurd, and this wasn't the life she had planned for herself at all.

"Can you figure it out?" she would ask, usually at night and after a few drinks. "Bring myself up from peasant stock, put myself through college, take a lousy little job on a suburban paper because it seemed a good-enough way to mark time for a year or two, and now look. Look. Can you figure it out?"

Nobody could. Her friends—and she always had admiring friends—could only agree that she'd had rotten luck. Elizabeth was much too good for the kind of work she did and for the inhibiting, stifling environment it had forced on her.

Back in the twenties, as a girl and a daydreaming reporter on the New Rochelle *Standard-Star*, she had looked up from her desk one day to see a tall, black-haired, shy-looking young man being shown around the office, a new staff member named Hugh Baker. "And the minute he walked in," she would say later, many times, "I thought: There's the man I'm going to marry." It didn't take long. They were married within a year and had a daughter two years later; then, soon, everything

fell apart in ways Elizabeth never cared to discuss. Hugh
Baker moved alone to New York, where he eventually
became a feature writer for one of the evening dailies
and was often praised for what the editors called his light
touch. And even Elizabeth never disparaged that: over
the years, embittered or not, she always said Hugh Baker
was the only man she had ever known who could really
make her laugh. But now she was thirty-six, with nothing
to do at the end of most days but go home to an upstairs
apartment in New Rochelle and pretend to take pleasure
in her child.

A stout middle-aged woman named Edna, whose slip
seemed always to hang at least an inch below the hem of
her dress all the way around, was working at the kitchen
stove when Elizabeth let herself in.

"Everything seems to be under control, Mrs. Baker,"
Edna said. "Nancy's eaten her supper, and I was just
putting this on the low heat so you can have it whenever
you're ready. I made a nice casserole; it turned out very
nice."

"Good, Edna, that's fine." And Elizabeth pulled off
her worn leather driving gloves. She always did this with
an unconscious little flourish, like that of a cavalry officer
just dismounted and removing his gauntlets after a long,
hard ride.

Nancy appeared to be ready for bed when they looked
in on her: she was in her pajamas and fooling around on
the floor of her room in some aimless game that involved
the careful alignment of a few old toys. She was nine, and
she would be tall and dark like her father. Edna had
recently cut out the soles of the feet in her Dr. Denton
pajamas to give her more freedom—she was growing out
of everything—but Elizabeth thought the pouches of ex-
cess cloth at her ankles looked funny; besides, she was

fairly sure that children of nine weren't supposed to wear that kind of pajamas anymore. "How was your day?" she inquired from the doorway.

"Oh, okay." And Nancy looked up only briefly at her mother. "Daddy called."

"Oh?"

"And he said he's coming out to see me Saturday after next and he's got tickets for *The Pirates of Penzance* at the County Center."

"Well, that's nice," Elizabeth said, "isn't it."

Then Edna stepped crouching into the room with her arms held wide. Nancy scrambled up eagerly, and they stood hugging for a long time. "See you tomorrow, then, funny-face," Edna said against the child's hair.

It often seemed to Elizabeth that the best part of the day was when she was alone at last, curled up on the sofa with a drink, with her spike-heeled shoes cast off and tumbled on the carpet. Perhaps a sense of well-earned peace like this was the best part of life itself, the part that made all the rest endurable. But she had always tried to know enough not to kid herself—self-deception was an illness—and so after a couple of drinks she was willing to acknowledge the real nature of these evenings alone: she was waiting for the telephone to ring.

Some months ago she had met an abrupt, intense, sporadically dazzling man named Judd Leonard. He ran his own small public-relations firm in New York and would snarl at anyone who didn't know the difference between public relations and publicity. He was forty-nine and twice divorced; he was often weak with ambition and anger and alcohol, and Elizabeth had come to love him. She had spent three or four weekends in his chaotic apartment in the city; once he had shown up here in New

Rochelle, laughing and shouting, and they'd talked for hours and he'd taken her on this very sofa, and he'd been nicely obedient about getting out of the place before Nancy woke up in the morning.

But Judd Leonard hardly ever called her now—or rather, hardly ever called her when he was able to speak coherently—and so Elizabeth had begun to wait here, one night after another.

When the phone rang at last she was dozing off on the sofa, having just decided to let the casserole dry out in the oven and to sleep right here, in her clothes—the hell with it—but it wasn't Judd.

It was Lucy Towers, one of her most admiring friends, and this meant she would be on the damned phone for at least an hour.

"... Well, sure, Lucy," she said. "Just give me a second to sort of pull myself together, okay? I was taking a nap."

"Oh. Well, of course; I'm sorry. I'll wait." Lucy was a few years older than Elizabeth, and if self-deception was an illness she was well into its advanced stages. She described herself as being "in real estate," which meant she had worked in various real-estate offices around the county, but she seemed unable or unwilling to hold those jobs and was often idle for long periods; she lived mostly on what her former husband sent her every month. She had a daughter of thirteen or so and a son of Nancy's age. And she had groundless social aspirations—social pretensions—that Elizabeth found silly. Still, Lucy was sweet and comforting, and they had been friends for years.

When she'd made a new drink and settled into a weary sitting position, Elizabeth picked up the phone again. "Okay," she said. "I'm fine now, Lucy."

"I'm sorry if I called at the wrong time," Lucy Towers

said, "but the thing is I simply couldn't wait to tell you this marvelous *idea* I have. First of all, do you know those houses along the Post Road in Scarsdale? Oh, I mean it's *Scars*dale, I know, but none of those houses have much market value because they're on the Post Road, you see, so most of them are rental properties and one or two of them are really very nice. . . ."

This was the idea: If Elizabeth and Lucy were to pool their resources, they could share one of those houses— and Lucy thought she had just the right place picked out already, though of course Elizabeth would have to in- spect it first. There'd be plenty of room to combine both households—the children would love every minute of it —and with the money they'd save they could even hire a maid.

"Oh, and besides," Lucy concluded, coming to the real point at last, "besides, I'm awfully tired of living alone, Elizabeth. Aren't you?"

The house, on a highway that bore steady traffic even in 1935, was bulky and glistening in the autumn sun. It was a jumble of architectural styles and materials: much of it was mock-Tudor but there were other expanses of fieldstone and still others of pink stucco, as if several things had gone wrong with the building plans and the men had been obliged to finish the job as best they could. It might not be much to look at, the rental agent conceded, but it was sound and clean, it was "tight," and at a rent like this it was certainly a bargain.

Lucy Towers and her children were the first to arrive on the appointed day of occupancy. The girl, Alice, who would be starting junior high school next week, wanted everything to look as nice as possible, and so she was a great help to her mother in moving their old furniture around into new and "interesting" arrangements to suit the unfamiliar rooms.

"Russell, will you get out of my *way,* please?" she said to her brother, who had found an old rubber ball in one of the packing boxes and was bouncing it moodily on the floor. "He keeps getting in my way and getting in my *way,*" Alice explained, "just when I'm trying to—ugh!"

"All right." And Lucy Towers swept back her hair in an exasperated gesture that revealed a coating of house dust on the inside of her forearm, runneled with several clean, dry streaks from when she had last washed her hands. "Dear, if you're not going to work with us you'd better go outside," she told her son. "Please."

So Russell Towers stuffed the ball in his pocket and went down the short slope of weedy, uncropped grass to the edge of the highway with nothing to do but stand there, watching the cars. The Bakers would soon be coming along in their old Ford, either before or after their moving van, and he decided it might be nice to have them find him here, like a courteous sentinel posted at the driveway.

Russell's family had changed houses and towns many times, and he'd never liked moving, but this new venture was the least promising yet. He had occasionally been pressed into acquaintance with Nancy Baker since they'd both been six, but he'd always shied away from her, or she from him, because they both understood it was their mothers who were friends. Now, and perhaps for years to come, Nancy's bedroom and his own would be along the same short corridor, with a single bathroom; they would eat their meals together and might easily be stuck with nobody else for company the rest of the time. They had been assigned to separate sections of the third grade —a plan the principal had said was "wise"—but even so, there were bound to be other difficulties. If he ever brought somebody home from school (assuming he would make any friends at all, which was something he couldn't bring himself to think about yet), Nancy's presence in the house would be all but impossible to explain.

When the Model A did pull up and make its shuddering turn into the driveway, Mrs. Baker got out first and asked Russell to wait here until the van came, because she wasn't sure if the driver would know which house it was. Then Nancy got out of the car and came around to wait with him, carrying a suitcase and a small, grubby-looking teddy bear. She smiled uncertainly, Russell looked quickly down, and they both watched with apparent interest as Mrs. Baker ground out a cigarette with her shoe and made her way up to the kitchen door.

"Know why they call it the Post Road?" he asked, squinting off into the distance of it. "Because it goes all the way up to Boston. You're really supposed to call it the Boston Post Road, and I think the 'post' part is because they carry the mail on it."

"Oh," Nancy said. "Well, no, I didn't know that." Then she held up her teddy bear and said "His name's George. He's slept with me every night of my life since I was four years old."

"Oh yeah?"

Russell didn't see the van coming until it had slowed down to negotiate the turn. He waved vigorously anyway, but the driver didn't notice, or need to.

Within a very few weeks Nancy Baker turned out to be impossible. She was stubborn and sulky and a terrible crybaby; the empty feet of her mutilated Dr. Dentons were ludicrous, and one of her prominent front teeth crookedly overlapped another in a way appropriate only to homely, tiresome little girls. She was shameless in her pursuit of Alice Towers, even after Alice had tactfully discouraged her time and again ("Not *now*, Nancy, I *told* you, I'm *busy* with something."). And although Lucy Towers made occasional formal efforts to be kind, she too seemed always dismayed by her. "Nancy isn't a very —attractive child, is she?" she remarked once, thoughtfully, to her son. Russell needed no further evidence to know how awful Nancy was, but there was ample further evidence anyway: her own mother seemed to find her impossible too.

There were mornings when the Towers family had to sit embarrassed at breakfast and hear the noise of mother and daughter locked in quarreling upstairs. *"Nan*cy!" Elizabeth would cry, with the same stagey lilt in her voice that she sometimes used for reciting Irish poetry. *"Nan-*cy! I'm not putting up with this another *mo*ment. . . ." And through it all came the sound of Nancy's voice in tears. There would be a thump or two and a slamming of doors, and then the sharp, heavy tread of Elizabeth alone, coming downstairs in her spike-heeled pumps.

"Sometimes," she intoned through clenched teeth as she came into the dining room one morning, "sometimes I wish that child were at the bottom of the sea." She pulled out her chair and sat down with enough authority to suggest she was glad she'd said that, and would say it again. "Do you know what it was this time? It was shoelaces."

"Will you want something, Mrs. Baker?" asked the Negro maid, whose presence here was still a source of surprise to everyone.

"No, thanks, Myra, there isn't time. I'll just have coffee. If I don't have coffee I won't be responsible for my actions. Well. First it was shoelaces," Elizabeth went on. "She has only one flat shoelace and one round one, you see, and she's ashamed to go to school that way. Can you imagine? Can you imagine that? When half the children in the United States aren't getting enough to eat? Oh, and that was only the beginning. She then said she misses Edna. She wants Edna. So can someone please tell me what I'm expected to do? Am I expected to go over to New Rochelle and *get* the wretched woman and *bring* her here? And take her *home* again? Besides, I think she's working in the radio-tube factory now—a point I was *wholly* unable to get across."

Elizabeth took her coffee as if it were medicine and trudged out to the car. By then it was time for Alice and Russell to leave for school, and Lucy Towers found something to do in her bedroom. Nobody was there when Nancy came down at last to eat nothing, to put on her coat and hurry out between the borders of other people's lawns, through a broken fence and then along a gently curving suburban lane to the school building, where a frowning teacher would mark her "tardy" one more time.

But there was worse trouble by now in that Russell Towers had found himself ill-equipped to serve, even if only symbolically, as man of the house. There wasn't anything quiet or self-assured or dignified about him. He too, like Nancy, could throw dreadful fits of temper and crying that made him feel humiliated even while they were going on. When his mother came to his room one evening to announce that she was "going out to dinner in White Plains" with a man he had met only once before, a big, bald, red-faced man who had called him "Champ" and who was probably listening at the foot of the stairs right now, ready to learn in head-shaking wonderment what a snot-nosed little mother's boy he was, Russell went all the way. He faked a collapse on the floor as if tantrums were a form of epileptic seizure, then he faked a collapse on the bed, and he was appalled at the shrillness of his own voice: "You *can't* go! You *can't* go!"

". . . Oh, please," Lucy was saying. "Please, Russell. Listen. Listen. I'll bring you something nice, I promise, and you'll find it when you wake up, and that'll let you know I'm home."

". . . Ah! Oh! Oh! . . ."

"Please, now, Russell. Please . . ."

On waking ashamed the next morning he found a small, well-made stuffed toy in the form of a lamb beside his pillow—a gift for a baby, or a girl. He took it to the wooden chest against the wall that contained all the other toys he had outgrown, put it inside, and closed the lid. He was a mother's boy, all right, and at times like this it seemed useless ever to deny it.

"You sure made a racket last night," Nancy said to him later that day.

"Yeah, well, I've heard you make a lot of racket too. Plenty of times."

He might have added that he'd even heard Harry Snyder make a racket, and Harry was a year older, but she hadn't been present at Harry's tantrum and so would probably not have believed it, or even have cared.

School had as yet produced no real friends for Russell, and he worried about that, but Harry Snyder was the boy next door, and so a casual, loafing kind of friendship had been easy to achieve with him. One day they were intently hunkered down over many tin soldiers in the basement of Harry's house when Mrs. Snyder came to the stairs and called down "Russell, you'll have to go home now. Harry has to come up and get ready because we're all going for a drive to Mount Vernon."

"Aw, Mom, *now?* You mean *now?*"

"Certainly I mean 'now.' Your father wanted to get started an hour ago."

And that was when Harry went into action. In three swift, merciless kicks he sent soldiers flying in all directions, ruining formations that had been all afternoon in the making, and he howled and flailed and cried like someone half his age, while Russell looked away in a wincing smile of embarrassment.

"Harry!" Mrs. Snyder called. "Harry, I want you to stop this right now. Do you hear me?"

But he didn't stop until long after she'd come down and led him tragically upstairs; when Russell crept out for home he could still hear the terrible sound of it ringing across the yellow grass.

Even so, there was an important difference. Harry had cried because he wanted his mother to leave him alone; Russell had cried because he didn't—and therein lay the very definition of a mother's boy.

On some winter evenings Elizabeth would set up her typewriter in the living room and be lost in concentration for hours, hammering out her newspaper features or trying for something more substantial that she might submit to a magazine. She sat as straight as a stenographer at her work, her spine never touching the back of the chair, and she wore horn-rimmed glasses. Sometimes a lock of her pretty blond hair would dislodge itself and fall over one eye, and she'd put it back with impatient fingers—often the same fingers that held a short, burning cigarette. There was always a full ashtray on one side of her machine; on the other, near the paper supply, a big block of milk chocolate lay carefully broken apart in its torn-open wrapper—the kind of Hershey bar that cost almost fifty cents. Everyone understood, though, that this chocolate wasn't for passing around: it was the fuel Elizabeth needed when she wasn't drinking.

There were long intervals between spells of typing when she would hunch over a pencil to revise and correct her pages, and then the silence was broken only by the occasional *whack-whack-whack* of a car's loose tire chain whipping the underside of its fender along the packed snow and ice of the Post Road. During one such lull, on a night of heavy snowfall, the telephone rang for the first time in what seemed many weeks.

"I'll get it!" Alice Towers cried in headlong eagerness for the social life of junior high, but then she turned back and said "It's for you, Mrs. Baker." And they all listened as Elizabeth murmured and laughed into the phone in a way that could only have meant it was a man.

"My God," she told Lucy when she'd hung up, "I think Judd Leonard is insane. He's at the Hartsdale station and he says he'll be here in a taxi in ten minutes. Can you imagine anybody coming all the way out here on a night like this?" But moving uncertainly back toward her scattered work table, then turning and taking off her glasses, she couldn't hide a shy, pleased look that transformed her suddenly into a girl. "Well, Jesus, Lucy, is my hair all right?" she said. "Are my clothes all right? Do you think there's time to wash up and change?"

Judd Leonard arrived with gusts of laughter and a great stamping-off of snow in the vestibule. His thin city shoes weren't used to stuff like this and even his expensive overcoat looked forlorn, but he triumphantly displayed a heavy, snow-flecked paper bag that clinked with bottles of liquor. He gave Lucy Towers a kiss on the cheek to prove he had heard what a nice woman she was, and he was attentive to the children: he explained to them that he was an old broken-down word man and a very dear friend of Nancy's mother.

Everybody stayed up late that night. Lucy seemed to do most of the talking at first, telling Westchester anecdotes; then Elizabeth held forth at enthusiastic length on communism, and Judd Leonard went right along with her. Even though he earned his living in private enterprise, he said, he'd be happy to see every vestige of it down the drain if that meant humanity might then have a chance. These were times of inevitable change; only a fool could fail to recognize that. Long after the children were in bed upstairs his rolling, thunderous voice filled the snowbound house. They listened as long as they could, comprehending or not, until they fell asleep in the rhythms of it.

When the snow had stopped the following afternoon, Elizabeth and Judd departed quietly by taxi for the Hartsdale station. As they rode together on the train to New York he said "Your roommate's an imbecile. Give her three drinks and all she wants to talk about is garden parties."

"Oh, Lucy's all right," Elizabeth said. "She just takes a little getting used to. Besides, it's a nice arrangement, sharing that house. It suits me."

"Ah, funny little Irish Scarsdale Bolshevik," he said fondly, putting his arm around her. "You're really not a hell of a lot smarter than she is, you know that?"

By the third or fourth day of Elizabeth's absence, Lucy assumed she was staying with Judd in New York for a while, commuting out to New Rochelle for work and back to the city each night. But wouldn't it have been only considerate to let people know her plans? Wasn't it a little thoughtless not even to have told Nancy?

Russell Towers found it amazing that Nancy didn't

know where her mother was and gave no sign of being eaten alive with worry—seemed, in fact, not even to care. He hung around the open door of her room one day, after Elizabeth had been gone for a week or more, watching Nancy work on the floor with some art paper taken from school and with a colored-pencil set of her own.

At last he said "Heard from your mother yet?"

"Nope," she said.

"Any idea where she is or anything?"

"Nope."

He knew the next question might easily make him a fool in her eyes, but couldn't hold it back. "You worried about it?"

And Nancy looked up at him in a frank, thoughtful way. "No," she said. "I know she'll come back. She always does."

That was impressive. As he slouched away to his own room, Russell knew that an attitude like that was exactly what he needed in his own life. But he knew too, sitting on his bed to think it over, that it was out of the question. It was as far-fetched as trying to compare himself to the athletes shown on the backs of breakfast-cereal boxes. He was an anxious, skinny little kid, forever too young for his age, and anyone opening the lid of his toy chest would only find sickening proof of it.

Alice Towers was once again the first to reach the phone when it rang a few nights later. "Oh, sure," she said, and then, "It's for you, Nancy. It's your mother."

Nancy took the call standing up, with her back to the Towers family. After the opening "Hi" her words were indistinct; then she was silent, listening, holding her shoulders in a high, unnatural way. At last she turned and held out the phone to Lucy, who took it up quickly.

"Well, Elizabeth. Are you all right? We've all been a little—concerned about you."

"Lucy, I need my child," Elizabeth said in the old Irish-poetry voice. "I want you to send me my child to-night."

"Oh. Well, look. For one thing the last train's probably been gone for hours, and besides, I—"

"The last train leaves there at ten-thirty-something," Elizabeth said. "Judd looked it up on the timetable. That gives her plenty of time to get ready."

"Well, but Elizabeth, I really don't think this is a very good idea. Has she ever taken a train alone before? And at night?"

"Oh, nonsense. It's only a forty-minute ride, and Judd and I'll be there to meet her, or at least I will. She knows that. I've told her, all she has to do when she gets off the train is follow the crowd."

And Lucy hesitated. "Well," she said, "I suppose if you can promise to be there when she—"

" 'Promise'? Am I expected to make a 'promise'? To you? About something like this? You're beginning to make me tired, Lucy."

Russell thought his mother looked hurt and bewildered and a little foolish after she'd hung up the phone, but she recovered quickly, and from then on she did everything right. In a tone that came out as a nice mixture of authority and affection, she sent Nancy upstairs to change her clothes and to pack. Then she called for a station taxicab, explaining that a nine-year-old girl would be traveling alone and asking if the driver could see her safely aboard the train.

When Nancy came down in a fresh dress, with her winter coat and her overnight bag, Lucy Towers said

"Oh, good. You look very nice, dear." And Russell couldn't be sure, but he thought it was the first time he had ever heard his mother call her "dear."

"Oh, wait," Nancy said, "I forgot." And she ran upstairs again and came back with her grubby-looking teddy bear.

"Oh, well, of course," Lucy said. "And I'll tell you what we'll do." She took the small suitcase on her lap and unfastened the clasps of it. "We'll open this up and we'll put old George right in there on top; that way you'll know exactly where he is at all times." And the best part of that, which Nancy's bashful smile only confirmed, was that Lucy had remembered the teddy bear's name.

"Now," Lucy said, and busied herself with her purse. "Let's see about money. I only have about a dollar and a half over the price of your ticket, but I'm sure that'll be enough. Your mother'll be waiting in Grand Central, so there won't really be any need for money at all. You've been in Grand Central before, haven't you?"

"Yes."

"Well, the thing to remember when you're alone is that all you have to do is follow the crowd. There'll be a long platform and then a long ramp going up; then you'll come out inside the station and that's where your mother'll be."

"Okay."

The cab's horn sounded in the driveway then, and all three members of the Towers family went out over slick crusted snow, in a freezing wind, to wish Nancy goodbye.

She was gone for well over a week, and there were no telephone calls. When she came back, alone, having somehow arranged for her own taxi home from the Hartsdale station (and that in itself was something Russell wasn't at all sure he'd have known how to do) she didn't tell much about her trip.

"Did you have a nice time in the city, Nancy?" Lucy Towers asked at dinner, while the maid moved softly around the table with plates of spaghetti and meat sauce.

"It was cold most of the time," Nancy said. "One day it was warm enough to go up and sit on the roof, so I did that, but I was only up there about an hour—one hour —before I was covered with soot. My hands, my face, my clothes, everything. Black."

"Mm, yes," Lucy said, winding too thick a load of spaghetti onto her fork. "Well, the air in New York does get—very dirty."

Harry Snyder's tantrum over the tin soldiers had never been mentioned, but the long aftermath of it seemed to have made him a little testy in Russell's presence. He had become hard to please and quick to find fault, and he stood around a lot looking "tough" with his thumbs hooked into the belt of his corduroy knickers.

"Whaddya got in there?" he asked one afternoon in Russell's room, indicating the toy chest.

"Nothing much. Just old stuff my mother hasn't thrown away."

But that didn't stop Harry from going over and opening the thing. "Jeez," he said. "You like stuff like this? You play with stuff like this?"

" 'Course not," Russell said. "I told you, it's just that my mother hasn't ever gotten around to throwing—"

"So why don't you throw it away yourself, if you don't like it? Huh? How come you have to wait for your mother to do it?"

It was a bad moment, and the only thing to do was get Harry out of the room at once. But there was no getting

RICHARD YATES

him downstairs and outside, because he seemed to think it might be more interesting to stand for a while at the doorway of Nancy's room, looking in.

"Whaddya doing, Nancy?" he asked her.

"Nothing; just putting my programs away."

"Your what?"

"These, look. Theater programs. I've been to five different Gilbert and Sullivan operettas with my father, and I always save the programs. The next one we're going to see is *The Mikado.*"

"The McWhat?"

"It means the emperor of Japan," she explained. "It's supposed to be very good. But my favorite so far is *The Pirates of Penzance,* and I think that's Daddy's favorite too. He sent me all the sheet music for it, the whole score."

Russell had never known her to be this talkative and high-spirited except when she brought a girl home from school, and even then what little could be heard of the conversation seemed mostly to be uncontrolled giggles. Now she was summarizing the libretto to the best of her ability, careful not to dwell on any aspect of it that might hamper Harry's grasp of the whole. Early in her monologue she had made some slight gesture of welcome to the boys, and soon they were in virtual possession of her room: Harry seated in the only chair with the sheaf of theater programs on his lap, Russell standing near the window with his thumbs in his belt.

". . . And I think the best part," she was saying, "the best part is this minor character of a policeman. He's very stiff and gruff." She paced a few steps and turned, pantomiming stiffness and gruffness. "He's wonderful, and he sings this wonderful song."

And she took up the song, trying for a deep male voice and a Cockney accent, trying mightily not to smile:

82

When a felon's not engaged in his employment
                                                                    —his employment

"Oh, I forgot to tell you that part," she said, smooth-
ing her hair with a nervous hand. "There's this whole
chorus of people on the stage, you see, and they always
come in and repeat the end of each line like that":

                                                                    —his employment
     Or maturing his felonious little plans
                                                                    —little plans
     His capacity for innocent enjoyment
                                                                    —cent enjoyment
     Is just as great as any honest man's
                                                                    —honest man's
     Our feelings we with difficulty smother
                                                                    —culty smother
     When constabulary duty's to be done
                                                                    —to be done
     Ah, taking one consideration with another—

Harry Snyder distorted his face and made a slow, loud
retching sound, as if this were the worst and most nau-
seating song he had ever heard, and to simulate vomiting
he spilled all the theater programs onto the floor with a
splat. That won him a tense little laugh of complicity
from Russell, and then there was silence in the room.
     The surprise and hurt in Nancy's face lasted only a few
seconds before she was furious. She might cry later, but
she certainly wasn't crying yet. "All right; out," she said.
"Get out of here. Both of you. Now."
     And they could only stumble deliriously from the
room like clowns, shoving each other and mugging, making it look like a mock retreat in order to make a mockery

of her anger. She slammed the door behind them so hard that flakes of paint fell from the hallway ceiling, and for the rest of the afternoon they found nothing to do but fool around in the backyard, avoiding each other's eyes, until it was time for Harry to go home.

When Elizabeth finally came back she looked "awful" —that was how Lucy described it to Alice.

"You think it's all over, then?" Alice asked. "With Judd?" She had come to rely on her mother for interpretations of adult behavior, because there was no one else to ask, but it wasn't always profitable: last month a girl in the ninth grade had dropped out of school because she was pregnant, and Lucy's revulsion at the news had precluded any interpretation at all.

"Oh, well, I don't know about *that,*" Lucy said now, "and I hope you won't start asking personal questions or anything, because it's really none of our—"

"Personal questions? Why would I do that?"

"Oh, well, it's just that you're always so inquisitive, dear, about other people's private business."

And Alice looked wounded, an expression even more frequent on her face lately than on her mother's, or her brother's.

The Towers family shied away from Elizabeth most of the time, and so did Nancy; it was like having a stranger in the house. Coming heavily downstairs in her spike heels, standing at the front windows to stare out at the Post Road as if in deep thought, picking at whatever food was set before her and drinking a lot after dinner as she paged impatiently through many magazines, Elizabeth didn't even seem to notice how uncomfortable she made everyone feel.

Then one night, long after the children were in bed,

she cast aside *The New Republic* and said "Lucy, I don't think this is working out. I'm sorry, because it did seem like a good idea, but I think we both ought to start looking for other places to live."

Lucy was stunned. "Well, but we signed a two-year lease," she said.

"Oh, come on. I've broken leases before and so have you. People break leases all the time. I don't think you and I are well suited to living like this, that's all, and the kids don't like it either, so let's call it off."

Lucy felt as if a man were leaving her. After a brief, intense effort to keep from crying—she knew it would be ridiculous to cry over something like this—she said, hesitantly, "Will you be moving into the city, then? With Judd?"

"Oh, *Jesus,* no." Elizabeth got up and began pacing the rug. "That loudmouth. That overbearing, posturing, drunken son of a bitch—and anyway, he broke off with me." She gave a harsh little laugh. "You ought to've *seen* the way he broke off with me. You ought to've *heard* it. No, I'll look for something like I had before, or maybe better, where I can just be quiet and go about my—go about my business alone."

"Well, Elizabeth, I wish you'd think it over. I know you've had a difficult time this winter, but it doesn't really seem fair of you to—oh, look: wait a few weeks or a month; then decide. Because there *are* advantages for you here, or can be, and besides, you and I are friends."

Elizabeth let the word "friends" hang in the air for a while, as if to examine it.

"Well," Lucy said, qualifying it, "I mean we certainly have a lot in common, and we—"

"No, we don't." And Elizabeth's eyes took on a glint of cruelty that Lucy had never seen in them before. "We don't have anything in common at all. I'm a communist and you'll probably vote for Alf Landon. I've worked all my life and you've scarcely lifted a finger. I've never even *believed* in alimony, and you live on it."

There was nothing for Lucy Towers to do then but sweep out of the room in silence, climb the stairs, get into bed and wait for convulsions of weeping to overcome her. But she fell asleep before it happened, probably because she too had drunk a good deal that night.

By then it was early spring. They had been together in the house for six months, and now the end of it was in the air. It wasn't discussed much, but the days took on a quality of last times for everyone.

On one side of the house, away from the side where Harry Snyder lived, lay a vacant lot that made a good theater for war games: some of its weeds were tall enough to hide in, and there were trails and open spaces of packed dirt for the enactment of infantry combat. Russell was fooling around the lot alone one afternoon, perhaps because it might be the last time he'd be able to, but there wasn't much point in it without Harry. He was on his way home when he looked up and found Nancy watching him from the back porch.

"What were you *doing* out there?" she asked him.

"Nothing."

"Looked like you were walking around in circles and talking to yourself."

"Oh, I was," he said, pulling a goofy face. "I do that all the time. Doesn't everybody?"

And to his great relief she seemed to think that was funny; she even rewarded him with an agreeable little laugh.

In no time at all they were strolling the vacant lot

together while he pointed out the landmarks of recent military action. Here was the clump of weeds where Harry Snyder had concealed his machine-gun emplacement; here was the trail down which Russell had led a phantom patrol, and the first burst of fire had caught him right across the chest.

To recapture the scene he reeled back in shock and crumpled to the dirt, lying still. "There's nothing much you can do if you get it in the chest that way," he explained as he got up to brush off his clothes. "But the worst thing is taking a grenade in the belly." And that called for another performance of agony and dusty sprawling.

After the third time he died for her, she looked at him thoughtfully. "You really like the falling down part, don't you," she said.

"Huh?"

"Well, I mean the best part of it for you is getting killed, right?"

"No," he said defensively, because her tone had implied something unwholesome in such a preference. "No, I just—I don't know."

That took the edge off the pleasure, though they remained on cordial terms as they walked back to the house; still, it couldn't be denied that for a little while they had been companions.

And it was on the strength of that, during their lunch break from school the following day, that Russell came thumping in from the back porch with something important to tell her.

She had gotten home first; she was settled back in the cushions of the living-room sofa, gazing out a window and wrapping a lock of her black hair around her index finger.

"Hey," he said, "this is pretty funny. You know that real big guy in your class? Carl Shoemaker?"

"Sure," she said. "I know him."

"Well, I was coming out of school just now and Carl Shoemaker was there on the playground with these two other guys and he called me over. He said 'Hey, Towers, you gonna try out for the race?'

"I said 'What race?'

"He said 'The human race. But I better warn you, they don't let sissies in.'

"I said 'So who's the sissy?'

"And he said 'Aren't you one? I heard you were. That's why I'm warning you.'

"So I said 'Look, Shoemaker. Find somebody else to warn, okay?' I said 'You want somebody to warn, you better keep looking.' "

It was a fairly accurate rendering of the dialogue, and Nancy seemed to have followed it with interest. But the last line of it now had an inconclusive ring, as if leaving open a chance that there might be further trouble when he went back to school. "So then after that," he told her, "after that they just sort of smiled and walked away, Shoemaker and the two other guys. I don't think they'll mess with me anymore. But I mean the whole thing was really kind of—kind of funny."

He wondered now why he had told her about it at all, instead of finding other things to discuss. Watching her there on the sofa, in the noon light, he could see how she would probably look when she grew up and got pretty.

"Said he'd heard you were a sissy, uh?" she said.

"Well, that's what he said he'd *heard*, but I think I—"

And she gave him a long, infuriatingly sly look. "Well," she said. "I wonder where he ever heard that."

The thumbs came out of Russell's belt as he backed

slowly away from her across the rug, round-eyed, aghast at her betrayal. Just before he reached the doorway he saw the slyness in her face give way to fear, but it was too late: they both knew what he would do next, and there was no stopping him.

At the foot of the stairs he called "Mom? Mom?"

"What *is* it, dear?" Lucy Towers appeared on the landing, looking unsettled and wearing what she called her tea dress.

"Nancy told Carl Shoemaker I'm a sissy and he told a lot of other guys and now everybody's saying it and it's a lie. It's a lie."

In a stately manner appropriate to the tea dress, Lucy came downstairs. "Oh," she said. "Well. This is something we can discuss at lunch."

Elizabeth never came home for lunch and Alice ate in the junior high school cafeteria, so there were only the three of them at the table: Russell and his mother on one side, Nancy on the other. There was nobody to deflect the force of Lucy's slow, impassioned, relentless voice.

"I'm surprised at what you did, Nancy, and I'm deeply troubled by it. People don't do things like that. People don't spread malicious gossip and lies about their friends behind their backs. It's as bad as stealing, or cheating. It's disgusting. Oh, I suppose there are people who behave that way, but they aren't the kind of people I'd want to sit at a table with, or live in a house with, or ever have as friends of my own. Do you understand me, Nancy?"

The maid came in with their plates—there would be small portions of veal, mashed potatoes, and peas today —and she lingered to give Lucy a look of veiled reproach before going back to the kitchen. She had never worked in a house like this before, and didn't want to again. A nice lady, a crazy lady, and three sad-looking kids: what kind of a house was that? Well, it would most likely be over soon—she had already put the agency on the lookout for a new job—but meanwhile, somebody ought to shut that crazy lady's mouth before she scolded that little girl to death.

"Russell is your friend, Nancy," Lucy Towers was saying, "and he's a person you share your home with. When you spread vicious lies about him at school, behind his back, you're inflicting great damage. Oh, I'm sure you know that; you've known it from the start. But I wonder if you ever stopped to think of me. Because do you want to know something, Nancy? *I* found this house. *I* asked your mother to join me in it, so we could all live together. *I* was the one who kept hoping and hoping there'd be a little peace and harmony in our lives here—yes, and I went on hoping even after I knew there wouldn't be. So you see it isn't only Russell you've hurt, Nancy; it's me. It's me. You've hurt me terribly, Nancy. . . ."

There was more, and it came to an end exactly as Russell knew it would. All through the upbraiding Nancy had sat silent, with a rigid face and downcast eyes—she had even managed to eat a little, as if to show she was above all this—but eventually her mouth began to fall apart. There were telltale twitches of the lips, increasingly difficult to control; then it came open and was locked in a shape of despair around two partly chewed green peas, and she was crying wretchedly but making no sound.

They were both late for school that afternoon, though Nancy had a head start of at least a hundred yards. Walking out between the borders of other people's lawns and through the broken fence and then along the gently curving lane, Russell could catch only an occasional glimpse of her far ahead, a tall, slim girl with a way of walking that suggested she was older than nine. She would grow up and get pretty; she would get married and have boys and girls of her own; so it was probably a dumb and even a sissy thing to be afraid she would always remember what Russell Towers had done to her today. Still, there would now be no way of knowing, ever, if she would forget it.

"Well, I don't see any point in prolonging this," Elizabeth said the next day, setting two packed suitcases on the living-room floor. "Nancy and I'll go up to White Plains and stay in a hotel for a few days; then when we're settled somewhere I'll send back for the rest of our stuff."

"You're putting me in a very awkward position," Lucy said solemnly.

"Oh, come on; I don't see that at all. Here, look, I'll leave you an extra month's rent, okay?" She sat briefly at her old work table with her checkbook, and scribbled on it. "There," she said when it was done. "That ought to take care of the suffering." And she and Nancy carried their bags out to the Model A.

None of the Towers family went to the front windows to wave goodbye, but it didn't matter because neither of the Bakers looked back.

"Know something?" Elizabeth said when she and Nancy were heading north on the Post Road. "I couldn't really afford to write that check. It won't bounce, but it's going to give us a tight month. Still, maybe there are times when you have to buy your way out of something whether you can afford it or not."

After another mile or so she glanced from the road to

Nancy's serious profile and said "Well, Jesus, can't we even have a couple of laughs in this car? Why don't you sing me Gilbert and Sullivan or something?"

And Nancy gave her a brief, shy smile before turning away again. Slowly, Elizabeth removed the driving glove from her right hand. She reached across her daughter's lap, clasped the outer thigh and brought her sliding over, careful to keep her small knees clear of the shuddering gear shift. She held the child's thighs pressed fast against her own for a long time; then, in a voice so soft it could scarcely be heard over the sound of the car, she said "Listen, it'll be all right, sweetheart. It'll be all right."

# LIARS
# IN LOVE

WHEN Warren Mathews came to live in London, with his wife and their two-year-old daughter, he was afraid people might wonder at his apparent idleness. It didn't help much to say he was "on a Fulbright" because only a few other Americans knew what that meant; most of the English would look blank or smile helpfully until he explained it, and even then they didn't understand.

"Why tell them anything at all?" his wife would say. "Is it any of their business? What about all the Americans living here on *private* incomes?" And she'd go back to work at the stove, or the sink, or the ironing board, or at the rhythmic and graceful task of brushing her long brown hair.

She was a sharp-featured, pretty girl named Carol, married at an age she often said had been much too young, and it didn't take her long to discover that she hated London. It was big and drab and unwelcoming; you could walk or ride a bus for miles without seeing anything nice, and the coming of winter brought an evil-smelling sulphurous fog that stained everything yellow, that seeped through closed windows and doors to hang in your rooms and afflict your wincing, weeping eyes.

Besides, she and Warren hadn't been getting along well for a long time. They may both have hoped the adventure of moving to England might help set things right, but now it was hard to remember whether they'd hoped that or not. They didn't quarrel much—quarreling had belonged to an earlier phase of their marriage—but they hardly ever enjoyed each other's company, and there were whole days when they seemed unable to do anything at all in their small, tidy basement flat without getting in each other's way. "Oh, sorry," they would mutter after each clumsy little bump or jostle. "Sorry . . ."

The basement flat had been their single stroke of luck: it cost them only a token rent because it belonged to Carol's English aunt, Judith, an elegant widow of seventy who lived alone in the apartment upstairs and who often told them, fondly, how "charming" they were. She was very charming too. The only inconvenience, carefully discussed in advance, was that Judith required the use of their bathtub because there wasn't one in her own place. She would knock shyly at their door in the mornings and come in, all smiles and apologies, wrapped in a regal floor-length robe. Later, emerging from her bath in billows of steam with her handsome old face as pink and fresh as a child's, she would make her way slowly into the front room. Sometimes she'd linger there to talk for a while, sometimes not. Once, pausing with her hand on the knob of the hallway door, she said "Do you know, when we first made this living arrangement, when I agreed to sublet this floor, I remember thinking Oh, but what if I don't *like* them? And now it's all so marvelous, because I do like you both so very much."

They managed to make pleased and affectionate replies; then, after she'd gone, Warren said "That was nice, wasn't it."

"Yes; very nice." Carol was seated on the rug, struggling to sink their daughter's heel into a red rubber boot. "Hold still, now, baby," she said. "Give Mommy a break, okay?"

The little girl, Cathy, attended a local nursery school called The Peter Pan Club every weekday. The original idea of this had been that it would free Carol to find work in London, to supplement the Fulbright income; then it turned out there was a law forbidding British employers to hire foreigners unless it could be established that the foreigner offered skills unavailable among British applicants, and Carol couldn't hope to establish anything like that. But they'd kept Cathy enrolled in the nursery school anyway because she seemed to like it, and also—though neither parent quite put it into words—because it was good to have her out of the house all day.

And on this particular morning Carol was especially glad of the prospect of the time alone with her husband: she had made up her mind last night that this was the day she would announce her decision to leave him. He must surely have come to agree, by now, that things weren't right. She would take the baby home to New York; once they were settled there she would get a job—secretary or receptionist or something—and make a life of her own. They would keep in touch by mail, of course, and when his Fulbright year was done they could—well, they could both think it over and discuss it then.

All the way to The Peter Pan Club with Cathy chattering and clinging to her hand, and all the way back, walking alone and faster, Carol tried to rehearse her lines just under her breath; but when the time came it proved to be a much less difficult scene than she'd feared. Warren didn't even seem very surprised—not, at least, in ways that might have challenged or undermined her argument.

"Okay," he kept saying gloomily, without quite looking at her. "Okay . . ." Then after a while he asked a troubling question. "What'll we tell Judith?"

"Well, yes, I've thought of that too," she said, "and it *would* be awkward to tell her the truth. Do you think we could just say there's an illness in my family, and that's why I have to go home?"

"Well, but your family is *her* family."

"Oh, that's silly. My father was her brother, but he's dead. She's never even met my mother, and anyway they'd been divorced for God knows how many years. And there aren't any other lines of—you know—lines of communication, or anything. She'll never find out."

Warren thought about it. "Okay," he said at last, "but I don't want to be the one to tell her. You tell her, okay?"

"Sure. Of course I'll tell her, if it's all right with you."

And that seemed to settle it—what to tell Judith, as well as the larger matter of their separation. But late that night, after Warren had sat staring for a long time into the hot blue-and-pink glow of the clay filaments in their gas fireplace, he said "Hey, Carol?"

"What?" She flapping and spreading clean sheets on the couch, where she planned to sleep alone.

"What do you suppose he'll be like, this man of yours?"

"What do you mean? *What* man of mine?"

"You know. The guy you're hoping to find in New York. Oh, I know he'll be better than me in about thirteen ways, and he'll certainly be an awful lot richer, but I mean what'll he be like? What'll he *look* like?"

"I'm not listening to any of this."

"Well, okay, but tell me. What'll he look like?"

"I don't know," she said impatiently. "A dollar bill, I guess."

Less than a week before Carol's ship was scheduled to sail, The Peter Pan Club held a party in honor of Cathy's third birthday. It was a fine occasion of ice cream and cake for "tea," as well as the usual fare of bread and meat paste, bread and jam, and cups of a bright fluid that was the English equivalent of Kool-Aid. Warren and Carol stood together on the sidelines, smiling at their happy daughter as if to promise her that one way or another they would always be her parents.

"So you'll be here alone with us for a while, Mr. Mathews," said Marjorie Blaine, who ran the nursery school. She was a trim, chain-smoking woman of forty or so, long divorced, and Warren had noticed a few times that she wasn't bad. "You must come round to our pub," she said. "Do you know Finch's, in the Fulham Road? It's rather a scruffy little pub, actually, but all sorts of nice people go there."

And he told her he would be sure to drop by.

Then it was the day of the sailing, and Warren accompanied his wife and child as far as the railroad station and the gate to the boat train.

"Isn't Daddy coming?" Cathy asked, looking frightened.

"It's all right, dear," Carol told her. "We have to leave Daddy here for now, but you'll see him again very soon." And they walked quickly away into the enclosing crowd.

One of the presents given to Cathy at the party was a cardboard music box with a jolly yellow duck and a birthday-card message on the front, and with a little crank on one side: when you turned the crank it played a tinny rendition of "Happy Birthday to You." And when Warren came back to the flat that night he found it, among several other cheap, forgotten toys, on the floor beneath Cathy's stripped bed. He played it once or twice as he sat drinking whiskey over the strewn books and papers on his desk; then, with a child's sense of pointless experiment, he turned the crank the other way and played it backwards, slowly. And once he'd begun doing that he found he couldn't stop, or didn't want to, because the dim, rude little melody it made suggested all the loss and loneliness in the world.

RICHARD YATES

> Dum *dee* dum da da-da
> Dum *dee* dum da da-da . . .

He was tall and very thin and always aware of how ungainly he must look, even when nobody was there to see—even when the whole of his life had come down to sitting alone and fooling with a cardboard toy, three thousand miles from home. It was March of 1953, and he was twenty-seven years old.

"Oh, you poor man," Judith said when she came down for her bath in the morning. "It's so *sad* to find you all alone here. You must miss them terribly."

"Yeah, well, it'll only be a few months."

"Well, but that's awful. Isn't there someone who could sort of look after you? Didn't you and Carol meet any young people who might be company for you?"

"Oh, sure, we met a few people," he said, "but nobody I'd want to—you know, nobody I'd especially want to have around or anything."

"Well then, you ought to get out and make *new* friends."

Soon after the first of April, as was her custom, Judith went to live in her cottage in Sussex, where she would stay until September. She would make occasional visits back to town for a few days, she explained to Warren, but "Don't worry; I'll always be sure to ring you up well in advance before I sort of *descend* on you again."

And so he was truly alone. He went to the pub called Finch's one night with a vague idea of persuading Marjorie Blaine to come home with him and then of having her in his own and Carol's bed. And he found her alone at the crowded bar, but she looked old and fuddled with drink.

"Oh, I say, Mr. Mathews," she said. "Do come and join me."

"Warren," he said.

"What?"

"People call me Warren."

"Ah. Yes, well, this is England, you see; we're all dreadfully formal here." And a little later she said "I've never quite understood what it is you do, Mr. Mathews."

"Well, I'm on a Fulbright," he said. "It's an American scholarship program for students overseas. The government pays your way, and you—"

"Yes, well of course America *is* quite good about that sort of thing, isn't it. And I should imagine you must have a very clever mind." She gave him a flickering glance. "People who haven't lived often do." Then she cringed, to pantomime evasion of a blow. "Sorry," she said quickly; "sorry I said that." But she brightened at once. "Sarah!" she called. "Sarah, do come and meet young Mr. Mathews, who wants to be called Warren."

A tall, pretty girl turned from a group of other drinkers to smile at him, extending her hand, but when Marjorie Blaine said "He's an American," the girl's smile froze and her hand fell.

"Oh," she said. "How nice." And she turned away again.

It wasn't a good time to be an American in London. Eisenhower had been elected and the Rosenbergs killed; Joseph McCarthy was on the rise, and the war in Korea, with its reluctant contingent of British troops, had come to seem as if it might last forever. Still, Warren Mathews suspected that even in the best of times he would feel alien and homesick here. The very English language, as spoken by natives, bore so little relation to his own that there were far too many opportunities for missed points in every exchange. Nothing was clear.

He went on trying, but even on better nights, in happier pubs than Finch's and in the company of more agreeable strangers, he found only a slight lessening of discomfort—and he found no attractive, unattached girls. The girls, whether blandly or maddeningly pretty, were always fastened to the arms of men whose relentlessly witty talk could leave him smiling in bafflement. And he was dismayed to find how many of these people's innuendoes, winked or shouted, dwelt on the humorous aspects of homosexuality. Was all of England obsessed with that topic? Or did it haunt only this quiet, "interesting" part of London where Chelsea met South Kensington along the Fulham Road?

Then one night he took a late bus for Piccadilly Circus. "What do you want to go *there* for?" Carol would have said, and almost half the ride was over before he realized that he didn't have to answer questions like that anymore.

In 1945, as a boy on his first furlough from the Army after the war, he had been astonished at the nightly promenade of prostitutes then called Piccadilly Commandos, and there had been an unforgettable quickening of his blood as he watched them walk and turn, walk and turn again: girls for sale. They seemed to have become a laughingstock among more sophisticated soldiers, some of whom liked to slump against buildings and flip big English pennies onto the sidewalk at their feet as they passed, but Warren had longed for the courage to defy that mockery. He'd wanted to choose a girl and buy her and have her, however she might turn out to be, and he'd despised himself for letting the whole two weeks of his leave run out without doing so.

He knew that a modified version of that spectacle had still been going on as recently as last fall, because he and Carol had seen it on their way to some West End theater. "Oh, I don't believe this," Carol said. "Are they really all whores? This is the saddest thing I've ever seen."

There had lately been newspaper items about the pressing need to "clean up Piccadilly" before the impending Coronation, but the police must have been lax in their efforts so far, because the girls were very much there.

Most of them were young, with heavily made-up faces; they wore bright clothes in the colors of candy and Easter eggs, and they either walked and turned or stood waiting in the shadows. It took him three straight whiskeys to work up the nerve, and even then he wasn't sure of himself. He knew he looked shabby—he was wearing a gray suit coat with old Army pants, and his shoes were almost ready to be thrown away—but no clothes in the world would have kept him from feeling naked as he made a quick choice from among four girls standing along Shaftesbury Avenue and went up to her and said "Are you free?"

"Am I free?" she said, meeting his eyes for less than a second. "Honey, I've been free all my life."

The first thing she wanted him to agree on, before they'd walked half a block, was her price—steep, but within his means; then she asked if he would mind taking a short cab ride. And in the cab she explained that she never used the cheap hotels and rooming houses around here, as most of the other girls did, because she had a six-month-old daughter and didn't like to leave her for long.

"I don't blame you," he said. "I have a daughter too."

And he instantly wondered why he'd felt it necessary to tell her that.

"Oh yeah? So where's your wife?"

"Back in New York."

"You divorced then, or what?"

"Well, separated."

"Oh yeah? That's too bad."

They rode in an awkward silence for a while until she said "Listen, it's all right if you want to kiss me or anything, but no big feely-feely in the cab, okay? I really don't go for that."

And only then, kissing her, did he begin to find out what she was like. She wore her bright yellow hair in ringlets around her face—it was illuminated and darkened again with each passing streetlamp; her eyes were pleasant despite all the mascara; her mouth was nice; and though he tried no big feely-feely his hands were quick to discover she was slender and firm.

It wasn't a short cab ride—it went on until Warren began to wonder if it might stop only when they met a waiting group of hoodlums who would haul him out of the back seat and beat him up and rob him and take off in the cab with the girl—but it came to an end at last on a silent city block in what he guessed was the northeast of London. She took him into a house that looked rude but peaceful in the moonlight; then she said "Shh," and they tiptoed down a creaking linoleum corridor and into her room, where she switched on a light and closed the door behind them.

She checked the baby, who lay small and still and covered-up in the center of a big yellow crib against one wall. Along the facing wall, not six feet away, stood the reasonably fresh-looking double bed in which Warren was expected to take his pleasure.

"I just like to make sure she's breathing," the girl explained, turning back from the crib; then she watched him count out the right number of pound and ten-shilling notes on the top of her dresser. She turned off the ceiling light but left a small one on at the bedside as she began to undress, and he managed to watch her while nervously taking off his own clothes. Except that her cotton-knit underpants looked pitifully cheap, that her brown pubic hair gave the lie to her blond head, that her legs were short and her knees a little thick, she was all right. And she was certainly young.

"Do you ever enjoy this?" he asked when they were clumsily in bed together.

"Huh? How do you mean?"

"Well, just—you know—after a while it must get so you can't really—" and he stopped there in a paralysis of embarrassment.

"Oh, no," she assured him. "Well, I mean it depends on the *guy* a lot, but I'm not—I'm not a block of ice or anything. You'll find out."

And so, in wholly unexpected grace and nourishment, she became a real girl for him.

Her name was Christine Phillips and she was twenty-two. She came from Glasgow, and she'd been in London for four years. He knew it would be gullible to believe everything she told him when they sat up later that night over cigarettes and a warm quart bottle of beer; still, he wanted to keep an open mind. And if much of what she said was predictable stuff—she explained, for example, that she wouldn't have to be on the street at all if she were willing to take a job as a "hostess" in a "club," but that she'd turned down many such offers because "all those places are clip joints"—there were other, unguarded remarks that could make his arm tighten around her in tenderness, as when she said she had named her baby Laura "because I've always thought that's the most beautiful girl's name in the world. Don't you?"

And he began to understand why there was scarcely a trace of Scotch or English accent in her speech: she must have known so many Americans, soldiers and sailors and random civilian strays, that they had invaded and plundered her language.

"So what do you do for a living, Warren?" she asked. "You get money from home?"

"Well, sort of." And he explained, once again, about the Fulbright program.

"Yeah?" she said. "You have to be smart for that?"

"Oh, not necessarily. You don't have to be very smart for anything in America anymore."

"You kidding me?"

"Not wholly."

"Huh?"

"I mean I'm only kidding you a little."

And after a thoughtful pause she said "Well, I wish *I* could've had more schooling. I wish I was smart enough to write a book, because I'd have a hell of a book to write. Know what I'd call it?" She narrowed her eyes, and her fingers sketched a suggestion of formal lettering in the air. "I'd call it *This Is Piccadilly.* Because I mean people don't really *know* what goes on. Ah, Jesus, I could tell you things that'd make your—well, never mind. Skip it."

". . . Hey, Christine?" he said later still, when they were back in bed.

"Uh-huh?"

"Want to tell each other the stories of our lives?"

"Okay," she said with a child's eagerness, and so he

had to explain again, shyly, that he was only kidding her a little.

The baby's cry woke them both at six in the morning, but Christine got up and told him he could go back to sleep for a while. When he awoke again he was alone in the room, which smelled faintly of cosmetics and piss. He could hear several women talking and laughing nearby, and he didn't know what he was expected to do but get up and dressed and find his way out of here.

Then Christine came to the door and asked if he would like a cup of tea. "Whyn't you come on out, if you're ready," she said as she carefully handed him the hot mug, "and meet my friends, okay?"

And he followed her into a combination kitchen and living room whose windows overlooked a weed-grown vacant lot. A stubby woman in her thirties stood working at an ironing board with the electrical cord plugged into a ceiling fixture, and another girl of about Christine's age lay back in an easy chair, wearing a knee-length robe and slippers, with her bare, pretty legs ablaze in morning sunlight. A gas fireplace hissed beneath a framed oval mirror, and the good smells of steam and tea were everywhere.

"Warren, this is Grace Arnold," Christine said of the woman at the ironing board, who looked up to say she was pleased to meet him, "and this is Amy." Amy licked her lips and smiled and said "Hi."

"You'll probably meet the kids in a minute," Christine told him. "Grace has six kids. Grace and *Alfred* do, I mean. Alfred's the man of the house."

And very gradually, as he sipped and listened, mustering appropriate nods and smiles and inquiries, Warren was able to piece the facts together. Alfred Arnold was an interior housepainter, or rather a "painter and decorator." He and his wife, with all those children to raise, made ends meet by renting out rooms to Christine and Amy in full knowledge of how both girls earned their living, and so they had all become a kind of family.

How many polite, nervous men had sat on this sofa in the mornings, watching the whisk and glide of Grace Arnold's iron, helplessly intrigued with the sunny spectacle of Amy's legs, hearing the talk of these three women and wondering how soon it would be all right to leave? But Warren Mathews had nothing to go home to, so he began to hope this pleasant social occasion might last.

"You've a nice name, Warren," Amy told him, crossing her legs. "I've always liked that name."

"Warren?" Christine said. "Can you stay and have something to eat with us?"

Soon there was a fried egg on buttered toast for each of them, served with more tea around a clean kitchen table, and they all ate as daintily as if they were in a public place. Christine sat beside him, and once during the meal she gave his free hand a shy little squeeze.

"If you don't have to rush off," she said, while Grace was stacking the dishes, "we can get a beer. The pub'll be open in half an hour."

"Good," he said. "Fine." Because the last thing he wanted to do was rush off, even when all six children came clamoring in from their morning's play down the street, each of them in turn wanting to sit on his lap and poke fun at him and run jam-stained fingers through his hair. They were a shrill, rowdy crowd, and they all glowed with health. The oldest was a bright girl named Jane who looked oddly like a Negro—light-skinned, but with African features and hair—and who giggled as she backed away from him and said "Are you Christine's fella?"

"I sure am," he told her.

And he did feel very much like Christine's fella when he took her out alone to the pub around the corner. He liked the way she walked—she didn't look anything at all like a prostitute in her fresh tan raincoat with the collar turned up around her cheeks—and he liked her sitting close beside him on a leather bench against the wall of an old brown room where everything, even the mote-filled shafts of sunlight, seemed to be steeped in beer.

"Look, Warren," she said after a while, turning her bright glass on the table. "Do you want to stay over another night?"

"Well, no, I really—the thing is I can't afford it."

"Oh, I didn't mean that," she said, and squeezed his hand again. "I didn't mean for money. I meant—just stay. Because I want you to."

Nobody had to tell him what a triumph of masculinity it was to have a young whore offer herself to you free of charge. He didn't even need *From Here to Eternity* to tell him that, though he would always remember how that novel came quickly to mind as he drew her face up closer to his own. She had made him feel profoundly strong. "Oh, that's nice," he said huskily, and he kissed her. Then, just before kissing her again, he said "Oh, that's awfully nice, Christine."

And they both made frequent use of the word "nice" all afternoon. Christine seemed unable to keep away from him except for brief intervals when she had to attend to the baby; once, when Warren was alone in the living room, she came dancing slowly and dreamily across the floor, as if to the sound of violins, and fell into his arms like a girl in the movies. Another time, curled fast against him on the sofa, she softly crooned a popular song called "Unforgettable" to him, with a significant dipping of her eyelashes over the title word whenever the lyrics brought it around.

"Oh, you're nice, Warren," she kept saying. "You know that? You're really nice."

And he would tell her, again and again, how nice she was too.

When Alfred Arnold came home from work—a compact and tired and bashfully agreeable-looking man—his wife and young Amy were quick to busy themselves in the ritual of making him welcome: taking his coat, readying his chair, bringing his glass of gin. But Christine held back, clinging to Warren's arm, until the time came to take him up for a formal introduction to the man of the house.

"Pleased to meet you, Warren," Alfred Arnold said. "Make yourself at home."

There was corned beef with boiled potatoes for supper, which everyone said was very good, and in the afterglow Alfred fell to reminiscing in a laconic way about his time as prisoner of war in Burma. "Four years," he said, displaying the fingers of one hand with only the thumb held down. "Four years."

And Warren said it must have been terrible.

"Alfred?" Grace said. "Show Warren your citation."

"Oh, no, love; nobody wants to bother with that."

"Show him," she insisted.

And Alfred gave in. A thick black wallet was shyly withdrawn from his hip pocket; then from one of its depths came a stained, much-folded piece of paper. It was almost falling apart at the creases, but the typewritten message was clear: it conveyed the British Army's

recognition that Private A. J. Arnold, while a prisoner of
war of the Japanese in Burma, had been commended by
his captors as a good and steady worker on the construc-
tion of a railroad bridge in 1944.

"Well," Warren said. "That's fine."

"Ah, you know the women," Alfred confided, tucking
the paper back where it came from. "The women always
want you to show this stuff around. I'd rather forget the
whole bloody business."

Christine and Warren managed to make an early escape, under Grace Arnold's winking smile, and as soon
as the bedroom door was shut they were clasped and
writhing and breathing heavily, eager and solemn in lust.
The shedding of their clothes took no time at all but
seemed a terrible hindrance and delay; then they were
deep in bed and reveling in each other, and then they
were joined again.

"Oh, Warren," she said. "Oh, God. Oh, Warren. Oh,
I love you."

And he heard himself saying more than once, more
times than he cared to believe or remember, that he
loved her too.

Sometime after midnight, as they lay quiet, he wondered how those words could have spilled so easily and
often from his mouth. And at about the same time, when
Christine began talking again, he became aware that
she'd had a lot to drink. A quarter-full bottle of gin stood
on the floor beside the bed, with two cloudy, finger-
printed glasses to prove they had both made ample use
of it, but she seemed to be well ahead of him now. Pour-
ing herself still another one, she sat back in comfort
against the pillows and the wall and talked in a way that
suggested she was carefully composing each sentence for

dramatic effect, like a little girl pretending to be an actress.

"You know something, Warren? Everything I ever wanted was taken away from me. All my life. When I was eleven I wanted a bicycle more than anything in the world, and my father finally bought me one. Oh, it was only second-hand and cheap, but I loved it. And then that same summer he got mad and wanted to punish me for something—I can't even remember what—and he took it away. I never saw it again."

"Yeah, well, that must've felt bad," Warren said, but then he tried to steer the talk along less sentimental lines. "What kind of work does your father do?"

"Oh, he's a pen-pusher. For the gas works. We don't get along at all, and I don't get along with my mother either. I never go home. No, but it's true what I said: everything I ever wanted was—you know—taken away from me." She paused there, as if to bring her stage voice back under control, and when she began to speak again, with greater confidence, it was in the low, hushed tones appropriate for an intimate audience of one.

"Warren? Would you like to hear about Adrian? Laura's father? Because I'd really like to tell you, if you're interested."

"Sure."

"Well, Adrian's an American Army officer. A young major. Or maybe he's a lieutenant colonel by now, wherever he is. I don't even know where he is, and the funny part is I don't care. I really don't care at all anymore. But Adrian and I had a wonderful time until I told him I was pregnant; then he froze up. He just froze up. Oh, I suppose I didn't really think he'd ask me to marry him or anything—he had this rich society girl waiting for him back in the States; I knew that. But he got very cold and he told me to get an abortion, and I said no. I said 'I'm going to have this baby, Adrian.' And he said 'All right.' He said 'All right, but you're on your own, Christine. You'll have to raise this child any way you can.' That was when I decided to go and see his commanding officer."

"His commanding officer?"

"Well, *somebody* had to help," she said. "*Somebody* had to make him see his responsibility. And God, I'll never forget that day. The regimental commander was this very dignified man named Colonel Masters, and he just sat there behind his desk and looked at me and listened, and he nodded a few times. Adrian was there with me, not saying a word; there were just the three of us in the office. And in the end Colonel Masters said 'Well, Miss Phillips, as far as I can see it comes down to this. You made a mistake. You made a mistake, and you'll have to live with it.'"

"Yeah," Warren said uneasily. "Yeah, well, that must've been—"

But he didn't have to finish that sentence, or to say anything else that might let her know he hadn't believed a word of the story, because she was crying. She had drawn up her knees and laid the side of her rumpled head on them as the sobs began; then she set her empty glass carefully on the floor, slid back into bed, and turned away from him, crying and crying.

"Hey, come on," he said. "Come on, baby, don't cry." And there was nothing to do but turn her around and take her in his arms until she was still.

After a long time she said "Is there any more gin?"

"Some."

"Well, listen, let's finish it, okay? Grace won't mind, or if she wants me to pay her for it I'll *pay* her for it."

In the morning, with her face so swollen from emotion

and sleep that she tried to hide it with her fingers, she said "Jesus. I guess I got pretty drunk last night."

"That's okay; we both drank a lot."

"Well, I'm sorry," she said in the impatient, almost defiant way of people accustomed to making frequent apologies. "I'm sorry." She had taken care of the baby and was walking unsteadily around the little room in a drab green bathrobe. "Anyway, listen. Will you come back, Warren?"

"Sure. I'll call you, okay?"

"No, there's no telephone here. But will you come back soon?" She followed him out to the front door, where he turned to see the limpid appeal in her eyes. "If you come in the daytime," she said, "I'll always be home."

For a few days, idling at his desk or wandering the streets and the park in the first real spring weather of the year, Warren found it impossible to keep his mind on anything but Christine. Nothing like this could ever have been expected to happen in his life: a young Scotch prostitute in love with him. With a high, fine confidence that wasn't at all characteristic of him, he had begun to see himself as a rare and privileged adventurer of the heart. Memories of Christine in his arms whispering "Oh, I love you" made him smile like a fool in the sunshine, and at other moments he found a different, subtler pleasure in considering all the pathetic things about her —the humorless ignorance, the cheap, drooping underwear, the drunken crying. Even her story of "Adrian" (a name almost certainly lifted from a women's magazine) was easy to forgive—or would be, once he'd found some wise and gentle way of letting her know he knew it wasn't true. He might eventually have to find a way of telling her he hadn't really meant to say he loved her, too, but all that could wait. There was no hurry, and the season was spring.

"Know what I like most about you, Warren?" she asked very late in their third or fourth night together. "Know what I really love about you? It's that I feel I can trust you. All my life, that's all I ever wanted: somebody to trust. And you see I keep making mistakes and making mistakes because I trust people who turn out to be—"

"Shh, shh," he said, "it's okay, baby. Let's just sleep now."

"Well, but wait a second. Listen a minute, okay? Because I really do want to tell you something, Warren. I knew this boy Jack. He kept saying he wanted to marry me and everything, but this was the trouble: Jack's a gambler. He'll always be a gambler. And I suppose you can guess what that meant."

"What'd it mean?"

"It meant money, that's what it meant. Staking him, covering his losses, helping him get through the month until payday—ah, Christ, it makes me sick just to think of all that now. For almost a year. And do you know how much of it I ever got back? Well, you won't believe this, but I'll tell you. Or no, wait—I'll show you. Wait a second."

She got up and stumbled and switched on the ceiling light in an explosion of brilliance that startled the baby, who whimpered in her sleep. "It's okay, Laura," Christine said softly as she rummaged in the top drawer of her dresser; then she found what she was looking for and brought it back to the bed. "Here," she said. "Look. Read this."

It was a single sheet of cheap ruled paper torn from a

tablet of the kind meant for school children, and it bore
no date.

> Dear Miss Phillips:
>
> Enclosed is the sum of two pounds ten shillings.
> This is all I can afford now and there will be no more
> as I am being shipped back to the U.S. next week for
> discharge and separation from the service.
>
> My Commanding Officer says you telephoned him
> four times last month and three times this month
> and this must stop as he is a busy man and can not
> be bothered with calls of this kind. Do not call him
> again, or the 1st Sgt. either, or anyone else in this
> organization.
>
> Pfc. John F. Curtis

"Isn't that the damnedest thing?" Christine said. "I
mean really, Warren, isn't that the God damnedest
thing?"

"Sure is." And he read it over again. It was the sentence beginning "My Commanding Officer" that seemed
to give it all away, demolishing "Adrian" at a glance and
leaving little doubt in Warren's mind that John F. Curtis
had fathered her child.

"Could you turn the light off now, Christine?" he said,
handing the letter back to her.

"Sure, honey. I just wanted you to see that." And she
had undoubtedly wanted to see if he'd be dumb enough
to swallow the story too.

When the room was dark again and she lay curled
against his back, he silently prepared a quiet, reasonable
speech. He would say Baby, don't get mad, but listen.
You mustn't try to put these stories over on me anymore.

I didn't believe the one about Adrian and I don't believe Jack the Gambler either, so how about cutting this stuff out? Wouldn't it be better if we could sort of try to tell each other the truth?

What stopped his mouth, on thinking it over, was that to say all that would humiliate her into wrath. She'd be out of bed and shouting in an instant, reviling him in the ugliest language of her trade until long after the baby woke up crying, and then there would be nothing but wreckage.

There might still be an appropriate moment for inquiring into her truthfulness—there would have to be, and soon—but whether it made him feel cowardly or not he had to acknowledge, as he lay facing the wall with her sweet arm around his ribs, that this wasn't the time.

A few nights later, at home, he answered the phone and was startled to hear her voice: "Hi, honey."

"Christine? Well, hi, but how'd you—how'd you get this number?"

"You gave it to me. Don't you remember? You wrote it down."

"Oh, yeah, sure," he said, smiling foolishly into the mouthpiece, but this was alarming. The phone here in the basement flat was only an extension of Judith's phone upstairs. They rang simultaneously, and when Judith was home she always picked up her receiver on the first or second ring.

"So listen," Christine was saying. "Can you come over Thursday instead of Friday? Because it's Jane's birthday and we're having a party. She'll be nine. . . ."

After he'd hung up he sat hunched for a long time in the attitude of a man turning over grave and secret questions in his mind. How could he have been dumb enough to give her Judith's number? And soon he remembered something else, a second dumb thing that brought him to his feet for an intense, dramatic pacing of the floor: she knew his address too. Once in the pub he had run out of cash and been unable to pay for all the beer, so he'd given Christine a check to cover it.

"Most customers find it's a convenience to have their street addresses printed beneath their names on each check," an assistant bank manager had explained when Warren and Carol opened their checking account last year. "Shall I order them that way for you?"

"Sure, I guess so," Carol had said. "Why not?"

He was almost all the way to the Arnolds' house on Thursday before he realized he'd forgotten to buy a present for Jane. But he found a sweetshop and kept telling the girl at the counter to scoop more and more assorted hard candies into a paper bag until he had a heavy bundle of the stuff that he could only hope might be of passing interest to a nine-year-old.

And whether it was or not, Jane's party turned out to be a profound success. There were children all over that bright, ramshackle apartment, and when the time came for them to be seated at the table—three tables shoved together—Warren stood back smiling and watching with his arm around Christine, thinking of that other party at The Peter Pan Club. Alfred came home from work with a giant stuffed panda bear that he pressed into Jane's arms, laughing and then crouching to receive her long and heartfelt hug. But soon Jane was obliged to bring her delirium under control because the cake was set before her. She frowned, closed her eyes, made a wish, and blew out all nine candles in a single heroic breath as the room erupted into full-throated cheers.

There was plenty to drink for the grownups after that, even before the last of the party guests had gone home and all the Arnold children were in bed. Christine left the room to put her baby down for the night, carrying a drink along with her. Grace had begun fixing supper with apparent reluctance, and when Alfred excused himself to have a bit of a rest she turned the gas burners down very low and abandoned the stove to join him.

That left Warren alone with Amy, who stood meticulously applying her makeup at the oval mirror above the mantelpiece. She was really a lot better looking than Christine, he decided as he sat on the sofa with a drink in his hand, watching her. She was tall and long-legged and flawlessly graceful, with a firm slender ass that made you ache to clasp it and with plump, pointed little breasts. Her dark hair hung to her shoulderblades, and this evening she had chosen to wear a narrow black skirt with a peach-colored blouse. She was a proud and lovely girl, and he didn't want to think about the total stranger who would have her for money at the end of the night.

Amy had finished with her eyes and begun to work on her mouth, drawing the lipstick slowly along the yielding shape of each full lip until it glistened like marzipan, then pouting so that one lip could caress and rub the other, then parting them to inspect her perfect young teeth for possible traces of red. When she was finished, when she'd put all her implements back into a little plastic case and snapped it shut, she continued to stand at the mirror for what seemed at least half a minute, doing nothing, and that was when Warren realized she knew he'd been staring at her in all this privacy and silence, all this time. At last she turned around in such a quick, high-shouldered way, and with such a look of bravery conquering fear, that it was as if he might be halfway across the floor to make a grab for her.

"You look very nice, Amy," he said from the sofa.

Her shoulders slackened then and she let out a breath of relief, but she didn't smile. "Jesus," she said. "You scared the shit out of me."

When she'd put on her coat and left the house, Christine came back into the room with the languorous, self-indulgent air of a girl who has found a good reason for staying home from work.

"Move over," she said, and sat close beside him. "How've you been?"

"Oh, okay. You?"

"Okay." She hesitated then, as if constrained by the difficulty of making small talk. "Seen any good movies?"

"No."

She took his hand and held it in both of her own. "You miss me?"

"I sure did."

"The hell you did." And she flung down his hand as if it were something vile. "I went around to your place the other night, to surprise you, and I saw you going in there with a girl."

"No you didn't," he told her. "Come on, Christine, you know you didn't do that at all. Why do you always want to tell me these—"

Her eyes narrowed in menace and her lips went flat. "You calling me a liar?"

"Oh, Jesus," he said, "don't be like that. Why do you want to be like that? Let's just drop it, okay?"

She seemed to be thinking it over. "Okay," she said. "Look: It was dark and I was across the street; I could've had the wrong house; it could've been somebody else I saw with the girl, so okay, we'll drop it. But I want to tell you something: Don't ever call me a liar, Warren. I'm warning you. Because I swear to God"—and she pointed emphatically toward her bedroom—"I swear on that baby's life I'm not a liar."

"Ah, look at the lovebirds," Grace Arnold called, appearing in the doorway with her arm around her husband. "Well, you're not making *me* jealous. Me and Alfred are lovebirds too, aren't we, love? Married all these years and still lovebirds."

There was supper then, much of it consisting of partly burned beans, and Grace held forth at length on the unforgettable night when she and Alfred had first met. There'd been a party; Alfred had come alone, all shy and strange and still wearing his army uniform, and from the moment Grace spotted him across the room she'd thought: Oh, him. Oh, yes, he's the one. They had danced for a while to some phonograph records, though Alfred wasn't much of a dancer; then they'd gone outside and sat together on a low stone wall and talked. Just talked.

"What'd we talk about, Alfred?" she asked, as if trying in vain to remember.

"Oh, I don't know, love," he said, pink with pleasure and embarrassment as he pushed his fork around in his beans. "Don't suppose it could've been much."

And Grace turned back to address her other listeners in a lowered, intimate voice. "We talked about—well, about everything and nothing," she said. "You know how that can be? It was like we both knew—you know? —like we both knew we were made for each other." This last statement seemed a little sentimental even for Grace's taste, and she broke off with a laugh. "Oh, and the funny part," she said, laughing, "the funny part was, these friends of mine left the party a little after we did because they were going to the pictures? So they went up

to the pictures and stayed for the whole show, then they
went round to the pub afterwards and stayed there till
closing time, and it was practically morning when they
came back down that same road and found me and Alfred still sitting on the wall, still talking. Ah, God, they
still tease me about that, my friends do when I see them,
even now. They say 'Whatever were you two *talking*
about, Grace?' And I just laugh. I say 'Oh, never mind.
We were talking, that's all.' "

A respectful hush fell around the table.

"Isn't that wonderful?" Christine asked quietly. "Isn't
it wonderful when two people can just—find each other
that way?"

And Warren said it certainly was.

Later that night, when he and Christine sat naked on
the edge of her bed to drink, she said "Well, I'll tell you
one thing, anyway: I wouldn't half mind having Grace's
life. The part of it that came *after* she met Alfred, I mean;
not the part before." And after a pause she said "I don't
suppose you'd ever guess it, from the way she acts now
—I don't suppose you'd ever guess she was a Piccadilly
girl herself."

"Was she?"

"Ha, 'was she.' You better bet she was. For years, back
during the war. Got into it because she didn't know any
better, like all the rest of us; then she had Jane and didn't
know how to get out." And Christine gave him a little
glancing smile with a wink in it. "Nobody knows where
Jane came from."

"Oh." And if Jane was nine years old today it meant
she had been conceived and born in a time when tens of
thousands of American Negro soldiers were quartered in
England and said to be having their way with English
girls, provoking white troops into fights and riots that

ended only when everything went under in the vast upheaval of the Normandy Invasion. Alfred Arnold would still have been a prisoner in Burma then, with well over a year to wait for his release.

"Oh, she's never tried to deny it," Christine said. "She's never lied about it; give her credit for that. Alfred knew what he was getting, right from the start. She probably even told him that first night they met, because she would've known she couldn't hide it—or maybe he knew already because maybe that whole *party* was Piccadilly girls; I don't know. But I know he knew. He took her off the street and he married her, and he adopted her child. You don't find very many men like that. And I mean Grace is my best friend and she's done a lot for me, but sometimes she acts like she doesn't even know how lucky she is. Sometimes—oh, not tonight; she was showing off for you tonight—but sometimes she treats Alfred like dirt. Can you imagine that? A man like Alfred? That really pisses me off."

She reached down to fill their glasses, and by the time she'd settled back to sip he knew what his own next move would have to be.

"Well, so I guess you're sort of looking for a husband too, aren't you, baby," he said. "That's certainly understandable, and I'd like you to know I wish I could—you know—ask you to marry me, but the fact is I can't. Just can't."

"Sure," she said quietly, looking down at an unlighted cigarette in her fingers. "That's okay; forget it."

And he was pleased with the way this last exchange had turned out—even with the whopping lie of the "wish" in his part of it. His bewildering, hazardous advance into this strange girl's life was over, and now he could prepare for an orderly withdrawal. "I know you'll find the right guy, Christine," he told her, warm in the kindness of his own voice, "and it's bound to happen soon because you're such a nice girl. In the meantime, I want you to know that I'll always—"

"Look, I said *forget* it, okay? Jesus Christ, do you think *I* care? You think I give a shit about you? Listen." She was on her feet, naked and strong in the dim light, wagging one stiff forefinger an inch away from his wincing face. "Listen, skinny. I can get anybody I want, any time, and you better get that straight. You're only here because I felt sorry for you, and you better get that straight too."

"Felt sorry for me?"

"Well, *sure,* with all that sorrowful shit about your wife taking off, and your little girl. I felt sorry for you and I thought Well, why not? That's my trouble; I never learn. Sooner or later I always think Why not? and then I'm shit outa luck. Listen: Do you have any idea how much money I could've made all this time? Huh? No, you never even thought about that part of it, didja. Oh, no, you were all hearts and flowers and sweet-talk and bullshit, weren't-cha. Well, you know what I think you are? I think you're a ponce."

"What's a 'ponce'?"

"I don't know what it is where you come from," she said, "but in this country it's a man who lives off the earnings of a—ah, never mind. The hell with it. Fuck it. I'm tired. Move over, okay? Because I mean if all we're gonna do is sleep, let's sleep."

But instead of moving over he got up in the silent, trembling dignity of an insulted man and began to put his clothes on. She seemed either not to notice or not to care what he was doing as she went heavily back to bed, but before very long, when he was buttoning his shirt, he could tell she was watching him and ready to apologize.

"Warren?" she said in a small, fearful voice. "Don't go. I'm sorry I called you that, and I'll never say it again. Just please come back and stay with me, okay?"

That was enough to make his fingers pause in the fastening of shirt buttons; then, soon, it was enough to make him begin unfastening them again. Leaving now, with nothing settled, might easily be worse than staying. Besides, there was an undeniable advantage in being seen as a man big enough to be capable of forgiveness.

". . . Oh," she said when he was back in bed. "Oh, this is better. This is better. Oh, come closer and let me— there. There. Oh. Oh, I don't think anybody in the whole world ever wants to be alone at night. Do you?"

It was a fragile, pleasant truce that lasted well into the morning, when he made an agreeable if nervous departure.

But all the way home on the Underground he regretted having made no final statement to her. He went over the openings of several final statements in his mind as he rode—"Look, Christine, I don't think this is working out at all. . . ." or "Baby, if you're going to think of me as a ponce, and stuff like that, I think it's about time we . . ."—until he realized, from the uneasy, quickly averted glances of other passengers on the train, that he was moving his lips and making small, reasonable gestures with his hands.

"Warren?" said Judith's old, melodious voice on the telephone that afternoon, calling from Sussex. "I thought I might run up to town on Tuesday and stay for a week or two. Would that be a terrible nuisance for you?"

He told her not to be silly and said he'd be looking

forward to it, but he'd scarcely hung up the phone before it rang again and Christine said "Hi, honey."

"Oh, hi. How are you?"

"Well, okay, except I wasn't very nice to you last night. I get that way sometimes. I know it's awful, but I do. Can I make it up to you, though? Can you come over Tuesday night?"

"Well, I don't know, Christine, I've been thinking. Maybe we'd better sort of—"

Her voice changed. "You coming or not?"

He let her wait through a second or two of silence before he agreed to go—and he agreed then only because he knew it would be better to make his final statement in person than on the phone.

He wouldn't spend the night. He would stay only as long as it took to make himself clear to her; if the house were crowded he would take her around to the pub, where they could talk privately. And he resolved not to rehearse any more speeches: he would find the right words when the time came, and the right tone.

But apart from its having to be final, the most important thing about his statement—the dizzyingly difficult thing—was that it would have to be nice. If it wasn't, if it left her resentful, there might be any amount of trouble later on the phone—a risk that could no longer be taken, with Judith home—and there might be worse events even than that. He could picture Christine and himself as Judith's guests at afternoon tea in her sitting room ("Do bring your young friend along, Warren.") just as Carol and he had often been in the past. He could see Christine waiting for a conversational lull, then setting down her cup and saucer firmly, for emphasis, and saying "Listen, lady. I got news for you. You know what this big sweet nephew of yours is? Huh? Well, I'll tell you. He's a ponce."

He had planned to arrive well after supper, but they must have gotten a late start tonight because they were all still at the table, and Grace Arnold offered him a plate.

"No thanks," he said, but he sat down beside Christine anyway, with a drink, because it would have seemed rude not to.

"Christine?" he said. "When you've finished eating, want to come around to the pub with me for a while?"

"What for?" she asked with her mouth full.

"Because I want to talk to you."

"We can talk here."

"No we can't."

"So what's the big deal? We'll talk later, then."

And Warren felt his plans begin to slide away like sand.

Amy seemed to be in a wonderful mood that night. She laughed generously at everything Alfred and Warren said; she sang a chorus of "Unforgettable" with at least as much feeling as Christine had brought to it; she backed away into the middle of the room, stepped out of her shoes, and favored her audience with a neat, slow little hip-switching dance to the theme music of the movie *Moulin Rouge*.

"How come you're not going out tonight, Amy?" Christine inquired.

"Oh, I don't know; I don't feel like it. Sometimes all I want to do is stay home and be quiet."

"Alfred?" Grace called. "See if there's any lime juice, love, because if there's lime juice we can have gin and lime."

They found dance music on the radio and Grace

melted into Alfred's arms for an old-fashioned waltz. "I love a waltz," she explained. "I've always loved a waltz" —but it stopped abruptly when they waltzed into the ironing board and knocked it over, which struck everyone as the funniest thing they had ever seen.

Christine wanted to prove she could jitterbug, perhaps in rivalry with Amy's dance, but Warren made a clumsy partner for her: he hopped and shuffled and worked up a sweat and didn't really know how to send her whirling out to their arms' length and bring her whirling back, the way it was supposed to be done, so their performance too dissolved into awkwardness and laughter.

". . . Oh, isn't it nice that we're all such good friends," Grace Arnold said, earnestly breaking the seal on a new bottle of gin. "We can just be here and enjoy ourselves tonight and nothing else matters in the world as long as we're together, right?"

Right. Sometime later Alfred and Warren sat together on the sofa discussing points of difference and similarity in the British and American armies, a couple of old soldiers at peace; then Alfred excused himself to get another drink, and Amy sank smiling into the place he had left, lightly touching Warren's thigh with her fingertips to establish the opening of a new conversation.

"Amy," Christine said from across the room. "Take your hands off Warren or I'll kill you."

And everything went bad after that. Amy sprang to her feet in heated denial of any wrongdoing, Christine's rebuttal was loud and foul, Grace and Alfred stood with the weak smiles of spectators at a street accident, and Warren wanted to evaporate.

"You're *always* doing that," Christine shouted. "Ever since I got you *into* this house you've been waving it around and rubbing it up against every man I bring home. You're cheap; you're a tart; you're a little slut."

"And you're a *whore*," Amy cried, just before bursting into tears. She lurched for the door then, but didn't make it: she was obliged to turn back with her fist in her mouth, her eyes bright with terror, in order to witness what Christine was saying to Grace Arnold.

"All right, Grace, listen." Christine's voice was high and perilously steady. "You're my best friend and you always will be, but you've got to make a choice. It's her or me. I mean it. Because I swear on that baby's life"— and one arm made a theatrical sweep in the direction of her bedroom—"I swear on that baby's life I'm not staying in this house another day if she stays too."

"Oh," Amy said, advancing on her. "Oh, that was a rotten thing to do. Oh, you're a filthy—"

And the two girls were suddenly locked in combat, wrestling and punching, or trying to punch, tearing clothes and pulling hair. Grace tried to separate them, a shrill, quivering referee, but she only got pummeled and pushed around herself until she fell down, and that was when Alfred Arnold moved in.

"Shit," he said. "Break it up. Break it *up*." He managed to pull Christine away from Amy's throat and shove her roughly aside, then he prevented Amy from any further action by throwing her down full-length on the sofa, where she covered her face and wept.

"Cows," Alfred said as he stumbled and righted himself. "Fucking cows."

"Put some coffee on," Grace suggested from the chair she had crawled to, and Alfred blundered to the stove and set a pan of water on the gas. He fumbled around for a bottle of instant-coffee syrup and put a spoonful of the stuff into each of five clean cups, breathing hard; then he began stalking the room with the wide and glittering eyes of a man who never thought his life would turn out like this.

"Fucking cows," he said again. "Cows." And with all his strength he smashed his right fist against the wall.

"Well, I knew Alfred was upset," Christine said later, when she and Warren were in bed, "but I didn't think he'd go and hurt his hand that way. That was awful."

"Can I come in?" Grace asked with a timid knock on the door, and she came in looking happy and disheveled. She was still wearing her dress but had evidently removed her garter belt, for her black nylon stockings had fallen into wrinkles around her ankles and her shoes. Her naked legs were pale and faintly hairy.

"How's Alfred's hand?" Christine inquired.

"Well, he's got it soaking in hot water," Grace said, "but he keeps taking it out and trying to put it in his mouth. He'll be all right. Anyway, listen, though, Christine. You're right about Amy. She's no good. I've known that ever since you brought her here. I didn't want to say anything because she was your friend, but that's the God's truth. And I just want you to know you're my favorite, Christine. You'll always be my favorite."

Lying and listening, with the bedclothes pulled up to his chin, Warren longed for the silence of home.

". . . Remember the time she lost all the dry-cleaning tickets and lied about it?"

"Oh, and remember when you and me were getting ready to go to the pictures that day?" Grace said. "And there wasn't time to fix sandwiches so we had egg on toast instead because it was quicker? And she kept hanging around saying 'What're you making *eggs* for?' She was so mad and jealous because we hadn't asked her to

come along to the pictures she was acting like a little
kid."

"Well, she *is* a little kid. She doesn't have any—doesn't
have any maturity at all."

"Right. You're absolutely right about that, Christine.
And I'll tell you what I've decided to do: I'll tell her first
thing in the morning. I'll simply say 'I'm sorry, Amy, but
you're no longer welcome in my home. . . .' "

Warren got out of the house before dawn and tried to
sleep in his own place, though he couldn't hope for more
than an hour or two because he had to be up and dressed
and smiling when Judith came down for her bath.

"I must say you're certainly *looking* well, Warren,"
Judith told him. "You look as calm and fit as a man
thoroughly in charge of his life. There isn't a *trace* of that
haggard quality that used to worry me about you sometimes."

"Oh?" he said. "Well, thanks, Judith. You're looking
very well too, but then of course you always do."

He knew the phone was going to ring, and he could
only hope it would be silent until noon. That was when
Judith went out to lunch—or, on days when she'd decided to economize, it was the time she went out to do
her modest grocery shopping. She would carry a string
bag around the neighborhood to be filled by deferen-
tial, admiring shopkeepers—Englishmen and women
schooled for generations to know a lady when they saw
one.

At noon, from the front windows, he watched her
stately old figure descend the steps and move slowly
down the street. And it seemed no more than a minute
after that when the phone burst into ringing, his nerves
making it sound much louder than it was.

"You sure took off in a hurry," Christine said.

"Yeah. Well, I couldn't sleep. How'd it go with Amy this morning?"

"Oh, that's okay now. That's all over. The three of us had a long talk, and in the end I talked Grace into letting her stay."

"Well, good. Still, I'm surprised she'd *want* to stay."

"Are you kidding? Amy? You think she has anywhere else to go? Jesus, if you think *Amy* has anywhere else to go you're outa your mind. And I mean you know me, Warren: I get all upset sometimes, but I couldn't ever just turn somebody out on the street." She paused, and he could hear the faint rhythmic click of her chewing gum. He hadn't known, until then, that she ever chewed gum.

For a moment it occurred to him that having her in this placid, rational, gum-chewing frame of mind might be his best opportunity yet for breaking off with her, over the telephone or not, but he hadn't quite organized his opening remarks before she was talking again.

"So listen, honey, I don't think I'll be able to see you for a while. Tonight's out, and tomorrow night too, and all through the weekend." And she gave a quietly harsh little laugh. "I've got to make *some* money, don't I?"

"Well, *sure,*" he said. "*Sure* you do; I know that." And not until those agreeable words were out of his mouth did he realize they were exactly the kind of thing a ponce might say.

"I might be able to come around to your place some afternoon, though," Christine suggested.

"No, don't do that," he said quickly. "I'm—I'm almost always out at the library in the afternoons."

They settled on an evening in the following week, at her place, at five; but something in her voice made him suspect even then that she wouldn't be there—that intentionally failing to keep this appointment would be her inarticulate way of getting rid of him, or at least of making a start at it: nobody's ponce could expect to last forever. And so, when the day and the hour came, he wasn't surprised to find her gone.

"Christine's not here, Warren," Grace Arnold explained, backing politely away from the door to let him come in. "She said to tell you she'd call. She had to go up to Scotland for a few days."

"Oh? Is there—trouble at home, then?"

"How do you mean 'trouble'?"

"Well, I just mean is there an—" And Warren found himself mouthing the same lame alibi that Carol and he had once agreed would be good enough for Judith, in what now seemed another life. "Is there an illness in her family, or something like that?"

"That's right, yes." Grace was visibly grateful for his help. "There's an illness in her family."

And he said he was sorry to hear it.

"Can I get you something, Warren?"

"No thanks. I'll see you, Grace." Turning to leave, he found that the words for a cool, final exit line were already forming themselves in his mind. But he hadn't yet reached the door when Alfred came in from work, looking embarrassed, with his forearm encased in a heavy plaster cast from the elbow to the tips of the splinted fingers and hung in a muslin sling.

"Jesus," Warren said, "that sure looks uncomfortable."

"Ah, you get used to it," Alfred said, "like everything else."

"Know how many bones he broke, Warren?" Grace asked, almost as if she were boasting. "Three. Three bones."

"Wow. Well, but how can you do any work, Alfred, with a hand like that?"

"Oh, well." And Alfred managed a small, self-deprecating smile. "They give me all the cushy jobs."

At the door, holding the knob in readiness, Warren turned back and said "Tell Christine I stopped by, Grace, okay? And you might tell her too that I don't believe a word of anything you said about Scotland. Oh, and if she wants to call me, tell her I said not to bother. So long."

Riding home, he kept assuring himself that he would probably never hear from Christine again. He might have wished for a more satisfactory conclusion; still, perhaps no satisfactory conclusion would ever have been possible. And he was increasingly pleased with the last thing he'd said: "If she wants to call me, tell her I said not to bother." That, under the circumstances, had been just the right message, delivered in just the right way.

It was very late at night when the phone rang the next time; Judith was almost certainly asleep, and Warren sprang to pick it up before it could wake her.

"Listen," Christine said, her voice empty of all affection and even of all civility, like that of an informer in a crime movie. "I'm just calling because this is something you ought to know. Alfred's mad at you. I mean really mad."

"He is? Why?"

And he could almost see the narrowing of her eyes and lips. "Because you called his wife a liar."

"Oh, come on. I don't believe—"

"You don't believe me? All right, wait and see. I'm just telling you for your own good. When a man like Alfred feels his wife has been insulted, that's trouble."

The next day was Sunday—the man of the house

would be home—and it took Warren most of the morning to decide that he'd better go there and talk to him. It seemed a silly thing to do, and he dreaded meeting Christine; still, once it was done he could put all of them out of his mind.

But he didn't have to go near the house. Turning the corner into the last block he met Alfred and the six children walking up the street, all dressed up for some Sunday outing, possibly to the zoo. Jane seemed glad to see him: she was holding Alfred's good left hand and wearing a bright pink ribbon in her African hair. "Hi, Warren," she said as the younger ones came to a stop and clustered around.

"Hi, Jane. You look really nice." And then he faced the man. "Alfred, I understand I owe you an apology."

"Apology? What for?"

"Well, Christine said you were angry with me for what I said to Grace."

Alfred looked puzzled, as if contemplating issues too complex and subtle ever to be sorted out. "No," he said. "No, there was nothing like that."

"Okay, then. Good. But I wanted to tell you I didn't mean any—you know."

With a slight grimace, Alfred hitched his cast into a better position in the sling. "Piece of advice for you, Warren," he said. "You don't ever want to listen to the women too much." And he winked like an old comrade.

When Christine called him again it was in a rush of girlish ebullience, as if nothing had ever gone wrong between them—but Warren would never know what brought about the change, nor ever need to weigh its truth or falsehood.

"Honey, listen," she said, "I think it's mostly all blown

over at home now—I mean he's all calmed down and everything—so if you want to come over tomorrow night, or the next night or whenever you can, we can have a nice—"

"Now, wait a minute," he told her. "You just listen to me a minute, sweetheart—oh, and by the way I think it's about time we cut out all the 'honey' and the 'sweetheart' stuff, don't you? Listen to me."

He had gotten to his feet for emphasis, standing his ground, with the telephone cord snaked tight across his shirt and his free hand clenched into a fist that shook as rhythmically in the air as that of an impassioned public speaker as he made his final statement.

"Listen to me. Alfred didn't even know what the hell I meant when I tried to apologize. Didn't even know what the hell I was talking about, do you understand me? All right. That's one thing. Here's the other thing. I've had enough. Don't be calling me anymore, Christine, do you understand me? Don't be *calling* me anymore."

"Okay, honey," she said in a quick, meek voice that was almost lost in the sound of her hanging up.

And he was still gripping the phone at his cheek, breathing hard, when he heard the slow and careful deposit of Judith's receiver into its cradle upstairs.

Well, all right, and who cared? He walked over to a heavy cardboard box full of books and kicked it hard enough to send it skidding three or four feet away and release a shuddering cloud of dust; then he looked around for other things to kick, or to punch, or to smash and break, but instead he went back and sat bouncingly on the couch again and socked one fist into the palm of the other hand. Yeah, yeah, well, the hell with it. So what? Who cared?

After a while, as his heart slowed down, he found he

could think only of the way Christine's voice had flickered to nothingness with the words "Okay, honey." There had never been anything to fear. All this time, if he had ever before taken a stern tone with her, she would have vanished from his life in an instant—"Okay, honey" —even, perhaps, with an obliging, cowering smile. She was only a dumb little London streetwalker, after all.

A few days later there was a letter from his wife that changed everything. She had mailed hasty, amicable letters once a week or so since she'd been back in New York, typed on the rattling stationery of the business office where she'd found her job, but this one was in handwriting, on soft blue paper, and gave every sign of having been carefully composed. It said she loved him, that she missed him terribly and wanted him to come home—though it added quickly that the choice would have to be entirely his own.

". . . When I think back over our time together I know the trouble was more my fault than yours. I used to mistake your gentleness for weakness—that must have been my worst mistake because it's the most painful to remember, but oh there were so many others . . ."

Characteristically, she devoted a long paragraph to matters of real estate. The apartment shortage in New York was terrible, she explained, but she'd found a fairly decent place: three rooms on the second floor in a not-bad neighborhood, and the rent was surprisingly . . .

He hurried through the parts about the rent and the lease and the dimensions of the rooms and windows, and he lingered over the end of her letter.

"The Fulbright people won't object to your coming home early if you *want* to, will they? Oh, I do hope you will—that you'll want to, I mean. Cathy keeps asking me when her daddy is coming home, and I keep saying 'Soon.'"

"I have a terrible confession," Judith said over tea in her sitting room that afternoon. "I listened in to your talk on the phone the other night—and then of course I made the silly mistake of hanging up before you did, so you certainly must have known I was there. I'm frightfully sorry, Warren."

"Oh," he said. "Well, that doesn't matter."

"No, I don't suppose it does, really. If we're going to live in close quarters I suppose there'll always be these small invasions of privacy. But I did want you to know I'm—well, never mind. You know." Then after a moment she gave him a sly, teasing look. "I wouldn't have expected you to have such a temper, Warren. So harsh. So loud and domineering. Still, I must say I didn't much care for the girl's voice. She sounded a bit vulgar."

"Yeah. Well, it's a long story." And he looked down at his teacup, aware that he was blushing, until he felt it would be all right to look up again and change the subject. "Judith, I think I'll be going home pretty soon. Carol's found a place for us to live in New York, so as soon as I—"

"Oh, then you've settled it," Judith said. "Oh, that's marvelous."

"Settled what?"

"Whatever it was that was making you both so miserable. Oh, I'm so glad. You didn't ever really think I believed the nonsense about the illness in the family, did you? Has any young wife ever crossed the ocean alone for a reason like that? I was even a little annoyed with Carol for *assuming* I'd believe it. I kept wanting to say Oh, tell me, dear. Tell me. Because you see when you're old,

Warren—" Her eyes began to leak and she wiped them ineffectually with her hand. "When you're old, you want so much for the people you love to be happy."

On the night before his sailing, with his bags packed and with the basement flat as clean as a whole day's scrubbing could make it, Warren set to work on the final task of clearing his desk. Most of the books could be thrown away and all the necessary papers could be stacked and made to fit the last available suitcase space —Christ, he was getting out of here; Oh, Christ, he was going home—but when he gathered up the last handful of stuff it uncovered the little cardboard music box.

He took the time to play it backwards, slowly, as if to remind himself forever of its dim and melancholy song. He allowed it to call up a vision of Christine in his arms whispering "Oh, I love you," because he would want to remember that too, and then he let it fall into the trash.

# A
# COMPASSIONATE
# LEAVE

NOTHING ever seemed to go right for the 57th Division. It had come overseas just in time to take heavy casualties in the Battle of the Bulge; then, too-quickly strengthened with masses of new replacements, it had plodded through further combat in eastern France and in Germany, never doing badly but never doing especially well, until the war was over in May.

And by July of that year, when service with the Army of Occupation had begun to give every promise of turning into the best time of their lives—there were an extraordinary number of unattached girls in Germany then —all the men of the luckless 57th were loaded into freight trains and hauled back to France.

Many of them wondered if this was their punishment for having been indifferent soldiers. Some of them even voiced that question, during the tedious ride in the box-cars, until others told them to shut up about it. And there was little hope of welcome or comfort in their destination: the people of France were famous, at the time, for detesting Americans.

When the train carrying one battalion came to a stop at last in a sunny field of weeds near Rheims, which nobody even wanted to learn how to pronounce, the men dropped off and struggled with their equipment into trucks that drove them to their new place of residence— an encampment of olive-drab squad tents hastily pitched a few days before, where they were told to stuff muslin mattress covers with the clumps of straw provided for that purpose, and to cradle their empty rifles upside-down in the crotches formed by the crossed wooden legs of their canvas cots. Captain Henry R. Widdoes, a gruff and hard-drinking man who commanded C company,

143

explained everything the next morning when he addressed his assembled men in the tall yellow grass of the company street.

"Way I understand it," he began, taking the nervous little backward and forward steps that were characteristic of him, "this here is what they call a redeployment camp. They got a good many of 'em going up all through this area. They'll be moving men out of Germany according to the point system and bringing 'em through these camps for processing on their way home. And what we're gonna do, we're gonna do the whaddyacallit, the processing. We're the permanent party here. I don't know what our duties'll be, mostly supply work and clerical work, I imagine. Soon as I have more information I'll let you know. Okay."

Captain Widdoes had been awarded the Silver Star for leading an attack through knee-deep snow last winter; the attack had gained him an excellent tactical advantage and lost him nearly half a platoon. Even now, many of the men in the company were afraid of him.

A few weeks after their arrival in the camp, when their straw mattresses had flattened out and their rifles were beginning to speckle with rust from the dew, there was a funny incident in one of the squad tents. A buck sergeant named Myron Phelps, who was thirty-three but looked much older, and who had been a soft-coal miner in civilian life, delicately tapped the ash from a big PX cigar and said "Ah, I wish you kids'd quit talking about Germany. I'm tired of all this Germany, Germany, Germany." Then he stretched out on his back, causing his flimsy cot to wobble on the uneven earth. He folded one arm under his head to suggest a world of peace, using the other to gesture lazily with the cigar. "I mean what the hell would you be doing if you *was* in Germany? Huh?

Well, you'd be out getting laid and getting the clap and getting the syphilis and getting the blue balls, that's all, and you'd be drinking up all that schnapps and beer and getting soft and getting out of shape. Right? Right? Well, if you ask me, this here is a whole lot better. We got fresh air, we got shelter, we got food, we got discipline. This is a *man's* life."

And at first everybody thought he was kidding. It seemed to take at least five seconds, while they gaped at Phelps and then at each other and then at Phelps again, before the first thunderclap of laughter broke.

"Jee-sus *Christ*, Phelps, 'a man's life,'" somebody cried, and somebody else called "Phelps, you're an asshole. You've always *been* an asshole."

Phelps had struggled upright under the attack; his eyes and mouth were pitiably angry, and there were pink blotches of embarrassment in both cheeks.

". . . How about your fucking *coal* mine, Phelps? Was that 'a man's life' too? . . ."

He looked helpless, trying to speak and not being heard, and soon he began to look wretched. It was clear in his face that he knew the phrase "a man's life" would now be passed around to other tents, to other explosions of laughter, and that it would haunt him as long as he stayed in this company.

Private First Class Paul Colby was still laughing along with the others when he left the tent that afternoon on his way to an appointment with Captain Widdoes, but he wasn't sorry when the laughter dwindled and died behind him. Poor old Myron Phelps had made buck sergeant because he'd been one of the only two men left in his squad after the Bulge, and he would almost certainly lose the stripes soon if he went on making a fool of himself.

And there was more to it than that. Whether Paul Colby was quite able to admit it to himself or not, he had agreed with at least one element in Phelps's outburst: he too had come to like the simplicity, the order, and the idleness of life in these tents in the grass. There was nothing to prove here.

Colby had been one of the many replacements who joined the company in Belgium last January, and the few remaining months of the war had taken him through pride and terror and fatigue and dismay. He was nineteen years old.

At Captain Widdoes's desk in the orderly room tent, Colby came to attention, saluted, and said "Sir, I want to request permission to apply for a compassionate leave."

"For a what?"

"For a compassionate—"

"At ease."

"Thank you, sir. The thing is, back in the States you could sometimes get a compassionate leave if you had trouble at home—if there'd been a death, or if somebody was very sick or something like that. And now over here, since the war ended, they've been giving them out for guys just to visit close relatives in Europe—I mean nobody has to be sick or anything."

"Oh, yeah?" Widdoes said. "Yeah, I think I read that. You got relatives here?"

"Yes, sir. My mother and my sister, in England."

"You English?"

"No, sir. I'm from Michigan; that's where my father lives."

"Well, then, I don't get it. How come your—"

"They're divorced, sir."

"Oh." And Widdoes's frown made clear that he still didn't quite get it, but he began writing on a pad. "Okay,

uh, Colby," he said at last. "Now, you write down your
—you know—your mother's name here, and her address,
and I'll get somebody to put the rest of the shit together.
You'll be informed if it comes through, but I better tell
you, all the paperwork's so fucked up throughout this
area I don't think you better count on it."

So Colby decided not to count on it, which brought a
slight easing of pressure in his conscience. He hadn't
seen his mother or sister since he was eleven, and knew
almost nothing of them now. He had applied for the
leave mostly from a sense of duty, and because there had
seemed no alternative. But now there were two possibili-
ties, each mercifully beyond his control:

If it came through there might be ten days of excessive
politeness and artificial laughter and awkward silences,
while they all tried to pretend he wasn't a stranger.
There might be slow sight-seeing tours of London in
order to kill whole afternoons; they might want to show
him "typically English" things to do, like nibbling fish
and chips out of twisted newspaper, or whatever the hell
else it was that typically English people did, and there
would be repeated expressions of how nice everything
was while they all counted the days until it was over.

If it didn't come through he might never see them
again; but then he had resigned himself to that many
years ago, when it had mattered a great deal more—
when it had, in fact, amounted to an almost unendurable
loss.

"Well, your mother was one of these bright young
English girls who come over to America thinking the
streets are paved with gold," Paul Colby's father had
explained to him, more than a few times, usually walking
around the living room with a drink in his hand. "So we

got married, and you and your sister came along, and then pretty soon I guess she started wondering, well, where's the great promise of this country? Where's all the happiness? Where's the gold? You follow me, Paul?"

"Sure."

"So she started getting restless—damn, she got restless, but I'll spare you that part of it—and pretty soon she wanted a divorce. Well, okay, I thought, that's in the cards, but then by Jesus she said 'I'll take the children.' And I told her, I said 'Way-*hait* a minute.' I said 'Hold your *horses* a minute here, Miss Queen of England; let's play *fair.*'

"Well, fortunately, I had this great friend of mine at the time, Earl Gibbs, and Earl was a crackerjack lawyer. He told me 'Fred, she wouldn't have a leg to stand on in a custody dispute.' I said 'Earl, just get me the kids.' I said 'Let me have the kids, Earl, that's all I ask.' And he tried. Earl did his best for me, but you see by then she'd moved down to Detroit and she had both of you there with her, so it wasn't easy. I went down there once to take you both to a ballgame, but your sister said she didn't like baseball and wasn't feeling very well anyway— Christ, what grief a little thing like that can cause! So it was just you and me went out to Briggs Stadium that day and watched the Tigers play—do you remember that? Do you remember that, Paul?"

"Sure."

"And then afterwards I brought you back up here to stay with me. Well, your mother threw a fit. That's the only word for it. She was wholly irrational. She already had boat tickets to England, you see, for the three of you, and she came storming up here in this rattletrap little Plymouth that she didn't even know how to drive, and she started yelling and screaming that I'd 'kidnapped' you. Do you remember?"

"Yes."

"Well, that was one God-awful afternoon. Earl Gibbs and his wife happened to be here with me at the time, and that saved the day—or half-saved it, I guess. Because once we'd all managed to get your mother calmed down a little, Earl went to her and talked to her for a long time, and in the end he said 'Vivien, count your blessings. Settle for what you can get.'

"So you see, she had no choice. She drove away in that crummy car with your sister riding beside her, and I guess a couple weeks later they were in London, and that was it. That was it.

"Well, but the point I'm trying to make here, Paul, is that things did work out pretty much for the best after all. I was fortunate enough to meet your stepmother, and we're right for each other. Anybody can see we're right for each other, right? As for your mother, I know she was never happy with me. Any man, Paul—*any* man—oughta know when a woman isn't happy with him. And what the hell, life's too short: I forgave her long ago for the pain she caused me as my wife. There's only one thing I can't forgive her for. Ever. She took away my little girl."

Paul Colby's sister, Marcia, was almost exactly a year younger than he. At five she had taught him how to blow steady bubbles in bath water; at eight she had kicked over his electric train in order to persuade him that paper dolls could be more entertaining, which was true; a year or so after that, trembling in fear together, they had dared each other to jump from a high limb of a maple tree, and they'd done it, though he would always remember that she went first.

On the afternoon of their parents' hysteria, and of the lawyer's sonorous entreaties for order in the living room, he had watched Marcia from the house as she waited in the passenger seat of the mud-spattered Plymouth in the driveway. And because he was fairly sure nobody would notice his absence, he went out to visit with her.

When she saw him coming she rolled down her window and said "What're they doing in there, anyway?"

"Well, they're—I don't know. There's a lot of—I don't really know what they're doing. I guess it'll be okay, though."

"Yeah, well, I guess so too. Only, you better get back inside, Paul, okay? I mean I don't think Daddy'd want to see you out here."

"Okay." On his way to the house he stopped and looked back, and they exchanged quick, shy waves.

At first there were frequent letters from England— jolly, sometimes silly, hastily written ones from Marcia, careful and increasingly stilted ones from his mother.

During the "Blitz" of 1940, when every American radio news commentator implied that all London was in rubble and on fire, Marcia wrote at some length to suggest that perhaps the reports might be exaggerated. Things were certainly terrible in the East End, she said, which was "cruel" because that was where most of the poor people lived, but there were "very extensive areas" of the city that hadn't been touched. And the suburb where she and their mother were, eight miles out, had been "perfectly safe." She was thirteen when she wrote that, and it stayed in his mind as a remarkably intelligent, remarkably thoughtful letter for someone of that age.

Over the next few years she drifted out of the habit of writing, except for Christmas and birthday cards. But his mother's letters continued with dogged regularity, whether he'd answered the last one or not, and it became an effort of will to read them—an effort even to open the flimsy blue envelopes and unfold the notepaper. Her strain in the writing was so clear that it could only make for strain in the reading; her final, pointedly cheerful paragraph always came as a relief, and he could sense her own relief at having brought it off. She had married again within a year or two after going back to England; she and her new husband soon had a son, "your little half brother," of whom she said Marcia was "enormously fond." In 1943 she wrote that Marcia was "with the American Embassy in London now," which seemed a funny thing to say about a sixteen-year-old girl, and there were no supporting details.

He had written to his sister from Germany once, managing to work in a few deft references to his combat infantry service, and had received no reply. It could have been because military mail was unreliable at the time, but it could also have meant she'd simply neglected to write back—and that had left a small, still-open wound in his feelings.

Now, after leaving the orderly room, he wrote a quick letter to his mother explaining his helplessness in the matter of the leave; when it was done and mailed he felt he could easily afford to stretch out on his cot in the drowsing, mildewed, half-deserted tent. He wasn't far across the aisle of trampled dirt from where poor old Myron Phelps lay sleeping off his shame—or, more likely, still ashamed and so pretending to sleep.

The big news of the following month was that three-day passes to Paris would now be issued in C company, a few at a time, and the tents began to ring with shrill and lubricious talk. Sure, the French hated Americans—everybody knew that—but everybody knew what "Paris" meant too. All you had to do in Paris, it was said, was walk up to a girl on the street—well-dressed, high-class-looking, *any* kind of girl—and say "Are you in business, baby?" If she wasn't she'd smile and say no; if she was —or maybe even if she wasn't but just sort of happened to feel like it—then oh, Jesus God.

Paul Colby arranged to take his pass with George Mueller, a quiet, thoughtful boy who had become his best friend in the rifle squad. Several nights before they went to Paris, in one of the soft-voiced conversations that were characteristic of their friendship, he haltingly confided to George Mueller what he'd never told anyone else and didn't even want to think about: he had never gotten laid in his life.

And Mueller didn't laugh. He'd been a virgin too, he said, until one night in a bunker with a German girl a week before the war ended. And he wasn't even sure if that counted: the girl had kept laughing and laughing— he didn't know what the hell she was laughing about— and he'd been so nervous that he didn't really get inside her before he came, and then she'd pushed him away.

Colby assured him that it did count—it certainly counted a great deal more than any of his own dumb fumblings. And he might have told Mueller about a few of those, but decided they were better kept to himself.

Not long before they'd left Germany, C company had been placed in charge of two hundred Russian "displaced persons"—civilian captives whom the Germans had put to work as unpaid laborers in a small-town plastics factory. On Captain Widdoes's orders, the newly freed Russians were soon quartered in what looked like the best residential section of town—neat, attractive houses on a hill well away from the factory—and the

Germans who'd lived up there (those, at least, who hadn't fled the advancing army days or weeks before) were assigned to the barracks in the old slave-laborers' compound.

There wasn't much for the riflemen to do in that pleasant, partially bombed-out town but stroll in the gentle spring weather and make occasional gestures at keeping things, as Widdoes said, "under control." Paul Colby was on guard duty alone at the very top of the residential hill one afternoon at sunset when a Russian girl came out and smiled at him, as though she'd been watching him from a window. She was seventeen or so, slim and pretty, wearing the kind of cheap, old, wash-ruined cotton dress that all the Russian women wore, and her breasts looked as firm and tender as ripe nippled peaches. Apart from knowing he would absolutely have to get his hands on her, he didn't know what to do. Far down the hill, and on either side, there was no one else in sight.

He made what he hoped was a courtly little bow and shook hands with her—that seemed an appropriate opening for an acquaintance that would have to take place without language—and she gave no sign of thinking it silly or puzzling. Then he bent to put his rifle and helmet on the grass, straightened up again and took her in his arms—she felt marvelous—and kissed her mouth, and there was a thrilling amount of tongue in the way she kissed back. Soon he had one splendid breast naked in his hand (he fondled it as impersonally as if it *were* a nippled peach) and blood was flowing heavily in him; but then the old, inevitable shyness and the terrible awkwardness set in, as they'd set in with every girl he had ever touched.

And as always before, he was quick to find excuses: he couldn't take her back into the house because it would

be crowded with other Russians—or so he imagined—
and he couldn't have her out here because someone
would be sure to come along; it was almost time for the
guard truck to pick him up anyway.

There seemed nothing to do, then, but release the girl
from their clasping embrace and stand close beside her,
one arm still around her, so they could gaze together
down the long hill at the sunset. It occurred to him, as
they lingered and lingered in that position, that they
might make an excellent scene for the final fadeout of
some thunderous Soviet-American movie called *Victory
over the Nazis*. And when the guard truck did come for
him, he couldn't even lie to himself that he felt anger and
frustration: he was relieved.

There was a taciturn, illiterate rifleman in the second
squad named Jesse O. Meeks—one of the four or five
men in the platoon who had to mark X instead of signing
the payroll every month—and within two days after the
fadeout of the great Soviet-American movie, Jesse O.
Meeks took full possession of that sweet girl.

"Ain't no use lookin' around for old Meeks tonight,"
somebody said in the platoon quarters. "No use lookin'
for him tomorra, either, or the day after that. Old Meeks
got himself shacked up re-eal fine."

But here in France, on a morning bright with promise,
Colby and George Mueller presented themselves at the
first sergeant's desk to claim their three-day passes. At
the left-hand edge of the desk, on a metal base screwed
into the wood, stood an ample rotary dispenser of linked,
foil-wrapped condoms: you could reel off as many as you
thought you might need. Colby let Mueller go first, in
order to watch how many he took—six—then he self-
consciously took six himself and stuffed them into his
pocket, and they set out together for the motor pool.

They wore their brand-new Eisenhower jackets, with
their modest display of ribbons and the handsome blue-
and-silver panels of their Combat Infantry Badges, and
they had carefully darkened and shined their combat
boots. They walked clumsily, though, because each of
them carried two cartons of stolen PX cigarettes inside
his trouserlegs: cigarettes were said to bring twenty dollars a carton on the Paris black market.

Coming into the city was spectacular. The Eiffel
Tower, the Arch of Triumph—there it all was, just the
way it looked in *Life* magazine, and it went on for miles
in all directions: there was so much of it that you couldn't
stop turning and looking, turning and looking again.

The truck let them off at the American Red Cross
Club, which would serve as a homely base of operations.
It provided dormitories and showers and regular meals,
and there were rooms for Ping-Pong and for drowsing in
deep upholstered chairs. Only some kind of a twerp
would want to spend much time in this place, when there
was such a wealth of mystery and challenge beyond its
doors, but Colby and Mueller agreed to have lunch here
anyway, because it was lunchtime.

And the next thing, they decided, was to get rid of the
cigarettes. It was easy. A few blocks away they met a
small, tight-faced boy of about fourteen who led them
upstairs to a triple-locked room that was packed to the
ceiling with American cigarettes. He was so intimidating
in his silence and so impatient to conclude the deal,
paying them off from a huge roll of lovely French bank-
notes, as to suggest that in three or four more years he
might be an important figure in the European under-
world.

George Mueller had brought his camera and wanted
snapshots to send to his parents, so they took a guided

155

bus tour of major landmarks that went on until late in the afternoon.

"We ought to have a map," Mueller said when they were rid of the boring, chattering tour guide at last. "Let's get a map." There were shabby old men everywhere selling maps to soldiers, as if selling toy balloons to children; when Colby and Mueller opened the many folds of theirs and spread it flat against the side of an office building, jabbing their forefingers at different parts of it and both talking at once, it was their first discord of the day.

Colby knew, from having read *The Sun Also Rises* in high school, that the Left Bank was where everything nice was most likely to happen. Mueller had read that book too, but he'd been listening to the guys in the tent for weeks, and so he favored the area up around the Place Pigalle.

"Well, but it's all prostitutes up there, George," Colby said. "You don't want to settle for some prostitute right away, do you? Before we've even tried for something better?" In the end they reached a compromise: they would try the Left Bank first—there was plenty of time —and then the other.

"Wow," Mueller said in the Metro station; he had always been good at figuring things out. "See how this works? You push the button where you are and the one where you want to go, and the whole fucking route lights up. You'd have to be an idiot to get lost in this town."

"Yeah."

And Colby soon had to admit that Mueller was right about the Left Bank. Even after a couple of hours its endless streets and boulevards failed to suggest that anything nice might happen. You could see hundreds of people sitting bright with talk and laughter in each of the long, deep sidewalk cafés, with plenty of good-looking girls among them, but their cool and quickly averted glances established at once their membership in the majority of French who detested Americans. And if you did occasionally see a pretty girl walking alone and tried to catch her eye, however bashfully, she looked capable of pulling a police whistle out of her purse and blowing it, hard, on being asked if she was in business.

But oh, Jesus God, the area up around the Place Pigalle. It throbbed in the new-fallen darkness with the very pulse of sex; it had a decidedly sinister quality, too, in the shadows and in the guarded faces of everyone you saw. Steam rose from iron manhole lids in the street and was instantly turned red and blue and green in the vivid lights of gas and electric signs. Girls and women were everywhere, walking and waiting, among hundreds of prowling soldiers.

Colby and Mueller took their time, watching everything, seated at a café table and nursing highballs of what the waiter had promised was "American whiskey." Dinner was out of the way—they had made a quick stop at the Red Cross to wash up and to eat, and Mueller had left his camera there (he didn't want to look like some tourist tonight)—so there was nothing to do for a while but watch.

"See the girl coming out of the door with the guy across the street?" Mueller inquired, narrowing his eyes. "See 'em? The girl in the blue? And the guy's walking away from her now?"

"Yeah."

"I swear to God it wasn't five minutes ago I saw them going *in* that door. Son of a bitch. She gave him five minutes—*less* than five minutes—and she probably charged him twenty bucks."

"Jesus." And Colby took a drink to help him sort out a quick profusion of ugly pictures in his mind. What could be accomplished in five minutes? Wouldn't it take almost that long just to get undressed and dressed again? How miserably premature could a premature ejaculation be? Maybe she had blown him, but even that, according to exhaustive discourse in the tent, was supposed to take a hell of a lot longer than five minutes. Or maybe—this was the possibility that brought a chill around his heart—maybe the man had been stricken with panic up there in the room. Maybe, watching her get ready, he had suddenly known he couldn't do what was expected—known it beyond all hope of trying or even of pretending to try—and so had blurted some apology in high-school French and shoved money into her hands, and she'd followed him closely downstairs talking all the way (Coarse? Contemptuous? Cruel?) until they were free to separate in the street.

For himself, Colby decided it would be best not to go with a streetwalker—even one he might spend a long time choosing for qualities of youth and health and the look of a gentle nature. The thing to do was find a girl in a bar—this bar or one of the others—and talk with her for a while, however brokenly, and go through the pleasant ritual of buying drinks. Because even if the girls in the bars *were* only streetwalkers at rest (or could they be whores of a higher caliber, with higher prices? And how could you possibly find out about distinctions like that?) —even so, you might at least have some sense of acquaintance before arriving at the bed.

It took Colby a minute or two to catch the waiter's eye for another round, and when he turned back he found George Mueller conversing with a woman who sat alone at the next table, a few inches away. The woman—you couldn't call her a girl—was trim and pleasant-looking, and from the stray phrases Colby overheard she seemed to be speaking mostly in English. Mueller had turned his chair away for talking, so his face was partly obscured, but Colby could see the heavy blush of it and the tense, shy smile. Then he saw the woman's hand moving slowly up and down Mueller's thigh.

"Paul?" Mueller said when he and the woman got up to leave. "Look, I may not see you again tonight, but I'll see you back in the whaddyacallit in the morning, okay? The Red Cross. Or maybe not in the morning, but you know. We'll work it out."

"Sure; that's okay."

In no other bar of the entire area around the Place Pigalle could a girl or a woman be found sitting alone. Paul Colby made certain of that because he tried them all—tried several of them twice or three times—and he drank so much in the course of his search that he wandered miles from where he'd started; he was in some wholly separate part of Paris when the sound of a rollicking piano brought him in off the street to a strange little American-style bar. There he joined five or six other soldiers, most of them apparently strangers to one other; they stood with their arms around each other's Eisenhower jackets and sang all ten choruses of "Roll Me Over" at the top of their lungs, with the piano thumping out the melody and the flourishes. Somewhere in the sixth or seventh verse it struck Colby that this might be considered a fairly memorable way to conclude your first night in Paris, but by the time it ended he knew better —and so, plainly, did all the other singers.

George Mueller had said you would have to be an idiot to get lost in this town, but Paul Colby stood for half an hour in some Metro station, pushing buttons, making more and more elaborate route patterns light up in many colors, until a very old man came along and told him how to get to the Red Cross Club. And there, where everybody knew that only some kind of a twerp would want to spend much time, he crawled into his dormitory bed as if it were the last bed in the world.

Things were even worse the next day. He was too sick with hangover to get his clothes on until noon; then he crept downstairs and looked into each of the public rooms for George Mueller, knowing he wouldn't find him. And he walked the streets for hours, on sore feet, indulging himself in the bleak satisfactions of petulance. What the hell was supposed to be so great and beautiful about Paris anyway? Had anybody ever had the guts to say it was just another city like Detroit or Chicago or New York, with too many pale, grim men in business suits hurrying down the sidewalks, and with too much noise and gasoline exhaust and too much plain damned uncivilized rudeness? Had anybody yet confessed to being dismayed and bewildered and bored by this whole fucking place, and lonely as a bastard too?

Late in the day he discovered white wine. It salved and dispelled his hangover; it softened the rasp of his anger into an almost pleasant melancholy. It was very nice and dry and mild and he drank a great deal of it, slowly, in one quietly obliging café after another. He found various ways to compose himself at the different tables, and soon he began to wonder how he must look to casual observers; that, for as long as he could remember, had been one of his most secret, most besetting, least admirable habits of mind. He imagined, as the white wine wore on and on, that he probably looked like a sensitive young man in wry contemplation of youth and love and death—an "interesting" young man—and on that high wave of self-regard he floated home and hit the sack again.

The final day was one of stunted thought and shriveled hope, of depression so thick that all of Paris lay awash and sinking in it while his time ran out.

Back in the Place Pigalle at midnight and drunk again —or more likely feigning drunkenness to himself—he found he was almost broke. He couldn't afford even the most raucous of middle-aged whores now, and he knew he had probably arranged in his secret heart for this to be so. There was nothing left to do but make his way to the dark part of the city where the Army trucks were parked.

You weren't really expected to make the first truck; you could even miss the last truck, and nobody would care very much. But those unspoken rules of conduct no longer applied to Paul Colby: he was very likely the only soldier in Europe ever to have spent three days in Paris without getting laid. And he had learned beyond question now that he could no longer attribute his trouble to shyness or awkwardness; it was fear. It was worse than fear: it was cowardice.

"How come you didn't pick up my messages?" George Mueller asked him in the tent the next day. Mueller had left three notes for Colby on the Red Cross message board, he said—one on the morning after they'd split up that first night, and two others later.

"I guess I didn't even notice there was a message board."

"Well, Christ, it was right there in the front room, by the desk," Mueller said, looking hurt. "I don't see how you could've missed it."

And Colby explained, despising himself and turning away quickly afterwards, that he hadn't really spent all that much time in the Red Cross Club.

Less than a week later he was summoned to the orderly room and told that the papers for his compassionate leave were ready. And a very few days after that, abruptly deposited somewhere in London, he checked into a murmurous, echoing Red Cross Club that was almost a duplicate of the one in Paris.

He spent a long time in the shower and changed meticulously into his other, wholly clean uniform—stalling and stalling; then, with his finger trembling in the dial of a cumbersome British coin telephone, he called his mother.

"Oh, my dear," her voice said. "Is this really you? Oh, how very strange . . ."

It was arranged that he would visit her that afternoon, "for tea," and he rode out to her suburb on a clattering commuters' train.

"Oh, well, how nice!" she said in the doorway of her tidy, semi-detached house. "And how fine you are in your marvelous American uniform. Oh, my dear; oh, my dear." As she pressed the side of her head against the ribbons and the Combat Badge she seemed to be weeping, but he couldn't be sure. He said it certainly was good to see her too, and they walked together into a small living room.

"Well, my goodness," she said, having apparently dried her tears. "How can I possibly hope to entertain a great big American soldier in a scruffy little house like this?"

But soon they were comfortable—at least as comfortable as they would ever be—sitting across from each other

in upholstered chairs while the clay filaments popped
and hissed and turned blue and orange in a small gas
fireplace. She told him her husband would soon be
home, as would their son, who was now six and "dying"
to meet him.

"Well, good," he said.

"And I did try to reach Marcia on the phone, but I was
a fraction of a second too late at the Embassy switchboard; then later I rang her flat but there was no answer,
so I expect they're both out. She's been sharing a flat
with another girl for a year or so now, you see"—and
here his mother sniffed sharply through one nostril and
turned her face partly away, a mannerism that brought
her suddenly alive from his memory—"she's quite the
young woman of the world these days. Still, we can try
again later in the evening, and perhaps we'll—"

"No, that's okay," he said. "I'll call her tomorrow."

"Well, whatever you wish."

And it was whatever he wished for the rest of that
rapidly darkening afternoon, even after her husband had
come home—a drained-looking man in middle age
whose hat left a neat ridge around the crown of his flat,
well-combed hair, and who ventured almost no conversational openings—and their little boy, who seemed far
from dying to meet him as he peered from hiding and
stuck out his tongue.

Would Paul like another bread-and-butter sandwich
with his tea? Good. Would he like a drink? Oh, good.
And was he sure he wouldn't stay awhile longer and have
some sort of scrappy little supper with them—baked
beans on toast sort of thing—and spend the night? Because really, there was plenty of room. It was whatever
he wished.

He could hardly wait to get out of the house, though

he kept assuring himself, on the train back into town, that he hadn't been rude.

And he awoke barely able to face breakfast in his nervousness about calling the American Embassy.

"Who?" said a switchboard operator. "What department is that, please?"

"Well, I don't know; I just know she works there. Isn't there some way you can—"

"Just a moment . . . yes, here: we do have a Miss Colby, Marcia, in Disbursements. I'll connect you." And after several buzzings and clickings, after a long wait, a voice came on the line as clear as a flute and happy to hear from him—a sweet-sounding English girl.

". . . Well, that'd be marvelous," she was saying. "Could you come round about five? It's the first building over from the main one, just to the left of the FDR statue if you're coming up from Berkeley Square; you can't miss it; and I'll be there in half a minute if you're waiting, or —you know—I'll be waiting there if you're late."

It took him a while to realize, after hanging up the phone, that she hadn't once spoken his name; she had probably been shy too.

There was an overheated shop in the Red Cross basement where two sweating, jabbering Cockneys in undershirts would steam-press your whole uniform for half a crown, while many soldiers waited in line for the service, and Colby chose to kill part of the afternoon down there. He knew his clothes didn't really need pressing, but he wanted to look nice tonight.

Then he was coming up from Berkeley Square, trying in every stride to perfect what he hoped would be a devil-may-care kind of walk. There was the FDR statue, and there was her office building; and there in the corridor, straggling alone behind a group of other women and girls, came a hesitant, large-eyed, half-smiling girl who could only have been Marcia.

"Paul?" she inquired. "Is it Paul?"

He rushed forward and enwrapped her in a great hug, pinning her arms and nuzzling her hair, hoping to swing her laughing off her feet—and he brought it off well, probably from his self-tutelage in the devil-may-care walk; by the time her shoes hit the floor again she *was* laughing, with every sign of having liked it.

". . . Well!" she said. "Aren't you something."

"So are you," he said, and offered her his arm for walking.

In the first place they went to, which she'd described as "a rather nice, smallish pub not far from here," he kept secretly congratulating himself on how well he was doing. His talk was fluent—once or twice he even made her laugh again—and his listening was attentive and sympathetic. Only one small thing went wrong: he had assumed that English girls liked beer, but she changed her order to "pink gin," which made him feel dumb for having failed to ask her; apart from that he couldn't find anything the matter with his performance.

If there had been a mirror behind the bar he would certainly have sneaked a happy glance into it on his way to the men's room; he had stamped twice on the old floor in the regulation manner for making his trouserlegs "blouse down" over his boots, then walked away from her through the smoke-hung crowd in the new devil-may-care style, and he hoped she was watching.

". . . What does Disbursements mean?" he asked when he got back to their table.

"Oh, nothing much. In a business firm I suppose you'd call it the payroll office. I'm a payroll clerk. Ah, I know," she said then, with a smile that turned wittily sour,

"Mother's told you I'm 'with the American Embassy.' God. I heard her saying that to people on the phone a few times, when I was still living there; that was about the time I decided to move out."

He had been so concerned with himself that he didn't realize until now, offering a light for her cigarette, what a pretty girl she was. And it wasn't only in the face; she was nice all the way down.

". . . I'm afraid our timing's been rather awkward, Paul," she was saying. "Because tomorrow's the last day before my vacation and I had no idea you were coming, you see, so I arranged to spend the week with a friend up in Blackpool. But we can get together again tomorrow night, if you like—could you come up to the flat for supper or something?"

"Sure. That'd be fine."

"Oh, good. Do come. It won't be much, but we can sort of fortify ourselves by having a real dinner tonight. Jesus, I'm hungry, aren't you?" And he guessed that a lot of English girls had learned to say "Jesus" during the war.

She took him to what she called "a good black-market restaurant," a warm, closed-in, upstairs room that did look fairly clandestine; they sat surrounded by American officers and their women, forking down rich slices of what she told him was horsemeat steak. They were oddly shy with each other there, like children in a strange house, but soon afterwards, in the next pub they visited, they got around to memories.

"It's funny," she said. "I missed Daddy terribly at first, it was like a sickness, but then it got so I couldn't really remember him very well. And lately, I don't know. His letters seem so—well, sort of loud and empty. Sort of vapid."

"Yeah. Well, he's a very—yeah."

"And once during the war he sent me a Public Health Service pamphlet about venereal disease. That wasn't really a very tactful thing to do, was it?"

"No. No, it wasn't."

But she remembered the electric train and the paper dolls. She remembered the terrifying jump from the maple tree—the worst part, she said, was that you had to clear another horrible big branch on the way down—and yes, she remembered waiting alone in the car that afternoon while their parents shouted in the house. She even remembered that Paul had come out to the car to say goodbye.

At the end of the evening they settled into still another place, and that was where she started talking about her plans. She might go back to the States and go to college next year—that was what their father wanted her to do —but then there was also a chance that she might go back and get married.

"Yeah? No kidding? Who to?"

The little smile she gave him then was the first disingenuous look he had seen in her face. "I haven't decided," she said. "Because you see there've been any number of offers—well, *almost* any number." And out of her purse came a big, cheap American wallet of the kind with many hinged plastic frames for photographs. There was one smiling or frowning face after another, most of them wearing their overseas caps, a gallery of American soldiers.

". . . and this is Chet," she was saying, "he's nice; he's back in Cleveland now. And this is John, he'll be going home soon to a small town in east Texas; and this is Tom; he's nice; he's . . ."

There were probably five or six photographs, but

there seemed to be more. One was a decorated 82nd Airborne man who looked impressive, but another was a member of service and support personnel—a "Blue-Star Commando"—and Colby had learned to express a veiled disdain for those people.

"Well, but what does that matter?" she inquired. "I don't care what he 'did' or didn't 'do' in the war; what's *that* got to do with anything?"

"Okay; I guess you're right," he said while she was putting the wallet away, and he watched her closely. "But look: are you in love with any of these guys?"

"Oh, well, certainly, I suppose so," she said. "But then, that's easy, isn't it?"

"What is?"

"Being in love with someone, if he's nice and you like him."

And that gave him much to think about, all the next day.

The following night, when he'd been asked to "come up for supper or something," he gravely inspected her white, ill-furnished apartment and met her roommate, whose name was Irene. She looked to be in her middle thirties, and it was clear from her every glance and smile that she enjoyed sharing a place with someone so much younger. She made Colby uneasy at once by telling him what a "nice-looking boy" he was; then she hovered and fussed over Marcia's fixing the drinks, which were a cheap brand of American blended whiskey and soda, with no ice.

The supper turned out to be even more perfunctory than he'd imagined—a casserole of Spam and sliced potatoes and powdered milk—and while they were still at the table Irene laughed heartily at something Colby said, something he hadn't meant to be all that funny.

Recovering, her eyes shining, she turned to Marcia and said "Oh, he's sweet, your brother, isn't he—and d'you know something? I think you're right about him. I think he *is* a virgin."

There are various ways of enduring acute embarrassment: Colby might have hung his blushing head, or he might have stuck a cigarette in his lips and lighted it, squinting, looking up at the woman with still-narrowed eyes and saying "What makes you think that?" but what he did instead was burst out laughing. And he went on laughing and laughing long after the time for showing what a preposterous assumption they had made; he was helpless in his chair; he couldn't stop.

". . . *Irene!*" Marcia was saying, and she was blushing too. "I don't know what you're *talking* about—*I* never said that."

"Oh, well, sorry; sorry; my fault," Irene said, but there was still a sparkle in her eye across the messy table when he pulled himself together at last, feeling a little sick.

Marcia's train would leave at nine, from some station far in the north of London, so she had to hurry. "Look, Paul," she said over the hasty packing of her suitcase, "there's really no need for you to come along all that way; I'll just run up there by myself."

But he insisted—he wanted to get away from Irene— and so they rode nervously together, without speaking, on the Underground. But they got off at the wrong stop —"Jesus, that was foolish," she said; "now we'll have to walk"—and when they were walking they began to talk again.

"I'll never know what possessed Irene to say such a silly thing," she said.

"That's okay. Forget it."

"Because I only said you seemed very young. Was that such a terrible thing to say?"

"I guess not."

"I mean who ever minded being *young,* for God's sake —isn't that what everyone wants to be?"

"I guess so."

"Oh, you guess not and you guess so. Well, it's true —everyone does want to be young. I'm eighteen now, and sometimes I wish I were *six*teen again."

"Why?"

"Oh, so I could do things a little more intelligently, I suppose; try not to go chasing after uniforms quite so much—British *or* American; I don't know."

So she had been laid at sixteen, either by some plucky little RAF pilot or some slavering American, and probably by several of both.

He was tired of walking and of carrying the suitcase; it took an effort of will to remind himself that he was an infantry soldier. Then she said "Oh, look: we've made it!" and they ran the last fifty yards into the railroad station and across its echoing marble floor. But her train had gone, and there wasn't another one due to leave for an hour. They sat uncomfortably on an old bench for a while; then they went out to the street again to get the fresh air.

She took the suitcase from him, placed it against the base of a lamppost and seated herself prettily on it, crossing her nice legs. Her knees were nice too. She looked thoroughly composed. She would leave tonight knowing he was a virgin—she would know it forever, whether she ever saw him again or not.

"Paul?" she said.

"Yeah?"

"Look, I was only sort of teasing you about those boys

in the photographs—I don't know why I did that, except to be silly."

"Okay. I knew you were teasing." But it was a relief to hear her say it, even so.

"They were just boys I met when I used to go to the Red Cross dances at Rainbow Corner. None of them ever really did propose to me except Chet, and that was only a kidding-around sort of thing because he said I was pretty. If I ever took him up on it he'd die."

"Okay."

"And it was silly just now to tell you about chasing uniforms when I was sixteen—God, I was *terrified* of boys at sixteen. Have you any idea what it is that makes people of our age want to claim more knowledge of—of sex and so forth than they really have?"

"No. No, I don't." He was beginning to like her more and more, but he was afraid that if he let her go on she would soon insist she was a virgin too, to make him feel better; that would almost certainly be a condescending lie, and so would only make him feel worse.

"Because I mean we have our whole *lives,*" she said, "isn't that right? Take you: you'll be going home soon and going to college and there'll be girls coming in and out of your life for years; then eventually you'll fall in love with someone, and isn't that what makes the world go around?"

She was being kind to him; he didn't know whether to be grateful or to sink even further into wretchedness.

"And then me, well I'm in love with someone now," she said, and this time there appeared to be no teasing in her face. "I've wanted to tell you about him ever since we met, but there hasn't been time. He's the man I'm going up to spend the week with in Blackpool. His name is Ralph Kovacks and he's twenty-three. He was a waist-

RICHARD YATES

gunner on a B-17 but he only flew thirteen missions because his nerves fell apart and he's been in and out of hospitals ever since. He's sort of small and funny-looking and all he wants to do is sit around in his underwear reading great books, and he's going to be a philosopher and I've sort of come to think I can't live without him. I may not go to the States at all next year; I may go to Heidelberg because that's where Ralph wants to go; the whole question is whether or not he'll let me stay with him."

"Oh," Colby said. "I see."

"What d'you mean, you 'see'? You really aren't much of a conversationalist, you know that? You 'see.' What can you possibly 'see' from what little I've told you? Jesus, how can you see anything at all with those big, round, virginal eyes of yours?"

He was walking away from her, head down, because there seemed nothing else to do, but he hadn't gone far before she came running after him, her little high-heeled shoes clicking on the sidewalk. "Oh, Paul, don't go away," she called. "Come back; please come back. I'm terribly sorry."

So they went back together to where the suitcase stood against the lamppost, but this time she didn't sit down. "I'm terribly sorry," she said again. "And look, don't come to the train with me; I want to say goodbye here. Only, listen. Listen. I know you'll be all right. We'll both be all right. It's awfully important to believe that. Well; God bless."

"Okay, and you too," he said. "You too, Marcia."

Then her arms went up and around his neck and the whole slender weight of her was pressed against him for a moment, and in a voice broken with tears she said "Oh, my brother."

He walked a great distance alone after that, and there wasn't anything devil-may-care about it. The heels of his boots came down in a calm, regular cadence, and his face was set in the look of a practical young man with a few things on his mind. Tomorrow he would telephone his mother and say he'd been called back to France, "for duty," a phrase she would neither understand nor ever question; then all that would be finished. And with seven days left in this vast, intricate, English-speaking place, there was every reason to expect he would have a girl.

# REGARDS___
## AT HOME

"WELL, I know it seems funny," the young man said, getting up from his drawing board, "but I don't think we've been formally introduced. My name's Dan Rosenthal." He was tall and heavy, and his face suggested the pain of shyness.

"Bill Grove," I told him as we shook hands, and then we could both pretend to settle down. We had just been hired at Remington Rand and assigned to share a glassed-in cubicle in the bright, murmurous maze of the eleventh floor; this was in the spring of 1949, in New York.

Dan Rosenthal's job was to design and illustrate the company's "external house organ," a slick and unreadable monthly magazine called *Systems;* mine was to write and edit the copy for it. He seemed able to talk and listen while executing even the subtlest parts of his work, and I soon fell to neglecting mine for hours and days at a time, so there began an almost steady flow of conversation over the small space between his immaculate drawing board and the ever-more dismaying clutter of my desk.

I was twenty-three that year; Dan was a year or so older, and there was a gruff, rumbling gentleness in his voice that seemed to promise he would always be good company. He lived with his parents and his younger brother in Brooklyn, "just around the corner from Coney Island, if that gives you a picture," and he was a recent graduate of the art school at Cooper Union—a school that charges no tuition but is famous for being highly selective. I'd heard that only one out of ten applicants is accepted there; when I asked him if that was true he said he didn't know.

"So where'd *you* go to school, Bill?" he asked, and that was always an awkward question.

I had come out of the Army with the wealth of the GI Bill of Rights at my disposal, but hadn't taken advantage of it—and I will never wholly understand why. It was partly fear: I'd done poorly in high school, the Army had assessed my IQ at 109, and I didn't want the risk of further failure. And it was partly arrogance: I planned to become a professional writer as soon as possible, and that made four years of college seem a wasteful delay. There was a third factor too—one that took too much explaining for comfort, but could in a greatly simplified form be easier to tell than all the fear-and-arrogance stuff —and this had become the reply I gave most often on being asked why I hadn't gone to college. "Well," I would say, "I had my mother to take care of."

"Oh, that's too bad," Dan Rosenthal said, looking concerned. "I mean, it's too bad you had to miss out on college." He seemed to be thinking it over for a while, trailing a delicate paintbrush back and forth under the clean scent of banana oil that always hung in his side of the cubicle. Then he said "Still, if the GI Bill gives allotments for dependent wives and children, how come they wouldn't do it for a dependent mother?"

That was something I had never looked into; worse, it was something that had never occurred to me. But whatever lame and evasive reply I made didn't matter much because he had already moved on to find another marshy place in the dark field of my autobiography.

"And you're married now?" he said.

"Uh-huh."

"Well, so who's taking care of Mother? You still doing that too?"

"No, she's—well, she's pretty much back on her feet now," I said, and that was a lie.

I knew he wouldn't press me on it, and he didn't. Office friendships don't work that way. But I knew too, as I fingered nervously through the *Systems* copy, that I had better watch my mouth around Dan Rosenthal from now on.

My mother, who had lived on alimony payments as long as I could remember, had been left with nothing after my father died in 1942. At first she'd taken a few harsh and degrading jobs—working in a lens-grinding shop, working in the cheap loft factories that make department-store mannequins—but work like that was pitifully wrong for a bewildered, rapidly aging, often hysterical woman who had always considered herself a sculptor with at least as much intensity as I brought to the notion of myself as a writer. During my time in the Army she had collected something from her status as a "Class A Dependent," but it couldn't have been much. For a while she lived with my older sister and her family in the Long Island suburbs, but the clash of personalities in that unhappy house soon brought her back to New York—and to me. My sister wrote me a letter about it, as if it were too delicate a matter for discussion on the phone, explaining that her husband's "views" on sharing his home with in-laws were "sound in theory, though terribly difficult in practice," and saying she was sure I would understand.

That was how it started. My mother and I lived on what little I earned at apprentice jobs, first on a trade journal and later as a rewrite man for the United Press, and we shared an apartment she had found on Hudson Street.

Except for a nagging sense that this wasn't a very adventurous or attractive way for a young man to live, I was comfortable there at first. We got along surprisingly well; but then, we always had.

All through childhood I had admired the way she made light of money troubles—that, perhaps even more than the art she doggedly aspired to or the love she so frequently invoked, was what had made her uncommon and fine for me. If we were occasionally evicted from our rented homes, if we seldom had presentable clothes and sometimes went hungry for two or three days while waiting for my father's monthly check, those hardships only enhanced the sweet poignance of her reading *Great Expectations* aloud to my sister and me in her bed. She was a free spirit. *We* were free spirits, and only a world composed of creditors or of "people like your father" could fail to appreciate the romance of our lives.

Now, she often assured me that this new arrangement was only temporary—she would surely find some way to get "back on her feet" in no time at all—but as the months wore on she made no effort, or any reasonable plans, and so I began to lose patience. This wasn't making any sense. I didn't want to listen to her torrential talk anymore or join in her laughter; I thought she was drinking too much; I found her childish and irresponsible—two of my father's words—and I didn't even want to look at her: small and hunched in tasteful clothes that were never quite clean, with sparse, wild, yellow-gray hair and a soft mouth set in the shape either of petulance or of hilarity.

Her teeth had been bad for years. They were unsightly, and they'd begun to hurt. I took her to the Northern Dispensary, an antique little triangular brick landmark of the Village that was said to be the oldest free dental clinic in New York. A pleasant young dentist examined her and told us that all her teeth would have to be removed.

"Oh, no!" she cried.

The work couldn't be done here in the clinic, he explained, but if she came to his private office in Queens he would do it there, equip her with dentures, and charge us only half his normal fee because she was a clinic patient.

It was a deal. We took a train out to Jamaica and I sat with her through it all, hearing her grunt and shudder with the shock of each extraction, watching the dentist drop one ugly old tooth after another onto his little porcelain tray. It made my toes clench and my scalp prickle; it was a terrible but oddly satisfying thing to watch. There, I thought as each tooth fell bloody on the tray. There . . . there . . . there. How could she make a romance out of this? Maybe now, at last, she would come to terms with reality.

All the way home that afternoon, with the lower half of her face so fallen-in that she wouldn't let anyone see it, she rode staring out the train window and pressed a wad of Kleenex to her mouth. She seemed utterly defeated. That night, when worse pain set in, she thrashed and moaned in her bed and pleaded with me for a drink.

"Well, I don't think that's too good an idea," I told her. "I mean alcohol warms your blood, and when you're bleeding, you see, it'll only make it worse."

"Call him up," she commanded. "Call what's-his-name, the dentist. Get the Queens information operator. I don't care what time it is. I'm dying. Do you understand me? I'm dying."

And I obeyed her. "I'm sorry to bother you at home, Doctor," I began, "but the thing is I wondered if it would be all right for my mother to have something to drink."

"Oh, certainly," he said. "Fluids are the best thing. Fruit juices, iced tea, any of the popular sodas and soft drinks; that'll be fine."

"No, I meant—you know—whiskey. Alcohol."

"Oh." And he explained, tactfully, that alcohol would not be advisable at all.

In the end I gave her a couple of drinks anyway and had three or four myself, standing alone and slumped at the window in a melodramatic posture of despair. I thought I would never get out of that place alive.

After she got her new teeth, and after the first discomfort of wearing them was over, she seemed to shed twenty years. She smiled and laughed frequently and spent a lot of time at the mirror. But she was afraid everyone would know they were false teeth, and that made her shy.

"Can you hear me clacking when I talk?" she would ask me.

"No."

"Well, *I* can hear it. And do you see this awful little *crease* under my nose, where they fit in? Is that very noticeable?"

"No, of course not. Nobody's going to notice that."

In her days as a sculptor she had joined three art organizations that required the paying of dues: the National Sculpture Society, the National Association of Women Artists, and something called Pen and Brush, which was a local Village women's club—a relic, I think, of the old, old Village of smocks and incense and monogrammed Egyptian cigarettes and Edna St. Vincent Millay. At my urging she had reluctantly agreed to let her dues lapse at the two uptown enterprises, but she clung to Pen and Brush because it was "socially" important for her.

That was all right with me; it didn't cost much, and they sometimes held group exhibitions of painting and sculpture—awful afternoons of tea and sponge cake, of heavily creaking wooden floors and clustering ladies in funny hats—at which a small, old, finger-smudged piece of my mother's sculpture might win an Honorable Mention.

"And you see, it's only recently that they've let sculptors *into* Pen and Brush," she explained, far more often than necessary. "It was always just writers and painters before that, and of course they can't change the *name* of it now, to include the sculptors, but we call ourselves 'the chiselers.'" And that always struck her as so funny that she'd laugh and laugh, either trying to hide her old teeth with her fingers or, later, happily displaying the gleam of her new ones.

I met almost nobody of my own age during that time, except by hanging around Village bars and trying to figure out what was going on; then once I was taken to a small party and met a girl named Eileen who turned out to be as lonely as I was, though she was better at concealing it. She was tall and slender with rich dark red hair and a pretty, bony face that could sometimes look warily stern, as if the world were trying to put something over on her. She too had come from what she called a "shabby-genteel" background (I had never heard that phrase before and added it at once to my vocabulary); her parents too had been long divorced; she hadn't gone to college either; and, again like me, she earned her living as a white-collar employee. She was a secretary in a business office. An important difference here was that she insisted she liked her work because it was "a good job," but I imagined there would be plenty of time for talking her out of that.

From the beginning, and for the whole of the next year, we were hardly ever apart except during working hours. It may not have been love, but we couldn't have been persuaded of that because we kept telling each other, and telling ourselves, that it was. If we often quarreled, the movies had proved time and again that love was like that. We couldn't keep away from each other, though I think we both came to suspect, after a while, that this might be because neither of us had anywhere else to go.

Eileen wanted to meet my mother, and I knew it would be a mistake but couldn't think of an acceptable way to say no. And my mother, predictably, didn't like her. "Well, she's a pleasant girl, dear," she said later, "but I don't see how you can find her so at*trac*tive."

Then once when Eileen was telling me about a boring middle-aged man who lived in her building, she said "He's been on the fringes of art for so many years, talking and talking about it, that he's come to expect all the prerogatives of being an artist without ever doing the work. I mean he's an *art* bum, like your mother."

"An art bum?"

"Well, you know. When you fool around with it all your life, trying to impress people with something that isn't really there and never really was—don't you think that's tiresome? Don't you think it's a waste of everybody's time?"

From old loyalty I tried to defend my mother against the art-bum charge, but it came out weak and lame and overstated, and there might have been yet another quarrel if we hadn't found some way to change the subject.

REGARDS AT HOME

Some mornings when I'd come home after daylight, with barely time to put on a clean shirt for work, my mother would greet me with a tragic stare—and once or twice she said, as if I were the girl, "Well, I certainly hope you know what you're doing." Then one evening late in the year she went into one of her uncontrollable rages and referred to Eileen as "that cheap little Irish slut of yours." But that wasn't really so bad because it enabled me to get up in a disdainful silence and walk out of the place and shut the door, leaving her to wonder if I would ever come back.

That winter I came down with pneumonia, which seemed only in keeping with the general run of our bad luck. And during my recovery in the hospital there was a time when my mother and Eileen, who had skillfully avoided each other until then, found themselves riding in the same elevator and came into the ward together for the afternoon visiting hour. They took chairs on opposite sides of the high steel bed and made hesitant conversation across my chest, while I turned my head on the pillow from one to the other of their remarkably different faces, the old and the new, trying to muster appropriate expressions for each of them.

Then Eileen pulled open one side of my hospital gown, peered beneath it, and began massaging the flesh on my ribs with her hand. "Isn't he a nice color?" she inquired with a bright false trill in her voice.

"Well, yes, I've always thought so," my mother said quietly.

"Do you know what the best part is, though?" Eileen said. "The best part is, he's the same color all over."

And it might have been funny if my mother hadn't chosen to take it in silence, slightly lowering her eyelids and lifting her chin, like a dowager obliged to confront an impudent scullery maid; all Eileen could do was put her hand back in her lap and look down at it.

I was released from the ward a few days later, though not before a mild and conscientious-looking doctor lectured me on the virtues of adequate nutrition and regular hours. "You're underweight," he explained as if I didn't know it, as if being skinny hadn't been a terrible source of embarrassment all my life. "And you've had several lung ailments, and your general physical type suggests a susceptibility to TB."

I didn't know what to make of that as I rode home on the subway with my grubby little brown paper bag of toilet articles, but I knew it was something that would have to wait. For now, and for God only knew how long a time to come, there were other troubles.

And the most dreaded, the worst conceivable trouble came within a month or two, one warm night in Eileen's apartment when she said she wanted to break off with me. We had been "courting"—her word—for a year, and there didn't seem to be any future in it. She said she was "still interested in other men," and when I said *What* other men?" she looked away and made some enigmatic reply that told me I was losing the argument.

I knew I had a point—she didn't know any other men; still, she had a good point too. She wanted the freedom to be lonely again, to wait at her telephone until somebody asked her to some place where there would *be* other men, and then from among several candidates she would choose one. He would probably be older than me, and better looking and better dressed, with a few dollars in the bank and some idea of where his life was going, and he certainly wouldn't have a mother on his hands.

So it was over; and for a little while, taking a tragic view of my situation, I thought I would probably die. I wasn't yet as old as John Keats, another ill-nourished tubercular type, but then I hadn't yet established any claim to genius, either, and so my death might well be poignant in its very obscurity—a youth consumed before his time, an unknown soldier mourned by no one, ever, except perhaps by a single girl.

But I was still expected to hammer out United Press copy eight hours a day, and to ride the subway and pay attention to where the hell I was walking on the street, and it doesn't take long to discover that you have to be alive to do things like that.

One evening I came home and found my mother barely able to suppress the joy of something she had to tell me. For a moment of unreasoning hope, looking into her happy face, I thought the good news might be that she'd found some decent work, but that wasn't it.

There was going to be an evening's entertainment at Pen and Brush, she said, and a party afterwards. Each category of the club's membership would present a humorous song or skit or something, and she had been chosen to do the turn for the sculpture contingent.

There was a mindless little commercial jingle on the radio then, advertising bananas. A girl with a South American accent would come on and sing, to a Latin beat:

I'm Chiquita Banana and I've—come to say
Bananas have to ripen in a—certain way . . .

And this was my mother's parody of it, composed for the pleasure of the Pen and Brush ladies and performed, with bright eyes and a brisk little hopping around on the floor of our wretched home, for me:

> Oh, we are the sculptors and we've—come to say
> You have to treat the sculptors in a—certain
> way . . .

She was fifty-seven years old. It had often occurred to me that she was crazy—there had been people who said she was crazy as long as I could remember—but I think it must have been that night, or very soon afterwards, that I decided to get out.

I borrowed three hundred dollars from the bank, gave it to my mother, explained that I would make all the payments on it, and told her, in so many words, that she was on her own.

Then I hurried to Eileen's place—hurried as if in fear that "other men" might get there first—and asked her if she would marry me right away, and she said yes.

"It's funny about us," she said later. "We're nothing alike, we don't really have any common interests or anything, but there certainly is a—chemical affinity, isn't there."

"Yeah."

And on chemical affinity alone, it seemed, in a crumbling apartment at the quiet waterfront edge of the Village, we survived the summer of 1948.

There were times when my mother would call up in meekness and urgency to ask me for twenty, or ten, or five, until Eileen and I came to dread the ringing of the phone; then before very long she began to earn most of her own living. She was sculpting the heads for department-store mannequins on a free-lance basis, working at home—at least there would be no more factory employment—but she wanted me to know that something much better might soon come through for her. She had learned that the National Association of Women Artists planned to hire an administrative and public-relations person. Wouldn't that be a wonderful kind of job? There was no requirement that the person be able to type, which was a blessing, but the trouble was they would probably want her to work as a volunteer for a while before they'd put her on a salary. And if she had to spend several months working full-time there without pay, how could she get her mannequin heads done? Wasn't it ironic how things never seemed to work out quite right?

Yeah.

Late that fall I was fired from the United Press—for general incompetence, I think, though that word wasn't used in the cordial little firing speech—and there were a few tense weeks until I found work on a labor union newspaper. Then in the spring I was hired at Remington Rand, and so began my time of sloth and talk in that dry little glassed-in cubicle with Dan Rosenthal.

Once I'd learned not to tell him too much about myself, we got along very well. And it became very important for me to earn and keep his good opinion.

Much of his talk was about his family. He told me his father was a cutter in the men's clothing industry and had "done a remarkable amount in the way of self-education," but then he said "Ah, shit. It's impossible to say something like that without demeaning the man. You get a picture of some funny little guy hunched over a machine all day and then talking Kierkegaard all night. That's not what I mean at all. Know something? When you're close to someone, when you love someone, you can only make a God damn fool of yourself trying to explain it. Same with my mother."

And he was greatly proud of his brother, Phil, who was then in one of the several city high schools established for gifted students. "I ordered him," he said once. "When I was seven years old I told my parents I wanted a kid brother and wouldn't take no for an answer. They had no choice. So they came through for me, and that was fine, but the trouble was I hadn't realized it'd be years before I could play with him, or talk to him, or teach him anything, or do anything at *all* with him, and that was hard to take. Still, ever since he was about six I haven't had many complaints. We got a piano in the house and Phil was playing classical music in a couple of months. I'm not kidding. When it was time for high school he had his pick of the finest schools in the city. He's still very shy with girls, and I think he worries about that, but the girls sure as hell aren't shy with him. The damn phone rings every night. Girls. Just calling up to have a little time with Phil. Oh, son of a bitch, this kid's got everything."

Several times Dan said he guessed he was about ready to move into a place of his own, and he asked me in a tentative way about rents in different parts of the Village, but these plans implied no difficulty with his family. It seemed rather that moving away was what he thought the world might now expect of him, in view of his age and education. He wanted to do the right thing.

Then one morning he called in to the office, hoarse with shock and lack of sleep, and said "Bill? Listen, I won't be in for a few days. I don't know how many days. My father died last night."

When he came back to work he was very pale and seemed to have shrunk a little. He said "fuck" a great many times in muttering over office problems; then after a week or so he wanted to tell me about his father's life.

"You know what a cutter does?" he asked. "Well, he operates a little machine all day. The machine's got an automatic blade, sort of like a jigsaw; the man takes maybe twenty-five layers of cloth—flannel or worsted or whatever the hell it happens to be—and he works the blade around through that whole stack of stuff according to some pattern, like maybe a sleeve or a lapel or a coat pocket. And there's lint everywhere. It gets up into your nose; it gets into your throat. You're living your whole life in fucking *lint.* And can you imagine a man of high intelligence—a man of high intelligence doing that kind of work for thirty-five years? For no better reason than that he's never had time to be trained in anything else? Ah, shit. Shit. It's enough to break your fucking heart. Fifty-two years old."

Dan took up cigars that summer, always carrying a cluster of them in his shirt pocket, chewing and smoking them all day as he bent over his work. It seemed to me that he didn't really enjoy them much—they sometimes drove him into coughing fits—but it was as if they were a necessary part of his preparation for the thick, premature middle age he had assigned himself at twenty-five.

"You know this guy in the office I've told you about?" I said to Eileen one night. "The artist? Dan Rosenthal? I think he's getting into practice for being an old man."

"Oh? How do you mean?"

"Well, he's getting so—ah, I can't explain it. I'm not even sure if I've got it right."

She could seldom explain anything to me about people in her office, either. Our conversations often dissolved into admissions that we weren't even sure if we had it right, and then there would be silence until a quarrel broke out over something else.

We weren't an ideal couple. We had been married at ages we both now considered too young, and for reasons we both now considered inadequate. There were times when we could talk long and pleasantly, as if to prove we were good companions; still, even then, some of her speech mannerisms made me wince. Instead of "yeah" she said "yaw," often while squinting against the smoke of a cigarette; she said "as per usual" too—an accounting-department witticism, I think—and instead of "everything" she often said "the works." That was the way smart, no-nonsense New York secretaries talked, and a smart, no-nonsense New York secretary was all she had ever allowed herself to want to be.

Well, almost ever. During the previous winter, to my great surprise, she had enrolled in an acting class at the New School. She would come home breathless with what she was learning, eager to talk without any secretarial rhetoric at all; those were the best of our times together. Nobody could have guessed, on those nights, that this sweet student of the dramatic arts devoted forty hours a week to toiling in the office of a fabric manufacturer called Botany Mills.

At the end of the New School year all members of her class performed, for an audience composed mostly of relatives and friends, in a dusty old theater on Second Avenue. There were two- and three-character scenes taken from familiar American plays; other students had chosen to act alone, as Eileen did. She had picked something light but not insubstantial—a long, subtle, self-contained monologue from *Dream Girl* by Elmer Rice—and everybody let her know she was wonderful to watch and to hear.

She did so well that night that the New School offered her a scholarship for the following year. And that was when the trouble began. She thought it over for a few days—there were long silences in the apartment while she peeled potatoes or worked at the ironing board—

and then she announced that she'd decided to turn down the scholarship. Going to school at night was too tiring after a full day's work. Oh, it had been all right this year —it had been "fun"—but to go on with it would be foolish: even if it was free, it would cost too much in other ways. Besides, nobody could learn much about acting from these little adult-education courses. If she really wanted to learn, in any professional sense, she would have to study full-time; and that, of course, was out of the question.

"Why?"

"What do you mean, 'why?'"

"Well, Jesus, Eileen, you don't need that job. You could quit that dumb little job tomorrow. *I* can take care of—"

"Oh, you can take care of *what*?" And she turned to face me with both small fists on her hips, a gesture that always meant we were in for a bad one.

I loved the girl who'd wanted to tell me all about "the theater," and the girl who'd stood calm and shy in the thunderclap of applause that followed her scene from *Dream Girl.* I didn't much like the dependable typist at Botany Mills, or the grudging potato peeler, or the slow, tired woman who frowned over the ironing board to prove how poor we were. And I didn't want to be married to anyone, ever, who said things like "Oh, you can take care of *what*?"

It was a bad one, all right. It went on until after we'd waked the neighbors, and it was never resolved, as none of our worst fights ever were. Our lives, by that time, seemed to be all torn nerves and open wounds; I think we might have broken up that summer, and maybe for good, if we hadn't learned that Eileen was pregnant.

Dan Rosenthal rose happily from his drawing board to

shake hands on hearing there was a baby on the way. But after that brief ceremony, when we'd both sat down again, he peered at me reflectively. "How can you be a father," he asked, "when you still look like a son?"

One weekend soon after that, on one of the first chilly days of fall, I was out gathering scrap lumber in a vacant lot near the river. Our apartment house was very old and badly kept, but we had a fireplace that "worked." I chose only boards that could be split and broken down to fireplace size, and when I had enough to last a few days I pitched them over the high wire fence that surrounded the lot. From a distance that fence might have looked difficult to scale, but there were enough sagging places in it to make easy footholds. I went up and over it, and had just dropped to the street when I saw Dan Rosenthal walking toward me.

"Well," he said. "You looked pretty good there, coming over the fence. You looked very nimble."

That was a pleasure. I remember being pleased too that he'd found me wearing an old Army field jacket and blue jeans. He was dressed in a suit and tie and a light, new-looking topcoat.

As we walked back to the house with the load of wood —Dan carried part of it, holding it carefully away from his coat—he explained that he'd come over to the city today to visit a Cooper Union friend; then he'd found he had a few hours on his hands, so he'd just been walking around the Village. He hoped I didn't mind his dropping by.

"Hell, no," I told him. "This is great, Dan. Come on up; I'd like you to meet my wife."

Except that we lived there, Eileen and I weren't really Village people at all. Bohemians made us nervous. The very word "hip" held vaguely frightening overtones for us, as did the idea of smoking pot—or "tea," as I think it was usually called then—and what few parties we went to were most often composed of other young office workers as square as ourselves.

Even so, when I brought Dan Rosenthal into the house and upstairs that afternoon, I found I was doing my best to slouch and mumble and squint for him. And Eileen couldn't have been more helpful if she'd tried: we discovered her reclining on the big studio couch, wearing her black turtleneck sweater and black slacks. I had always loved that outfit because it was vastly becoming, with her long red hair, and also because it seemed to loosen all her joints. She had worn it to the acting class sometimes, and she nearly always wore it on evenings when we'd sit quietly for hours in the San Remo or some other locally famous bar, trying to conquer our uneasiness among young men who slouched and mumbled and squinted with their pale, long-haired girls, whole crowds of them erupting now and then into roars of laughter over matters we were fairly sure we would never understand.

If you're young enough, there can be exhilaration in pretending to be something you're not. And if I'd been nimble in vaulting the fence, if I'd been a little hip on the stairs, it was time to be rugged now. Crouching, and with a good deal more force than necessary, I smashed and split those boards over the ringing iron knob of an andiron hauled from the fireplace; then, when they'd been reduced to manageable sticks, I broke each stick in half, or into thirds, one after another, against one straining knee. Some of the lumber had held rows of rusty nails, and Dan said "Watch those nails," but I told him without words that I could look out for myself. Hadn't I done stuff like this all my life? Hadn't I been a rifleman in the Army? Did he think I'd always been some indoor kind of

business-office guy in a white shirt? Hell, there wasn't
much you couldn't learn in knocking around the world;
how else did he think I had won this stunning girl, from
whom he seemed almost wholly unable to take his eyes?

Soon I had a nice fire going. Dan removed his suit coat
and loosened his tie; the three of us sat around in atti-
tudes of comfort, drinking beer, and my posturing en-
tered a quiet, "interesting" new phase. Well, no, I told
him, aiming a sad smile into the flames, I'd decided to
shelve the novel I'd been working on since last spring.
It didn't feel right. "And if a thing doesn't feel right," I
explained, "you're better off leaving it alone." I always
tried to use short, cryptic phrases in discussing the craft.

"Yeah," he said.

"I imagine it's the same in painting, in a different
way."

"Well, sort of."

"Besides, I've got a few old stories I want to fix up and
send around. You have to fix them up, you know. You
have to keep taking 'em apart and putting 'em together.
They don't write themselves."

"Uh-huh."

I held forth at some length, then, on how hard it was
to get any real writing done when you were stuck in a
full-time job. We'd been trying to save a little money so
we could live in Europe, I explained, but now, with the
baby coming, there wasn't much chance of that.

"You want to live in Europe?" he asked.

"Well, it's a thing we've always talked about. Paris,
mostly."

"Why?"

Like some of his other questions, this one was disqui-
eting. There weren't any real reasons. Part of it was the
legend of Hemingway, and that of Joyce; the other part

was that I wanted to put three thousand miles of sea between my mother and myself. "Oh, well," I said, "it's mostly just that the cost of living's much lower there; we could probably get by on a lot less, and I'd have more time to work."

"You speak any French?"

"No; still, I suppose we could learn. Ah, hell, it's just —you know—the whole thing's probably just a day-dream." From the very sound of my voice I could tell I was faltering, so I stopped talking as soon as I could.

"Dan?" Eileen inquired, and her face in the firelight was a masterpiece of innocent flirtation. Nobody ever had to tell her when she'd made a conquest. "Is it true that only one applicant out of ten is accepted at Cooper Union?"

"Well, you hear different figures," he said bashfully, not quite meeting her eyes, "but it's something like that."

"That's wonderful. I mean that's really impressive. It must have made you very proud to go there."

She had thoroughly destroyed my act, if not the whole of my weekend; even so, their talk gave me the beginnings of what seemed a pretty good idea.

There was a lot more talk, and more beer; then she said "Will you stay and have supper with us, Dan?"

"Oh, that's a very nice thought," he said, "but maybe it'd better wait for another time; I should've been home long ago. Mind if I use your phone?"

He called his mother and talked agreeably for a few minutes; later, after he'd left with many thanks and apologies and promises to come again soon, Eileen said the phone call had sounded like a husband talking to his wife.

"Yeah, well, that's the thing, you see," I told her.

"Ever since his father died he's been acting sort of as if his mother *were* his wife. And he's got a younger brother, seven or eight years younger, and now he acts as if the brother were their son."

"Oh," she said. "Well, that's sort of sad, isn't it. Does he have a girl?"

"I don't think so. If so, he never mentions her."

"I really like him a lot, though," she said as she began to clatter pots and pans in the kitchen area of the room, getting dinner started. "I like him better than anyone I've met in a long time. He's very—kind."

It was such a carefully chosen word that I wondered why she'd chosen it, and I was quick to assume it was because that particular word could not, very readily, be applied to me.

But the hell with it. I could hardly wait to get into the alcove formed by a folding screen in the corner, where my work table was. The partly typed, partly scribbled abortion of my novel lay there, as did the several stories I planned to take apart and put together, to fix up and send around. My new idea, though, had nothing to do with writing at all.

I had always had a knack for drawing simple cartoons, and that night I filled many sheets of typing paper with caricatures of people who worked on the eleventh floor at Remington Rand. They were people Dan and I had to be patient with and nice to every day, and I was almost certain, as I chuckled over a few of the better ones, that the pictures would appeal to him.

It took me several more nights to weed out the crude ones, and to clean up the better ones; then one morning, as casually as possible, I dropped the finished stack of them on his drawing board.

"What's this?" he said. "Oh, I get it: Arch Davenport.

And poor old Gus Hoffman. And who's this? Jack Sheridan, right? Oh, and I guess this is Mrs. Jorgensen in the typing pool. . . ."

When he'd inspected them all he said "Well, these are clever, Bill." But I'd heard him use "clever" in a disparaging sense too many times to take it as a compliment.

"Ah, they're nothing much," I assured him. "I just thought they might—you know—give you a laugh."

The truth was that I'd hoped they might do a great deal more. I had worked out a scheme in which these drawings were only the opening move, and now his lukewarm response seemed to prohibit telling him the rest of it. But my reticence didn't last long. Before the day was over—even before lunch, I think—I'd spelled out the whole damned thing for him.

There were hundreds of Americans now enrolled in art schools in Paris on the GI Bill, I explained. Many of them were serious artists, of course, but many others weren't artists at all: they met few if any academic requirements; they were openly exploiting the GI Bill to subsidize their lives in Paris. And the art schools didn't care, because they were happy to have steady money coming in from the United States government. I had read about this in *Time* magazine, and the article had singled out one art school, by name, as being "perhaps the most casual of all in its handling of the matter."

I had now decided to apply for admission to that school as a way of getting on with my writing, I told Dan Rosenthal, but I would need a letter of recommendation. So here was the thing: Would he write the letter?

He looked puzzled and faintly displeased. "I don't get it," he said. "Me write the letter? They're supposed to've heard of me?"

"No. But you can be damn sure they've heard of Cooper Union."

It didn't go over very well—I'd have had to be blind not to see that—but he agreed. He wrote the letter quickly, using one of his drawing pencils, and passed it over to me for typing.

He had told the school authorities that I was a friend whose ability at line drawing showed promise, and that he wished to support my application; he had saved his Cooper Union credentials for the second and final paragraph.

"Well, this is fine, Dan," I said. "Thanks a lot. Really. There's just one thing: when you say I'm a 'friend,' don't you think that might tend to weaken the whole—"

"Ah, shit," he said without looking up, and I may have been wrong but I thought his neck was a darker pink than usual. "Shit, Bill. Come on. I said you were a friend. I didn't say we were brothers under the skin."

If he disliked me then, and I think he probably did, it wasn't a thing he allowed to show. After that first embarrassing day it began to appear that everything was all right between us again.

And now that he'd met my wife there was a new litany in the ritual of our acquaintance. Every night, or at least on nights when we left the building together and walked to the street corner where we'd have to separate for our different kinds of public transit, he would give me a shy little wave and say "Well. Regards at home."

He said it on so many nights that after a while he seemed to feel a need for variation: with a mock scowl he would say "How about some regards?" or "Let's have some regards there, huh?" But those weren't very satisfactory alternatives, so he went back to the original line.

I would always thank him and wave back and call "Same here," or "You too, Dan," and that small exchange came to seem a fitting conclusion to the day.

I never heard from the "casual" Paris art school—they didn't even acknowledge receipt of my application—so I was left to assume that the *Time* story must have brought them an avalanche of letters from other no-talent applicants all over America, misfits and losers and unhappy husbands for whom "Paris" had come to mean the last bright hope.

Dan came home with me for dinner several times during the next few months, and Eileen soon discovered he could make her laugh. That was nice, but I could almost never make her laugh myself—hadn't, it seemed, since the very early days of our time together—and so I was jealous. Then late one night after he'd gone and our place had grown uncomfortably quiet with only the two of us there, she pointed out that we had never really given a party. And she said she wanted to do it right away, before she got "too big," so we went through with it—both of us, I think, in terror of doing everything wrong.

Dan brought along one of his Cooper Union friends, an impeccably courteous young man named Jerry, who in turn brought a lovely, dead-silent girl. The party was all right—at least it was noisy and rapidly revolving—so Eileen and I were able to tell each other afterwards that it had been fine. A week or two later, in the office, Dan said "Know something? Jerry and his girl are getting married. And you want to know something else? It was your party that did the trick. I'm not kidding. Jerry told me they both thought the two of you were so—I don't know; who knows?—so romantic, I guess, that they figured what the hell; let's do it. And they're doing it.

Jerry's taken a job I don't think he ever would've considered otherwise, working for some commercial-art school way the hell up in the northern part of British Columbia. I don't know what the hell he'll be doing up there— teaching Eskimos how to hold a T-square, I guess—but there's no turning back now. It's done. The die is fucking cast."

"Well, that's great," I said. "Tell him congratulations for me."

"Yeah, I will; I will." Then he turned his chair away from his drawing board—he didn't often do that—and sat looking grave and thoughtful, examining the wet end of his cigar. "Well, hell, I'd like to get married too," he said. "I mean I'm not really *immune* to it or anything, but there are a few obstacles. Number one, I haven't met the right girl. Number two, I've got too many other responsibilities. Number three—or wait, come to think of it, who the hell needs number three?"

Soon after the year turned into 1950, and a few weeks before the baby was due, the National Association of Women Artists agreed at last to hire my mother at a starting salary of eighty a week. "Oh, Jesus, what a relief," Eileen said, and I couldn't have agreed more. Except for the smiling boredom entailed in having her over for dinner once, "to celebrate," it seemed now that we could stop thinking about her almost indefinitely.

Then our daughter was born. Dan Rosenthal paid a surprise visit to Eileen in the hospital afterwards, bringing flowers, and that made her blush. I walked him out into the corridor for a window-view of the baby, whom he solemnly pronounced a beauty; then we went back and sat at Eileen's bedside for half an hour or so.

"Oh, Dan," she said when he got up to leave, "it was *so* nice of you to come."

"My pleasure," he told her. "Entirely my pleasure. I'm very big on maternity wards."

The famous Long Island housing development called Levittown had recently been opened for business, and some of the younger married men around the eleventh floor began discussing at length—each of them explaining to the others, as if to convince himself—the many things that made it a good deal.

Then Dan told me he too had decided to buy into Levittown, and I might have said But you're not even *married*, if I hadn't checked myself in time. He and his mother and brother had gone out there last weekend.

What had won him over to Levittown was that the basement of the house they inspected was remarkably big and bright. "It might as well've been *designed* as a studio," he said. "I walked around that basement and all I could think was Wow. I'm gonna paint my ass off down here. And I can even make prints, set up a lithograph stone, whatever the hell I want. You know all this stuff about the perils of suburbia? How your life's supposed to fall apart when you move out of the city? I don't believe any of that. If your life's ready to fall apart, it'll fall apart anywhere."

Another time he said "You know anything about Harvard?"

"Harvard? No."

"Well, I think Phil's got a fairly good chance of getting in there, maybe even on a scholarship. It sounds fine; still, all I know about Harvard is the reputation, you know?—the outside view. And that's sort of like the Empire State Building, right? You see it from a distance, maybe at sunset, and it's this majestic, beautiful thing. Then you get inside, you walk around a couple of the lower floors, and it turns out to be one of the sleaziest

RICHARD YATES

office buildings in New York: there's nothing in there but small-time insurance agencies and costume-jewelry wholesalers. There isn't any *reason* for the tallest building in the world. So you ride all the way up to the top and your eardrums hurt and you're out there at the parapet looking out, looking down, and even that's a disappointment because you've seen it all in photographs so many times. Or take Radio City Music Hall, if you're a kid of about thirteen—same thing. I took Phil there once when I was home from the service, and we both knew it was a mistake. Oh, it's pretty nice to see seventy-eight good-looking girls come out and start kicking their legs up in unison—even if they're half a mile away, even if you happen to know they're all married to airline pilots and living in Rego Park—but I mean all you ever personally *find* in Radio City Music Hall is a lot of wrinkled old chewing gum stuck up underneath the arms of your fucking chair. Right? So I don't know; I think Phil and I'd better go up to Harvard for a couple of days and kind of snoop around."

And they did. Mrs. Rosenthal went along too. Dan came back to the office overflowing with enthusiasm for everything about Harvard, including the very sound of its name. "You can't imagine it, Bill," he told me. "You have to be there; you have to walk around and look, and listen, and take it all in. It's amazing: right there in the middle of a commercial city, this whole little world of ideas. It's like about twenty-seven Cooper Unions put together."

So it was arranged that Phil would be enrolled as a Harvard freshman the following fall, and Dan remarked more than a few times that the kid would certainly be missed at home.

One evening when we left the building together he

204

held our walk down to a stroll in order to get something off his chest that seemed to have been bothering him all day.

"You know all this 'need help' talk you hear around?" he inquired. " 'He needs help'; 'She needs help'; 'I need help'? Seems like almost everybody I know is taking up psychotherapy as if it were the new national craze, like Monopoly back in the thirties. And I've got this friend of mine from school—bright guy, good artist, married, holding down a pretty good job. Saw him last night and he told me he wants to be psychoanalyzed but can't afford it. Said he applied to this free clinic up at Columbia, had to take a lot of tests and write some half-assed essay about himself, and they turned him down. He said 'I guess they didn't think I was interesting enough.' I said 'Whaddya mean?' And he said 'Well, I got the impression they're up to their ass in overmothered Jewish boys.' Can you understand something like that?"

"No." We were strolling in the dusk past brilliant storefronts—a travel agency, a shoe store, a lunch counter—and I remember studying each one as if it might help me keep my brains together.

"Because I mean what's the deal on being 'interesting' in the first place?" Dan demanded. "Are we all supposed to lie on a couch and spill our guts to prove how 'interesting' we are? That's a degree of sophistication I don't care to attain. Well." We were at the corner now, and just before he moved away he waved his cigar at me. "Well. Regards at home."

I had felt terrible all that spring, and it was getting worse. I coughed all the time and had no strength; I knew I was losing weight because my pants seemed ready to fall off; my sleep was drenched in sweat; all I wanted during the day was to find a place to lie down, and there was no place like that in the whole of Remington Rand. Then one lunch hour I went to a free x-ray service near the office and learned I had advanced tuberculosis. A bed was found for me in a veterans' hospital on Staten Island, and so I retired from the business world, if not from the world itself.

I have since read that TB is high on the list of "psychosomatic" illnesses: people are said to come down with it while proving how hard they have tried under impossibly difficult circumstances. And there may be a lot of truth in that, but all I knew then was how good it felt to be encouraged—even to be ordered, by a grim ex-Army nurse wearing a sterile mask—to lie down and stay there.

It took eight months. In February of 1951 I was released as an outpatient and told I could get continuing treatment at VA-approved clinics "anywhere in the world." That phrase had a nice ring to it, and this was the best part: I was told my illness had qualified as a "service-connected disability," allowing me to collect two hundred dollars a month until my lungs were clean, and that there was a retroactive clause in the deal providing two thousand dollars in cash.

Eileen and I had never known such a glow of success. Late one night I was trying to make plans, wondering aloud whether to go back to Remington Rand or look for a better job,when Eileen said "Oh, listen: let's do it."

"Do what?"

"You know. Go to Paris. Because I mean if we don't do it now, while we're young enough and brave enough, when are we ever going to do it at all?"

I could scarcely believe she'd said that. She looked, then, very much the way she'd looked acknowledging the applause after her scene from *Dream Girl*—and there was a touch of the old secretarial "toughness" in her face too, suggesting that she might well turn out to be a sturdy traveler.

Because everything happened so fast after that, the next thing I remember clearly is the cramped farewell party in our cabin, or tourist-class "stateroom," aboard the S.S. *United States*. Eileen was trying to change the baby's diaper on an upper berth, but it wasn't easy because so many people were crowded into the small room. My mother was there, seated on the edge of a lower berth and talking steadily, telling everyone about the National Association of Women Artists. Several employees of Botany Mills were there, and several other random acquaintances, and Dan Rosenthal was there too. He had brought a bottle of champagne and an expensive-looking hand puppet, in the form of a tiger, which the baby wouldn't appreciate for another two years.

This tense gathering was what I'd heard Eileen describe on the phone a few times as "our little shipboard *soignée*"—I didn't think that word was right but didn't know enough French to correct her. There was plenty of liquor flowing, but most of it seemed to be going down my mother's throat. She wore a nice spring suit, with a rich little feathered hat that had probably been bought for the occasion.

". . . Well, but you see we're the only national organization in the country; our membership is up in the thousands now, and of course each member has to submit proof of professional standing as an artist before we'll even consider their application, so we're really a very . . ." And the deeper she settled into her monologue the farther she allowed her knees to move apart, with a forearm on each one, until the shadowy pouch of her underpants was visible to all guests seated across from her. That was an old failing: she never seemed to realize that if people could see her underpants they might not care what kind of hat she was wearing.

Dan Rosenthal was the first to leave, even before the first warning horn had sounded. He said it had been very nice to meet my mother, shaking hands with her; then he gravely turned to Eileen with both arms held out.

She had finished with the diapering—finished too, it seemed, with all concern for any of the other visitors. "Oh, *Dan,*" she cried, looking sad and lovely, and she melted fast against him. I saw his heavy fingers clap the small of her back three or four times.

"Take care of my friend the promising writer," he said.

"Well, sure, but *you* take care, Dan, okay? And promise to write?"

"Of course," he told her. "Of course. That goes without saying."

Then he let her go, and I sprang to his service as an escort upstairs to the main deck and the gangplank. We were both quickly winded in climbing, so we took our time on the sharply curving, paint-smelling staircase, but he talked a lot anyway.

"So you're gonna send back a whole bunch of stories, right?" he asked me.

"Right." And only dimly aware of paraphrasing his Levittown plans, I said "I'm gonna write my ass off over there."

"Well, good," he said. "So it turns out you didn't need that shitty little art school after all. You'll never have to sneak around pretending to be an artist and playing hooky all day, and conspiring with a bunch of very 'casual' Frenchmen to rob the United States. That's good. That's fine. You'll be doing this whole thing on your own, with money you've earned from your fucked-up lungs, and I'm proud of you. I mean it."

We were up on the open deck now, facing each other in the cluster of people near the gangplank.

"So okay," he said as we shook hands. "Keep in touch. Only, listen: do me a favor." He stepped back to pull on his topcoat, which flapped in the light wind, and to shrug and settle it around his neck; then he came up close and looked at me in stern admonishment. "Do me a favor," he said again. "Don't piss it all away."

I didn't know what he meant, even after he'd winked to show he was mostly kidding, until it occurred to me that I had everything he must ever have wanted—everything he'd resigned himself, since his father's death, never to wish for again. I had luck, time, opportunity, a young girl for a wife, and a child of my own.

A great, deep ship's horn blew then, frightening dozens of sea gulls into the sky. It was the sound of departure and of voyage, a sound that can make the walls of your throat fill up with blood whether you have anything to cry about or not. From the railing I saw his thick back descending slowly toward the pier. He wasn't yet far away: I could still call some final pleasantry that would oblige him to turn and smile and wave, and I thought of calling Hey, Dan? Regards at home! But for once I managed to keep my mouth shut, and I've always been glad of that. All I did was watch him walk away between fenced-off crowds and into the heavy shadows of the pier until he was gone.

Then I hurried back down those newly painted, seaworthy stairs to get my mother off the boat—there wouldn't be many more warning horns—and to take up the business of my life.

# SAYING GOODBYE TO SALLY

Jack Fields's first novel took him five years to write, and it left him feeling reasonably proud but exhausted almost to the point of illness. He was thirty-four then, and still living in a dark, wretchedly cheap Greenwich Village cellar that had seemed good enough for holing-up to get his work done after his marriage fell apart. He assumed he'd be able to find a better place and perhaps even a better life when his book came out, but he was mistaken: though it won general praise, the novel sold so poorly that only a scant, brief trickle of money came in during the whole of its first year in print. By that time Jack had taken to drinking heavily and not writing much—not even doing much of the anonymous, badly paid hackwork that had provided his income for years, though he still managed to do enough of that to meet his alimony payments—and he had begun to see himself, not without a certain literary satisfaction, as a tragic figure.

His two small daughters frequently came in from the country to spend weekends with him, always wearing fresh, bright clothes that were quick to wilt and get dirty in the damp and grime of his terrible home, and one day the younger girl announced in tears that she wouldn't take showers there anymore because of the cockroaches in the shower stall. At last, after he'd swatted and flushed away every cockroach in sight, and after a lot of coaxing, she said she guessed it would be okay if she kept her eyes shut—and the thought of her standing blind in there behind the mildewed plastic curtain, hurrying, trying not to shift her feet near the treacherously swarming drain as she soaped and rinsed herself, made him weak with remorse. He knew he ought to get out of here. He'd have had to be crazy not to know that—maybe he was crazy already, just for being here and continuing to inflict this squalor on the girls—but he didn't know how to begin the delicate, difficult task of putting his life back in order.

Then in the early spring of 1962, not long after his thirty-sixth birthday, there came a wholly unexpected break: he was assigned to write a screenplay based on a contemporary novel that he greatly admired. The producers would pay his way to Los Angeles to meet with the director, and it was recommended that he remain "out there" until he finished the script. It probably wouldn't take more than five months, and that first phase of the project alone, not to mention the dizzying prospect of subsequent earnings, would bring him more money than he'd made in any previous two or three years put together.

When he told his daughters about it, the older girl asked him to send her an inscribed photograph of Richard Chamberlain; the younger one had no requests.

In someone else's apartment a jolly, noisy party was held for him, closely attuned to the jaunty image of himself that he always hoped to convey to others, with a big hand-lettered banner across one wall:

GOODBYE BROADWAY
HELLO GRAUMAN'S CHINESE

And two nights later he sat locked alone and stiff with alcohol among strangers in the long, soft, murmurous tube of his very first jet plane. He slept most of the way across America and didn't wake up until they were floating low over the miles upon miles of lights in the darkness of outer Los Angeles. It occurred to him then, as he pressed his forehead against a small cold window and felt the fatigue and anxiety of the past few years beginning to fall away, that what lay ahead of him—good or bad—might easily turn out to be a significant adventure: F. Scott Fitzgerald in Hollywood.

For the first two or three weeks of his time in California, Jack lived as a guest in the sumptuous Malibu home of the director, Carl Oppenheimer, a dramatic, explosive, determinedly tough-talking man of thirty-two. Oppenheimer had gone straight from Yale into New York television during the years when there were still strictly disciplined "live" plays for the evening audience. When reviewers began to use the word "genius" in writing about his work on those shows he'd been summoned to Hollywood, where he'd turned down many more movie projects than he accepted, and where his pictures rapidly made a name for him as one of what somebody had decided to call The New Breed.

Like Jack Fields, Oppenheimer was a father of two and divorced, but he was never alone. A bright and pretty young actress named Ellis lived with him, prided herself on finding new ways to please him every day, often gave him long, rapturous looks that he seemed not to notice, and habitually called him "My love"—softly, with the stress on "my." And she managed to be an attentive hostess too.

"Jack?" she inquired at sunset one afternoon as she handed their guest a drink in a heavy, costly glass. "Did you ever hear what Fitzgerald did when he lived out here at the beach? He put up a sign outside his house that said 'Honi Soit Qui Malibu.' "

"Oh yeah? No, I'd never heard that."

"Isn't that wonderful? God, wouldn't it have been fun to be around then, when all the real—"

"Ellie!" Carl Oppenheimer called from across the room, where he was bent over and slamming cabinet doors behind a long, well-stocked bar of rich blond wood and leather. "Ellie, can you check the kitchen and find out what the fuck's happened to all the bouillon?"

"Well, certainly, my love," she said, "but I thought it was in the *mornings* that you liked bullshots."

"Sometimes yes," he told her, straightening up and smiling in a way that suggested exasperation and self-control. "Sometimes no. As it happens, I feel like making up a batch of them now. And the point is simply that I'd like to know how the fuck I can make bullshots without any fucking bouillon, you follow me?"

And as Ellis hurried obediently away, both men turned to watch the movement of firm, quivering buttocks in her skin-tight slacks.

By then Jack had grown eager to find a place of his own, and perhaps even a girl of his own, and so as soon as the screenplay was outlined—as soon as they'd agreed on what Oppenheimer called the thrust of it—he moved out.

A few miles down the coast highway, in the part of Malibu that looks from the road like nothing more than a long row of weatherbeaten shacks pressed together, he rented the lower half of a very small two-story beach house. It had a modest picture window overlooking the ocean and a sandy little concrete porch, but that was practically all it had. He didn't realize until after moving in—and after paying the required three months' rent in advance—that the place was very nearly as dismal and damp as his cellar in New York. Then, in a long-familiar pattern, he began to worry about himself: Maybe he was incapable of finding light and space in the world; maybe his nature would always seek darkness and confinement and decay. Maybe—and this was a phrase then popular in national magazines—he was a self-destructive personality.

To rid himself of those thoughts he came up with several good reasons why he ought to drive into town and see his agent right away; and once he was out in the afternoon sun, with his rented car purring along past masses of bright tropical foliage, he began to feel better.

The agent's name was Edgar Todd, and his office was near the top of a new high-rise building at the edge of Beverly Hills. Jack had been in to talk with him three or four times—the first time, when he asked how to go about getting the inscribed photograph of Richard Chamberlain, it had turned out to be a matter that Edgar Todd could settle with a single quick, casual phone call —and each time he'd grown more and more aware that Edgar's secretary, Sally Baldwin, was a strikingly attractive girl.

At first glance she might not quite have fallen into the "girl" category because her carefully coiffed hair was gray, with silver streaks, but the shape and texture of her face suggested she wasn't more than thirty-five, and so did the slender, supple, long-legged way she moved around. She had told him once that she "loved" his book and was certain it would make a wonderful movie some day; another time, as he was leaving the office, she'd said "Why don't we see more of you? Come back and visit us."

But today she wasn't there. She wasn't at her trim secretarial desk in the carpeted hall outside Edgar's office, nor was she anywhere else in sight. It was Friday afternoon; she had probably gone home early, and he felt a chill of disappointment until he saw that the door of Edgar's office was ajar. He knocked lightly, twice, then shoved it open and went inside—and there she was, love-lier than ever, seated at Edgar's enormous desk with the spines of at least a thousand shelved, bright-covered novels forming a backdrop to her sweet face. She was reading.

"Hello, Sally," he said.

"Oh, hi. Nice to see you."

"Edgar gone for the day?"

"Well, he said it was lunch, but I don't think we'll see him again till next week. It's nice to be interrupted though; I've been reading the worst novel of the year."

"You do Edgar's reading for him?"

"Well, most. He doesn't have the time, and anyway he hates to read. So I type up little one- and two-page sum-maries of the books that come in, and he reads those."

"Oh. Well, listen, Sally, how about coming out for a drink with me?"

"I'd love to," she said, closing the book. "I was begin-ning to think you'd never ask."

And in something less than two hours later, at a small shadowed table in the bar of a famous hotel, they were shyly but firmly holding hands because it was clear and settled that she would come home with him tonight—and, by implication, for the whole weekend. Looking at her, Jack Fields had begun to feel as calm and strong and full of blood as if the notion of his being a self-destruc-tive personality had never occurred to him. He was all right. The world was still intact, and everybody knew what made it go around.

"Only, look, Jack," she said. "Could we make another stop first? Here in Beverly? Because I'll have to pick up a few things, and anyway I'd like you to see where I live."

And she directed his driving up the shallow grade that forms the first residential part of Beverly Hills, before

the steeper slopes begin. He discovered that all the roads
there were arranged in graceful curves, as if their design-
ers had been unable to bear the thought of straight lines,
and that there were very tall, elegantly slender palm trees
at precisely measured intervals. Some of the big houses
along those roads were handsome, some were plain, and
some were ugly, but they all suggested wealth beyond
the comprehension of an ordinary man.

"Now if you take your next left," Sally said, "we're
practically home. Good. . . . Here."

"You live *here*?"

"Yup. I can explain everything."

It was a vast white mansion of the Old South, with at
least six columns rising from its porch to its lofty portico,
with a great many sun-bright windows, with a long extension of itself in the form of a wing on one side, and,
beyond a swimming pool, with several connected out-
buildings of the same color and style.

"We always go in this way, past the pool," Sally said.
"Nobody ever uses the front door."

And the ample room she led him into from the pool
terrace was what he guessed would be called a "den,"
though it might easily have been a library if she had
somehow contrived to bring Edgar Todd's thousand
novels home from the office. Its high walls were paneled
in pleasingly dark wood, there were deep leather sofas
and armchairs, and there was a fireplace with small
flames fluttering in it, though the day was mild. An arrangement of leather-padded wrought-iron benches was
built out around the hearth, and on one of the benches
sat a pale, sad boy of about thirteen, facing away from the
fire and holding his clasped hands between his thighs,
looking as though he had come to sit here because there
was nothing else to do.

"Hi, Kick," Sally said to him. "Kicker, I'd like you to meet Jack Fields. This is Kicker Jarvis."

"Hello, Kicker."

"Hi."

"You watch the Dodger game today?" Sally asked him.

"No."

"Oh? Why not?"

"I don't know; didn't feel like it."

"Where's your lovely mother?"

"I don't know. Getting dressed, I guess."

"Kicker's lovely mother is an old friend of mine," Sally explained. "She's the one who owns this tremendous place; I just live here."

"Oh?"

And when the boy's mother came into the room a minute later, Jack thought she *was* lovely—as tall and graceful as Sally and even better looking, with long black hair and with blue eyes that lighted up in automatic flirtation at the sound of her name: Jill.

But he didn't really want to meet a woman more desirable than Sally tonight—Sally would be plenty for the time being, even in Hollywood—so he looked closely enough at Jill Jarvis to find something blank or stunned in her heart-shaped face, though he scarcely had time to inspect it before she turned away.

"Sally, look at this," she said, and she thrust a heavy paperback book into Sally's hands. "Isn't it marvelous? I mean isn't it marvelous? I sent away for it weeks and weeks ago and I'd about given up, but it finally came in the mail today." Courteously peering, Jack saw that its title was *The Giant Crossword Puzzle Solving Book*. "Look how *thick* it is," Jill insisted. "I'll *never* get stuck in a puzzle again."

"Wonderful," Sally said, giving it back to her. Then

she said "Excuse me a couple of seconds, Jack, okay?"
She hurried into the living room, which looked as wide
as a lake, and he watched her pretty legs running up a
soundless staircase in a shaft of pale afternoon light.

Jill Jarvis told him to sit down and went away somewhere to "get drinks," leaving him alone with Kicker in
what seemed an increasingly awkward silence.

"You go to school around here?" Jack inquired.

"Yeah."

And that was the end of their talk. The funny-paper
section from last Sunday's *Los Angeles Times* lay on the
hearth bench and the boy turned sideways to hunch and
stare at it, but Jack was fairly sure he wasn't reading or
even looking at the pictures; he was only waiting for his
mother to come back.

Above the fireplace, in a space plainly meant for some
heavy old portrait or landscape, there hung instead a
small painting on black velvet, in harshly bright colors,
showing the face of a circus clown with a melancholy
expression; the artist's signature, so prominently written
in white that it might have been the title, read "Starr of
Hollywood." It was the kind of picture you can find on
the walls of third-rate bars and lunch counters all over
the United States, and in the airless waiting rooms of
failing doctors and dentists; it looked so foolishly out of
place in this room as to suggest that someone had stuck
it there as a joke—but then, so did *The Giant Crossword
Puzzle Solving Book,* which now lay displayed alone on a
coffee table that must have cost two thousand dollars.

"I can't imagine what's keeping Woody," Jill said as
she carried a liquor tray into the room.

"Want me to call the studio?" Kicker asked her.

"No, don't bother; he'll be along. You know Woody."

Then Sally came downstairs again with a Mexican

straw satchel that looked pleasingly full—she *did* plan to spend the weekend with him—and said "Let's just have one drink, Jack, and then we'll go."

But they had two, because Woody came smiling home during their first one and insisted that they stay for another. He was about Jack's age or younger, of medium height and lightly built, wearing jeans, fringed Indian moccasins, and a complicated shirt that fastened with metal snaps instead of buttons. He moved in a very limber way with a frequent dipping of the knees, and his face showed an unguarded eagerness to be liked.

"Well, it's certainly very nice out at Malibu," he said when he had come to rest at last in one of the armchairs. "I had a place out there for a few years—a small place, but very nice. Still, I've really come to love it here in Beverly. I feel at home here, that's the only way to put it, and you know a funny thing? I've never felt that way about any other place in my life. Get you a refill?"

"No thanks," Jack said. "We'd better be getting started."

"When'll we look for you, Sally?" Jill inquired.

"Oh, I don't know," Sally called back as she and Jack made for the terrace door, with Jack carrying the Mexican bag. "I'll give you a call sometime tomorrow, okay?"

"I won't let you take her away forever, Jack," Woody called. "You gotta promise you'll bring her back soon, okay?"

"Okay," Jack told him. "I promise."

And they were free, just the two of them, hurrying out past the swimming pool and down to the driveway and into his waiting car. All the way home—and the ride seemed to take no time at all in the new-fallen darkness of this still and fragrant night—he wanted to laugh aloud because this was the way things should always have been in his life; this was pretty nice: good money coming in, a weekend coming up, and a girl coming out to love him at the shore of the Pacific Ocean.

"Oh, I think it's sort of—cute," Sally said of his apartment. "Of course it's small, but you could really do a lot with it."

"Yeah, well, I probably won't be here long enough to do much. Can I get you a drink?"

"No thanks. Why don't you just—" She turned from her scrutiny of the black picture window to smile at him, looking bold and shy at the same time and then subtly averting her eyes. "Why don't you just come over here so we can sort of fall all over each other."

No other woman he'd known had made a more graceful passage from acquaintance to intimacy. There was nothing embarrassed in the way she undressed, and nothing of the show-off either: the clothes fell and were flung from her as if she'd waited all day to be rid of them; then she slipped into his bed and turned to welcome him with a look of desire that was as pretty as anything he'd ever seen in the movies. Her long body was strong and tender, and so was the pride she took in knowing what men believe a woman's flesh is for. It was a very long time before he could possibly have thought of any other woman, or girl, even if he'd wanted to.

"Oh, listen to the surf," she said later, when they were nestled together in peace. "Isn't that a wonderful sound?"

"Yeah."

But Jack Fields, curled close at her back with his arm around her and with one of her fine tits alive in his hand, wasn't paying attention to the surf at all. He was too

happy and sleepy to accomplish more than a single co-
herent, mercifully private thought: F. Scott Fitzgerald
meets Sheilah Graham.

Sally Baldwin had grown up as Sally Munk—"Jesus, I
couldn't *wait* to get rid of that name"—in an industrial
California town where her father had worked as an elec-
trician until his early death, and her mother had then
worked for many years as a seamstress in a department-
store fitting room. In high school Sally had been chosen
as a supporting actress in a series of grade-B movies
about adolescent life—"sort of like the old Andy Hardy
pictures, only nowhere near as good; still, they were a lot
better than all this dumb little beach-ball bikini stuff
they're fobbing off on the kids nowadays"—but her con-
tract had expired when she grew too tall for the roles
expected of her. She had put herself through college on
what was left of her movie earnings, and later by working
as a waitress. "Cocktail waitressing is the worst kind,"
she explained. "Pays the best, but it can be really—really
demoralizing work."

"Did you wear those hip-length black net stockings?"
he asked, thinking she must have looked terrific. "And
those little—"

"Yeah, yeah, all that," she said impatiently. "And then
pretty soon I got married. Lasted about nine years. He
was a lawyer—is a lawyer, I mean. You know how they say
never marry a lawyer because you'll never win an argument? Lot of truth in that. We didn't have any children
—at first he kept saying he didn't want any, then later it
turned out I couldn't have any anyway. I have a whaddyacallit, a fibroid."

And it was early afternoon, when they were lying back
in canvas deck chairs on his sandy little porch, before

Sally brought the story around to Jill Jarvis and her mansion.

". . . Well, I don't really *know* where all the money comes from," she said. "I know she gets an awful lot of it from her father, someplace in Georgia, and I know his family's had an awful lot of it down there for an awful long time, but I mean I don't really know where it *comes* from. Cotton or something, I guess. And of course Frank Jarvis is rich too, so she came out of that marriage with quite a nice settlement, as well as the house. So then you see when *my* marriage broke up she asked me to come and live there, and I was sort of—thrilled. I'd always loved that house—still do; probably always will. Besides, I didn't really have anywhere else to go. I knew the best I could do alone, on my salary, would've been some neat little place out in the Valley, and that's my definition of spiritual suicide. I'd rather eat worms than live in the Valley.

"Oh, and Jill really went out of her way to make it nice for me too. She hired a professional decorator to do my apartment, and God, you ought to see it, Jack. Well, you will see it. It's really only one big room but it's about as big as three rooms put together, and it's all bright and sunny and you can see green things all around. I love it. I love going in there after a day at the office and taking off my shoes and sort of dancing around for a minute thinking Wow. Look at me. Gawky Sally What's-her-name from No-place, California."

"Yeah," he said, "that does sound nice."

"Then after a while I began to figure out that she'd wanted me there mostly for—well, for protective coloration, sort of. She was living with a college boy then, or graduate student, I guess he was, and she seemed to think it'd sort of look better if there were two women in

the house. I finally found a way to ask her about that
once, and she was surprised I'd even had to ask—she
thought I'd understood from the beginning. Made me
feel a little—I don't know—made me feel funny."

"Yeah; I can see that."

"Anyway, the college boy only stuck around for a year
or two, and since then there's been quite a parade. I'll
just give you the highlights. There was a lawyer who was
a friend of her ex-husband's—a friend of my ex-husband's too, which was a little uncomfortable—and there
was a man from Germany named Klaus who runs a
Volkswagen agency in town. He was nice, and he was
very good with Kicker."

"How do you mean, 'good' with him?"

"Well, he'd take him to ballgames, or to the movies,
and he'd talk to him a lot. That's important for a boy
without a father."

"Does he see much of his father?"

"No. It's hard to explain, but no—not at all. Because
you see Frank Jarvis has always said he doesn't think he
*is* Kicker's father, so he's never wanted anything to do
with him."

"Oh."

"Well, you hear of situations like that; it's not uncommon. *Any*way, Klaus moved out after a while, and now
Woody's the man in residence. Did you happen to notice
the dopey little clown up over the fireplace? That's him
—I mean he painted it. Woody Starr. Starr of Hollywood. And I mean of course you can't call him an artist,
unless you want to be as dumb about it as Jill is. He's just
kind of an amiable guy trying to make a few dollars out
of the tourist trade. He has a shop down on Hollywood
Boulevard—he always calls it 'the studio'—with his corny

little sign hung out over the sidewalk; oh, and he doesn't just do clowns—he does black velvet moonlit lakes and black velvet winter scenes and black velvet mountains with waterfalls and God only knows what the hell else. So anyway, Jill wandered in there one day and thought all that black velvet trash was beautiful. It's always amazing to find out what crummy taste she has, in everything but clothes. And I guess she thought Woody Starr was beautiful too, because she brought him home the same night. That was about three years ago.

"And the funny part is he *is* sort of lovable. He can make you laugh. He's even—interesting, in his own way: been all over the world in the Merchant Marine, knows a lot of stories. I don't know. Woody grows on you. And it's really touching to watch him with Kicker: I think Kicker loves him even more than he loved Klaus."

"Where'd he get that name?"

"What name? Starr?"

"No, the boy."

" 'Kicker'? Oh, Jill started that. She used to say he almost kicked her to death before he was born. His real name's Alan, but you'd better not try calling him Al, or anything. Call him Kicker."

By the time Jack got up and went into the house for more drinks he'd decided it would be much better if Sally lived in a regular apartment, like a regular secretary. Still, maybe they could arrange to spend most of their time together out here at the beach; besides, it was too early to worry about stuff like that. All his life, it now seemed, he had spoiled things for himself by worrying too soon.

"Know what, Sally?" he said, carrying their full, cold glasses back outdoors, and he was going to say "You've got really great legs," but went back to the old topic instead. "It's beginning to sound like you live in a pretty fucked-up household."

"Oh, I know," she said. "Somebody else I knew called it 'degenerate.' That seemed too strong a word, but later I could see what he meant."

It was the first time she had made any reference to "somebody else I knew," or "he," and as Jack sipped at his clicking whiskey he gave in to a sulk of irrational jealousy. How many guys had she met in Edgar Todd's office and gone laughingly out for drinks with, over the years? And she had probably said, to each of them, "Could we make another stop first? Here in Beverly? Because I'll have to pick up a few things, and anyway I'd like you to see where I live." Worse: after thrashing and moaning in each man's bed all night she had probably told him, as she'd told Jack Fields in the small hours of this very morning, that he was "wonderful."

Had they all been writers? If so, what the hell were their names? Oh, there had probably been a few movie directors in there too, and movie technicians, and different kinds of people who had to do with the "packaging" of television shows.

He was making himself feel terrible, and the only way to stop it was to start talking again. "You know, you really look a lot younger than thirty-six, Sally," he said. "I mean except for the—"

"I know; except for the hair. I hate it. It's been gray since I was twenty-four and I used to dye it, but that didn't look right either."

"No, listen, it looks great. I didn't mean—" And hunching earnestly toward her on the lower part of his deck chair he launched into an apology that carried him helplessly from one lame line to another. He said her hair had been the first thing that attracted him, and when her look told him she knew that was a lie he dropped it quickly and tried something else. He said he'd always thought prematurely gray hair could make a pretty girl "interesting" and "mysterious"; he said he was surprised a lot of girls didn't *dye* their hair gray, and that was when she started laughing.

"God, you really like to apologize, don't you. If I let you go on with this, you'd probably go on and on."

"Well, okay," he said, "but listen: Let me tell you something else." He moved over to her deck chair, placed one haunch on the edge of it, and began massaging one of her warm, firm thighs with his hand. "I think you've got just about the greatest legs I've ever seen."

"Oh, that feels nice," she said, and her eyelids lowered very slightly. "That really feels nice. You know what, though, Jack? We're going to waste practically the whole afternoon if we don't get up pretty soon and go back in the house and play."

On Monday morning, sore-eyed and jittery from lack of sleep as he drove her back to Edgar Todd's office, he began to be afraid they would never have such a good time again. All future days and nights might wither under the strain of trying to recapture this first weekend. They would discover unpleasant, unattractive things in each other; they would seek and find small grievances; they would quarrel; they would get bored.

He licked his lips. "Can I call you?"

"Whaddya mean, can you call me?" she said. "If you don't, I'll never let you hear the end of it."

She spent several nights of that week with him, and the whole of the next weekend and much of the following week. Not until the end of that time was he obliged to visit Jill Jarvis's house again, and then it was only because

Sally insisted that she wanted him to see her apartment upstairs.

"Give me five minutes to get it looking decent, Jack, okay?" she told him in the den. "You wait here and talk to Woody, and I'll come down and get you when I'm ready." So he was left alone and smiling with Woody Starr, who seemed nervous too.

"Well, my only quarrel with you, Jack," Woody said as they sat down in leather armchairs, partly facing each other, "is that you've been keeping Sally away too much. We miss her. It's like losing a member of the family. Whyn't you bring her home more often?" Then, without waiting for an answer, he hurried on as if steady talking were the best known remedy for shyness. "No, but seriously, though, Sally's one of my favorite people. I think the world of her. She hasn't had an easy life, but nobody'd ever guess it. She's one of the finest human beings I know."

"Yeah," Jack said, making the leather creak as he shifted his weight. "Yeah, she's pretty nice, all right."

Then Kicker came hurrying in from the pool terrace for an intense, animated discussion with Woody Starr about a broken bicycle.

"Well, if the trouble's in the sprocket itself, Kick," Woody said when he'd sorted out the facts, "we'll have to take it into the shop. Be better to let those guys handle it than mess with it ourselves, right?"

"But the shop's *closed*, Woody."

"Well, it's closed for today, but we can take it in tomorrow. What's the big hurry?"

"Oh, I dunno. I was—gonna go down to the firehouse, is all. Some of the guys from school hang around there."

"Hell, I'll run you down there, Kick; no problem."

And the boy seemed to think it over for a few seconds,

looking at the rug, before he said "No, that's okay, Woody. I can go tomorrow, or some other time."

"Ready?" Sally called from the doorway. "Now, if you'll just step this way, sir, I'll take you up and show you my very own professionally decorated apartment."

She led him out into the main living room—all he could see of it was an acre of waxed floor, with mounds of cream-colored upholstery seeming to float in the pink evening light of tall windows—and up the elegant staircase. She took him down a second-story hallway past three or four closed doors; then she opened the final door, whirled inside with a theatrical flourish, and stood beaming there to welcome him.

It *was* as big as three rooms put together, and the ceiling was uncommonly high. The walls were a subtle shade of pale blue that the professional decorator must have considered "right" for Sally, though much of the wall space was given over to glass: huge gilt-framed mirrors on one side and an L-shaped display of French windows along two others, with heavy curtains poised to glide and sweep across their panes. There were two double beds, which Jack thought a little excessive even by professional-decorator standards, and on various chests or end tables around the expanse of deep white carpet stood big pottery lamps whose fabric shades were three or four feet tall. In one corner, at the far end of the room, was a very low, round, black-lacquered table with a floral centerpiece, and with cushions placed at intervals on the floor around it as if in readiness for a Japanese meal; in another, near the entrance, a ceramic umbrella stand held a bouquet of giant peacock feathers.

"Yeah," Jack murmured, turning around and squinting slightly in an effort to take it all in. "Yeah, this is really nice, honey. I can see why you like it."

"Go in and look at the bathroom," she commanded. "You've never seen such a bathroom in your life."

And after inspecting the flawless gleam and splendor of the bathroom, he came back and said "No, that's really true. You're right. I never have."

He stood peering down at the Japanese table for a moment; then he said "You ever use this?"

" 'Use' it?"

"Oh, well, I just thought you might call up five or six very close friends once in a while, get 'em all up here in their socks and sit 'em cross-legged around this thing, turn down the lights and break out the chopsticks and have yourselves a swell little evening in Tokyo."

There was a silence. "You're making fun of me, Jack," she said, "and I think you're going to find that's not a very good idea."

"Aw, baby, come on. I was only—"

"The *dec*orator put it there," she said. "I wasn't consulted on anything he did because Jill wanted the whole apartment to be a surprise for me. Besides, I've never thought it was funny at all. I think it makes a very nice *deco*ration."

And they hadn't yet recovered from that unpleasantness when they went back downstairs and found that a new guest had come to join in the cocktail hour. He was a short, stocky, faintly Oriental-looking young man named Ralph who gathered Sally close in a hug to which she responded with rapture, though she had to stoop for it, and who then held out a stubby hand and told Jack it was nice to meet him.

Ralph was an engineer, Jill Jarvis explained, pronouncing the word as if it were a title of rare distinction, and he'd just been telling of how he'd gone to work for a "marvelous" firm—still a small firm, but growing fast because they were bringing in "wonderful" new contracts. Wasn't that exciting?

"Well, it's my boss who makes it exciting," Ralph said, going back to his chair and his drink. "Cliff Myers. He's a dynamo. Founded the company eight years ago when he was fresh out of the Navy after the Korean war. Began with a couple of routine little Navy contracts, started branching out, and since then there's been no stopping him. Remarkable man. Oh, he drives his people hard, no question about that, but he drives himself harder than any man I've ever known. Give him two or three more years and he'll be the most prominent engineering executive in L. A., if not in all of California."

"Wonderful," Jill said. "And he's still young?"

"Well, thirty-eight; that's pretty young in this business."

"I always love to see that," Jill said fervently, narrowing her eyes. "I love to see a man go out and get what he's after."

And Woody Starr gazed down at his drink with a little smile of self-deprecation, suggesting that he knew perfectly well he hadn't ever gone out after much, or gotten much, except a dumb little souvenir shop on Hollywood Boulevard.

"Is he married?" Jill inquired discreetly.

"Oh yeah, very nice wife; no kids. They have a very nice home out in Pacific Palisades."

"Why don't you bring them over sometime, Ralph? You think they'd enjoy that? Because really, I'd love to meet them."

"Well, sure, Jill," Ralph said, though his face betrayed a flicker of embarrassment. "I'm sure they'd like that a lot."

The talk went on to other things, then—or rather it

sank for at least an hour into joshing and banter about nothing at all, or insiders' references to hilarious old times that Jack was unable to follow. He kept looking for opportunities to get Sally up and out of there, but she was so clearly enjoying herself, going along with the laughs, that he could only set his bite and smile to prove his patience.

"Hey, Jill?" Kicker said from the dining-room doorway, and that was the first time Jack noticed that the boy called his mother by her first name. "We ever gonna eat?"

"You go ahead, Kick," she told him. "Ask Nippy to fix you a plate. We'll be along in a while."

". . . And they go through that same dopey routine about dinner every *night*," Sally said later, when she and Jack were alone in his car on the way out to the beach. "Kicker always says 'We ever gonna eat?' and she always gives him that exact same answer, as if they're *both* trying to pretend it doesn't happen all the time. Sometimes it's ten-thirty or eleven before she feels like eating, and all the food's ruined, but by then everybody's so smashed they don't care. If you could *see* the beautiful cuts of meat that go to waste in that kitchen. Ah, God, if only she could have a little more—I don't know. It's just that I wish—well, never mind. I wish a lot of things."

"I know you do," he said, and reached over with one hand to hold her tense thigh. "So do I."

They rode in silence for what seemed a long time; then she said "No, but did you like Ralph, Jack?"

"I don't know; hardly had a chance to talk to him."

"Well, I hope you'll get to know him better. Ralph and I've been friends for years. He's a very—a very dear person."

And Jack winced in the darkness. He hadn't heard her use that phrase before, or any of its fudgy little show-business equivalents—"a very sweet man"; "a very gutsy lady." Still, she had been born and raised on the fringes of Hollywood; she had worked for years in a Hollywood agency, hearing Hollywood people talk all day. Was it any wonder that some of their language had seeped into her own?

"Ralph's a Hawaiian," she was saying. "He was a college friend of the other boy I told you about, the one Jill was living with when I moved in. And I think Jill felt sorry for him, this painfully shy Hawaiian kid who never seemed to have any fun. Then it turned out he needed a place to live, so she let him have the big ground-floor apartment in the main outbuilding—you know the one with all the French doors? Facing the pool? Well, wow, talk about having fun. It changed his life. He told me once—this was years later, after he'd moved away—he said 'Oh, it'd usually be like pulling teeth to get girls to go out with me, because I guess that's what you have to expect if you're a funny-looking little guy with the wrong kind of clothes, but once they saw where I lived, once they saw that *place*, it was magic.' He said 'Get two or three drinks into a girl and she'd be out skinny-dipping in the pool with me every time. And after that,' he said, 'after that, all the rest of it was a piece of cake.'" And Sally's voice dissolved in a rich little peal of lewd laughter.

"Yeah, well, that's nice," Jack said. "That's a nice story."

"And then," Sally went on, "then he told me, he said 'Oh, I always knew it was phony. I knew that whole setup at Jill's was phony. But I used to say to myself, Ralph, if you're gonna be a phony, you might as well be a *real* phony.' Isn't that sweet? I mean in its own kind of awkward, funny way, isn't that sweet?"

"Yeah. Sure is."

But later that night, lying awake while Sally slept, listening to the heavy gathering and pound and rumble and hiss of each wave on the beach, time and again, he wondered if Sheilah Graham had ever referred to someone as being "a very dear person." Well, maybe, or maybe she had used whatever other Hollywood jargon was current in her time, and Fitzgerald probably hadn't minded at all. *He* knew she would never be Zelda; that was one of the ways he knew he loved her. Holding himself together every day for her, dying for a drink but staying away from it, putting what little energy he had into those sketchy opening chapters of *The Last Tycoon,* he must have been humbly grateful just to have her there.

For weeks they were as domestic as a married couple. Except during her hours in the office they were always together at his place. They took long walks on the beach, finding new beachside places to have a drink when they were tired. They talked for hours—"You could *never* bore me," she said, making his lungs feel deeper than they'd felt in years—and he found he was making much better progress on the screenplay. He could look up from his manuscript after dinner and see her curled on the plastic sofa in the lamplight, knitting—she was making a heavy sweater for Kicker's birthday—and that vision never failed to please his sense of order and peace.

But it didn't last. Before the summer was half over, he was startled one evening to find her watching him in a keen, sad, bright-eyed way.

"What's the matter?"

"I can't stay here anymore, Jack, that's all. I mean it.

It's gotten so I absolutely can't bear this place. It's cramped and dark and damp—Jesus, it's not damp, it's *wet.*"

"*This* room's always dry," he said defensively, "and it's always light too, in the daytime. Sometimes it gets so bright I have to close the—"

"Well, but this room's only about five feet *square,*" she said, standing up for emphasis, "and the rest of it's a rotten old tomb. You know what I found on the floor of the shower stall this morning? I found this terrible little pale, transparent worm, sort of like a snail only without any shell, and I accidentally stepped on it about four times before I realized what the hell I was doing. Jesus!" She gave a profound shudder, letting the ragged gray clump of her knitting fall to the floor as she clasped and held herself with both arms, and Jack was reminded of his daughter in that other loathsome shower stall, back in New York.

"And the bedroom!" Sally said. "That mattress is about a hundred years old and it's all sour and it reeks of mildew. And no matter where I hang my clothes they're always clammy when I put them on in the morning. So I've had it, Jack, that's all. I'm never going into the office again wearing wet clothes and having to squirm around and *scratch* myself all day, and that's final."

And from the way she bustled around getting her things together after that speech, packing the Mexican bag and a small suitcase too, it was clear that she didn't even plan to stay for the night. Jack sat biting his lip, trying to think of something to say; then he got to his feet because that seemed better than sitting.

"I'm going home, Jack," she said. "You're perfectly welcome to come with me, and in fact I'd really like you to, but that part of it's entirely up to you."

It didn't take him long to make up his mind. He argued with her a little and feigned exasperation, for the sake of his rapidly diminishing pride, but in less than half an hour he was riding tense at the wheel of his car and following the taillights of hers at a respectful distance. He had even brought along the stacked pages of his screenplay and a supply of fresh paper and pencils, because she'd assured him there were any number of big, clean, well-appointed rooms in Jill's house where he could work all day in total privacy, if that was what he might decide he wanted to do. "And I mean really, wouldn't it be better to spend the rest of our time together at my place?" she'd said. "Come on. You know it would. And how much time do we have left anyway? Seven weeks or something? Six?"

So it happened that Jack Fields became, briefly, a resident of that Greek Revival mansion in Beverly Hills. Giving more thanks than he felt, he accepted the use of an upstairs room to work in—it even had a bathroom that was nearly as opulent as Sally's—and their nights together were spent in her "apartment," where neither of them ever mentioned the Japanese dinner table again.

During the cocktail hour each day it was necessary to associate with Jill Jarvis and to be drawn, however reluctantly, into her world, but at first, after a drink or two and an exchange of winks, they would manage to escape to a restaurant and an evening of their own. Later, though, more and more often and to Jack's increasing annoyance, Sally would go on drinking and talking with whatever guests of Jill's were there until they'd find themselves caught up in the ritual of the late, late dinner at home—until the plump uniformed Negro maid named Nippy appeared in the doorway saying "Miz Jarvis?

There isn't gonna be nothing left of this meat at all unless you folks come and eat it pretty soon."

Stiff and swaying, their eyes barely able to focus on their plates, the party would pick at blackened steak and shrunken, wrinkled vegetables until, as if in acknowledgment of a common revulsion, they would leave most of their dinner untouched and go back to the den to drink again. And the worst part was that Jack too, by this time, would find he wanted nothing more than more to drink. He and Sally, on some of those nights, were too drunk for anything but sleep as they climbed the reeling stairs; he would crawl alone into her bed and pass out, waking many hours later to lie listening to the slow, rasp of her breath, discovering more than once that it came from the other double bed.

He had learned that he didn't much like Sally when she drank. Her eyes would grow startlingly bright, her upper lip would loosen and bloat, and she'd laugh as stridently as an unpopular schoolgirl over things he didn't think were funny at all.

Late one afternoon the young Hawaiian, Ralph, dropped in again, but this time, despite happy cries of greeting and welcome from the girls, he was a solemn bearer of terrible news as he eased himself into a leather chair.

"You know the head of my firm I was telling you about?" he said. "Cliff Myers? His wife died this morning. Heart attack. Collapsed in the bathroom. Thirty-five years old." And lowering his eyes he took a hesitant sip of scotch as if it were a funereal sacrament.

Jill and Sally came urgently forward in their cushions to stare at him, their eyes round and their mouths instantly shaped for the syllable "Oh!" that burst from them in unison. Then Sally said "My God!" and Jill, slumping weakly with one wrist against her lovely forehead, said "Thirty-five years old. Oh, the poor man. The poor man."

Neither Jack nor Woody Starr had yet joined in the grief, but after quick self-conscious glances at each other they were able to murmur appropriate things.

"Was there any history of heart trouble at *all*?" Sally demanded.

"None at all," Ralph assured her. "None at all."

And for once, in these endless cocktail times, they had something substantial to talk about. Cliff Myers was a man of iron, Ralph told them. If he hadn't proved that in his professional career—and God knew he certainly had—then he'd proved it this morning. First he had tried and failed to administer mouth-to-mouth resuscitation on the bathroom floor; then he'd wrapped his wife in a blanket, carried her out to the car and driven her to the hospital, knowing she was probably dead all the way. The doctors there wanted to give him a sedative after they'd broken the news, but you didn't just go around giving sedatives to a man like Cliff Myers. He had driven home alone, and by nine-fifteen—nine-fifteen!—he had called the office to explain why he wouldn't be in for work today.

"Oh!" Sally cried. "Oh, God, I can't bear this. I can't bear this"—and she got up and ran from the room in tears.

Jack followed her quickly into the living room but she wouldn't let him put his arms around her, and he realized at once that he didn't really mind the refusal.

"Hey, come on, Sally," he said, standing several feet apart from her with his hands in his pockets while she wept, or seemed to weep. "Come on. Take it easy."

"Well, but things like this up*set* me, that's all; I can't help it. I'm *sen*sitive, that's all."

"Yeah, well, okay; okay."

"A girl with everything to live for," she said in a quavering voice, "and her whole life going out like that—click —and then *whump* on the bathroom floor; oh, God. Oh, God."

"Well, but look," he said. "Don't you think you're overdoing this a little? I mean you didn't even know the girl and you don't know the man either, so it's really like something you've read in the paper, right? And the point is you can read stuff like this in the paper every day, over your chicken-salad sandwich, and it doesn't necessarily make you—"

"Oh, Jesus, chicken-salad sandwich," she said with loathing, looking him harshly up and down as she backed away. "You really are a cold bastard, aren't you. You know something? You know what I've just begun to figure out about you? You're a cold, unfeeling son of a bitch and you don't care about anything in the world but yourself and your rotten self-indulgent scribbling and no *wonder* your wife couldn't stand the sight of you."

And she was halfway up the stairs before he decided that his best reply was to make no reply at all. He went back into the den to finish his drink and try to figure things out, and he was doing that when Kicker came in with a lumpy, badly rolled sleeping bag on his shoulder.

"Hey, Woody?" the boy said. "You ready?"

"Sure, Kick." Woody got quickly to his feet and knocked back his whiskey, and they left the house together. Jill, huddled with Ralph in an intense discussion of Cliff Myers's tragedy, barely glanced up to wish them good night.

After a while Jack went upstairs, walked on mincing

tiptoe past Sally's closed door and struck off down an adjoining hall to gather up the screenplay and the other personal stuff that had accumulated in "his" room; then he went back downstairs and made a nervous departure past Jill and Ralph, who paid him no attention.

He would wait a few days before calling Sally at the office. If they could make it up, that would be fine, though probably never as fine as before. And if not, well, hell, weren't there plenty of other girls in Los Angeles? Weren't there girls much younger than Sally who cavorted in marvelously scanty bathing suits on the sand beyond his window every day? Or couldn't he ask Carl Oppenheimer to introduce him to one of the many, many girls Carl Oppenheimer seemed to know? Besides, there were only a few weeks left before he'd be done with the script and back in New York, so who the hell cared?

But as his car hummed through the darkness toward Malibu he knew that line of reasoning was nonsense. Drunken and foolish or not, gray-haired or not, Sally Baldwin was the only woman in the world.

Until an hour before dawn that night he sat drinking in his chill, damp bedroom, hearing the surf and breathing the mildew from his hundred-year-old mattress, allowing himself to entertain the thought that he might be a self-destructive personality after all. What saved him, enabling him to lie down and cover himself with sleep at last, was his knowledge that any number of sanctimonious people had agreed to hang that bleak and terrible label on F. Scott Fitzgerald too.

Sally called up two days later and said, in a shy and guarded voice, "You still mad at me?"

And he assured her that he wasn't, while his right hand gripped the phone as if for life and his left made wide, mindless gestures in the air to prove his sincerity.

"Well, okay, I'm glad," she said. "And I'm sorry, Jack. Really. I know I drink too much and everything. And I've felt awful since you left, and I miss you an awful lot. So look: You think you might come in this afternoon and meet me at the Beverly Wilshire? You know? Where we had our first drink together, way back whenever it was?"

And all the way to that well-remembered bar he made heartfelt plans for the kind of reconciliation that might make them both feel young and strong again. If she could get a little time off from work they could take a trip together—up to San Francisco or down to Mexico—or else he could move out of the damned beach house and find a better place to stay with her in town.

But almost from the moment Sally sat down with him, when they were holding hands as tightly on the table as they'd done that other time, it was clear that Sally had other ideas.

"Well, I'm furious with Jill," she began. "Absolutely furious. It's been one ridiculous thing after another. First of all we went to the hairdresser yesterday—we always do that together—and on the way home she said she thought we ought to stop going places together. I said 'What do you mean? What're you talking about, Jill?' And she said 'I think people think we're lesbians.' Well, it made me sick, that's all. Made me sick.

"And then last night she called Ralph and asked him —oh, and in this very low, suggestive voice too—asked him to invite Cliff Myers over for dinner tonight. Can you believe that? I said 'Jill, that's tasteless.' I said 'Look: a month or two from now it might be a thoughtful gesture, but the man's wife's only been dead two *days*. Can't you see how—how tasteless that is?' And she said 'I don't care if it is.' She said 'I've got to meet that man. I'm helplessly attracted to everything that man stands for.'

"Oh, and it's even worse than that, Jack. Because you see Woody Starr has this lousy little apartment in the back of his studio? Where he used to live before he moved in with Jill? And I think it's against the law—I mean I think there's a city ordinance that merchants aren't supposed to sleep in their shops—but anyway, sometimes he takes Kicker down there to bunk in for a night or two with him, and they cook breakfast for themselves and stuff; I guess it's sort of like camping out. So they've spent the past couple of nights there, and today Jill called me at the office in this terrible fit of giggles— she sounded about sixteen—and said 'Guess what. I've just conned Woody into keeping Kicker in the studio another night. Isn't that neat?' I said 'What do you mean?' And she said 'Oh, don't be dense, Sally. Now they won't be here to spoil everything when Cliff *Myers* comes over.' I said 'Well, in the first place, Jill, what makes you think he'll come over at all?' And she said 'Didn't I tell you? Ralph called this morning and confirmed it. He's bringing Cliff Myers to the house at six o'clock.' "

"Oh," Jack said.

"And so listen, Jack. It'll probably be awful, watching her try to seduce that poor guy, but will you—will you come home with me? Because the point is I don't want to go through it alone."

"Why go through it at all? We can get a room some-where—hell, we can get a room right here, if you like."

"And not even have clean clothes in the morning?" she said. "Go to work in this same terrible dress? No thanks."

"That's dumb, Sally. Make a quick run up to the house, get your clothes and come back, and then we'll—"

"Look, Jack. If you don't want to come along with me

you certainly don't have to, but I'm going anyway. I mean everything may be sick and degenerate or whatever you want to call it in that house, but it's my home."

"Oh, shit, you know better than that. Whaddya mean 'home,' for Christ's sake? That fucking menagerie couldn't be *anybody's* home."

She looked at him in an offended, willfully humorless way, like someone whose religion has been held up to ridicule. "It's the only home I have, Jack," she said quietly.

*"Balls!"* And several people at neighboring tables looked quickly up and around at him, with startled faces. "I mean God damnit, Sally," he said, trying and failing to lower his voice, "if it gives you some kind of perverse pleasure to lie back and let Jill fucking Jarvis parade her depravity through your life, that's something you really ought to take up with some fucking psy*chi*atrist instead of me."

"Sir," a waiter said at his elbow, "I'll have to ask you to keep your voice down and watch your language. You can be heard all over this room."

"It's all right," Sally told the waiter. "We're leaving."

On the way out of the place, torn between more reckless shouting and abject apologies for having shouted at all, Jack hung his head and walked stiffly, in silence.

"Well," she said when they reached her parked car in the dazzling afternoon sun, "you were really attractive in there, weren't you? You really gave a memorable performance, didn't you? How can I ever go *in* there again without getting funny looks from the waiters and everyone else?"

"Yeah, well, you can write it all down in your memory book."

"Oh, good. And my memory book is getting so wonderfully full, isn't it? What a pleasure it'll be when I'm sixty years old. Look, Jack. You coming or staying?"

"I'll follow you," he said, and he wondered at once, as he moved away to his own car, why he hadn't had the guts to say "Staying."

Then he was following her among the slender palms of the first shallow rise of Beverly Hills, and then they were bringing their cars to a halt in Jill's big driveway, where the cars of two other visitors were already parked. Sally slammed her car door a little harder than necessary and stood waiting, ready to deliver a smiling speech that she'd probably prepared and rehearsed during the short drive from the hotel.

"Well, if nothing else," she said, "this should be interesting. I mean wouldn't any woman want to meet a man like Cliff Myers? He's young, he's rich, he's going places, and he's available. Wouldn't it be funny if I snare him away from Jill before she even gets her hands on him?"

"Ah, come on, Sally."

"Whaddya mean, 'come on'? Whadda *you* got to say about it? You really take a hell of a lot for granted, you know that?" They had made their way up onto the pool terrace and were approaching the big French doors of the den. "I mean in four more weeks you'll have gone back to wherever the hell you came from, so what am I supposed to do in the meantime? Am I really supposed to sit around and *knit* while every halfway decent man in the world passes me by?"

"Sally and Jack," Jill said solemnly from a leather sofa, "I'd like you to meet Cliff Myers." And Cliff Myers rose from his place close beside her to accept the introductions. He was tall and thick, in a rumpled suit, and his short hair stood upright in the blond bristles of a "crew cut" that made him look like a big, blunt-faced boy. Sally went to him first and told him of her sorrow for his terrible loss; Jack hoped a similar message might be conveyed in the dead-serious way he shook hands.

"Well, as I was just telling Jill," Cliff Myers said when they were all settled, "I've sure been racking up a lot of sympathy points. Walked into the office yesterday and a couple of the secretaries started crying; stuff like that. Went out to lunch with a client today and I thought the maiter dee was gonna start crying on me too. The waiter too. Funny business, this sympathy-getting bit. Too bad you can't put it in the bank, right? 'Course, it prob'ly won't last, so I may as well enjoy it while I can, right? Hey, Jill? Mind if I help myself to a little more of the Grand-dad?"

She told him to sit still, and she made the fixing and serving of his drink into a little ceremony of selfless admiration. When he took the first sip she watched carefully to make sure it was just to his liking.

Then Ralph came staggering into the room on rubber legs, comically exaggerating the heaviness of a load of firewood he held against his chest. "Hey, know what?" he said. "This really takes me back to old times. Jill used to work the hell out of me when I lived here, you see, Cliff," he explained as he crouched and dropped the wood in a neat pile on the hearth. "That was how I paid my rent. And I swear to God, you'd never guess how much work there is to do around a place like this."

"Oh, I can imagine," Cliff Myers said. "You got a really big—a really big place here."

Ralph straightened up and brushed shreds of bark from his rep tie and Oxford shirt, then from the lapels and sleeves of his trim hopsack jacket. He might still be a funny-looking little guy, but he no longer wore the wrong kind of clothes. Dusting his hands, he smiled shyly at his employer. "Nice, though, isn't it, Cliff?" he said. "I knew you'd like it here."

And Cliff Myers assured him that it was very nice, very fine indeed.

"I suppose it may seem funny to have a fire in the summertime," Jill said, "but it does get chilly here at night."

"Oh, yeah," Cliff said. "Out on the Palisades we used to light fires in the evening all year round. My wife always liked to have a fire." And Jill conspicuously squeezed his heavy hand.

Dinner was on time that night, but Jack Fields ate almost nothing. He brought a full drink to the table and went back once or twice to replenish it; as soon as the unusually elaborate meal was over he sank into a shadowed corner of the den, well away from the party, and went on drinking. He knew this was his third or fourth consecutive night of drunkenness, but he could worry about that some other time. He couldn't rid himself of Sally's saying "He's young, he's rich, he's going places, and he's available," and whenever he looked up now he could see the profile of her pretty head on its elegant neck, glowing in the firelight, smiling or laughing or saying "Oh, that's marvelous" in response to whatever dumb, dumb remark this bereaved stranger, this asshole Cliff Myers, had just made.

Soon he found he couldn't even watch her anymore because a heavy dark mist had closed in on all four sides of his vision, causing his head to droop and hang until the only thing he could see at all—and he saw it with the terrible clarity of self-hatred—was his own left shoe on the carpet.

". . . Hey, uh, Jack?"

"Uh?"

"I said wanna gimme a hand?" It was Ralph's voice. "Come on."

"Uh. Uh. Wai' second. Okay." And with energy that came from nowhere, or from the desperate last reserves of shame, he forced himself up and followed Ralph rapidly out into the kitchen and down the cellar stairs, nearly falling, until they came to a heap of firewood against the cellar wall. Off to one side, by itself, lay a log cut to fireplace length that must have been two feet thick: it looked like a sawed-off segment of telephone pole, and it held the full weight of Jack's drunken scrutiny. "Son of a bitch," he said.

"What'sa matter?"

"That's the biggest fucking log I ever saw in my life."

"Yeah, well, never mind that," Ralph said. "We just want the little stuff." And with double armloads of the little stuff piled to their chins they went back upstairs, all the way up to the second floor and into the high, wide emptiness of Jill's bedroom, or Jill's and Woody Starr's bedroom, which Jack had never seen before. At the far end of it, well away from the hearth where Ralph squatted to unload the wood, many yards of white cloth were hung from the ceiling and draped partly around the borders of a great "Hollywood" bed to form a bower that might have been dreamed by an adolescent girl as the last word in luxury and romance.

"Okay," Ralph said. "That'll do the job." And though he was plainly drunk himself, swaying on his haunches, he began the meticulous task of building and lighting a fire between the polished brass andirons.

Jack did his best to leave the room quickly but kept veering sideways against the near wall; then he decided it might be helpful to use the wall for support and guidance, letting one shoulder slide heavily along it while he gave his whole attention to lifting and placing his feet in the deep champagne-colored carpet. He knew dimly that Ralph had finished at the fireplace, had lurched past him muttering "Come on" and gone away into the hall, leaving him alone in this treacherously unstable but mercifully open room; he could see too that the bright doorway was very near now—only a few more steps—but his knees had begun to soften and buckle. He thought he could feel his shoulder sliding down the wall, rather than along it; then the tilting yellow carpet came slowly closer until it offered itself up as a logical, necessary surface for his hands, and for the side of his face.

Sometime later the sounds of low voices and laughter brought him awake. He lay staring at the open door and calculating whether he'd be able to make a run for it, knowing suddenly that Jill Jarvis and Cliff Myers were huddled together on this same carpet at the fireplace, ten or fifteen feet behind his head.

"So what's with this character on the floor?" Cliff Myers inquired. "He live here too?"

"Well, sort of," Jill said, "but he's harmless. He belongs to Sally. She'll come get him out in a minute, or else Ralph will, or else he'll get himself out. Don't worry about it."

"Hell, I'm not worried about anything. Just wondering how I can get this log settled in there without burning my mitts, is all. Sit back a second. There. That's got it."

And Jack took drunken, disdainful notice of Cliff Myers's saying "mitts" instead of hands. Only a dumb son of a bitch would say that, even when constricted with the shyness of flirtation, even if still in shock over his wife's death.

"Know something?" Jill said quietly. "You're quite a guy, Cliff."

"Yeah? Well, you're quite a girl."

There then began moist little sounds of kissing, and pleased, purring moans that suggested he was feeling her up. A zipper raced open (The back of her dress? The front of his pants?) and that was the last thing Jack Fields heard as he clambered to his feet and got the hell out of there and shut the door behind him.

He wasn't yet in good enough shape to find his way to Sally's room; all he could do was sit at the top of the stairs with his head in his hands, waiting for balance. After a few minutes he felt the whole staircase shuddering, and Ralph's voice called "Coming through! Coming through, please!" The sturdy little Hawaiian was climbing the stairs with remarkable speed and agility. His straining face gleamed with happiness, and in his arms he carried the single giant log from the cellar. "Coming through, please!" he called again as Jack made way for him, and without pausing to knock at the bedroom door he shouldered it open and lunged inside. There was just enough light to show that Jill Jarvis and Cliff Myers had left the fireplace; they were evidently in the bed. "Sorry, miss!" Ralph called as he hurried with his burden to the hearthside, "Sorry, sir! Compliments of the Company Commander!" And he dumped the great log onto the fire with a terrible thump that made the andirons ring and sent up a multitude of orange sparks.

"Oh, Ralph, you *idiot!*" Jill cried from within her bower. "Get *outa* here now!"

But Ralph was already leaving as quickly as he'd come, giggling at how funny it must have looked, and he was followed by rich, hearty peals of baritone laughter from the bed—the laughter of a man who might soon be the most prominent engineering executive in all of California, and who had always prided himself on knowing how to spot real talent in the young fellows he put on his payroll.

"Well, I guess neither of us were exactly at our best," Sally said the next morning, trying to do something about her hair at the mirror of her dressing table. It was Saturday: she wouldn't have to go to work, but she said she didn't know what else she wanted to do.

Jack was still in bed and wondering if it might be wise to drink nothing but beer, in moderation, for the rest of his life. "I guess I'll go back to the beach," he said. "Try and get some work done."

"Okay." She got up and drifted aimlessly to one of her many French windows. "Oh, Jesus, come and look at this," she said. "I mean really. Come and look." And he struggled up to join her at the window, which overlooked the swimming pool. Cliff Myers lay floating in the water, on his back, wearing a pair of maroon trunks that must surely have belonged to Woody Starr. Jill stood at the edge of the pool in a stunningly brief bikini, apparently calling to him, holding out a bright cocktail glass in either hand.

"Brandy Alexanders," Sally explained. "When I went down to the kitchen for coffee, Nippy gave me this big worried look and said 'Sally? You know how to make a brandy Alexander?' She said 'Miz Jarvis told me to make up a whole batch of 'em, and the trouble is I don't know how. We got a book on it somewhere?' " And Sally sighed. "Well, so everything worked out nicely, didn't it. Mr. Myers and Mrs. Jarvis are seen enjoying their breakfast cocktails at poolside, on the third morning after the late Mrs. Myers's death." After a silence she said "Still, I suppose this is a little healthier for Jill than the way she's spent all her *other* mornings as long as I've known her—lying in bed till noon with her coffee and her cigarettes and her endless, mindless fucking *cross*word puzzles."

"Yeah, well, look, Sally. You want to come home with me?"

And she answered him without taking her eyes from the window. "I don't know; I don't think so. We'd just start fighting again. I'll call you, Jack, okay?"

"Okay."

"Besides," she said, "I ought to be here when Woody and Kicker come home. I think I might be able to help. Oh, not Woody, of course, but Kicker. I mean Kicker loves me—or at least he used to. Sometimes he used to call me his 'proxy mother.' " She lingered silent at the window for a long time, looking jaded, her upper lip beginning to loosen the way it did when she was drunk. "Have you any idea," she asked, "of what it means to be a woman unable to have a child? Even if you don't necessarily want one, it's a terrible thing to discover you can't; and sometimes—oh, God, I don't know. Sometimes I think having a child is all I've ever really wanted in my whole life."

On his unsteady way out of the house, Jack went into the kitchen and said "Hey, uh, Nippy? Think you could find me a beer?"

"Well, I believe that can be arranged, Mr. Fields," the maid said. "Sit right here at the table." When he was settled with the beer she sat across from him and said "See that blender? Empty, right? Well, twenty minutes ago that blender was full to the top with brandy Alexanders. And I mean I don't think that's very sensible, do you? Giving a man all that drink first thing in the morning when he prob'ly doesn't even know where his brains are at anyway because it's only been three days since his wife passed away? I like to see a little restraint."

"Me too."

"Well, but then you never can tell with Miz Jarvis," Nippy said. "She's very—sophisticated, you know what I mean? Very kind of"—she fluttered the plump fingers of one hand to find the right word—"bohemian. Still, I don't care what anybody says—and I've heard a lot of people say a lot of things—I think the world of that lady, and that's the truth. I'd do anything for Miz Jarvis. Twice now, over the years, she's helped my husband get work in times we really needed it, and you know what she did for me, that I never can forget? She got me my contacts."

When he looked puzzled, Nippy pointed happily to the outer corners of her eyes with both index fingers, blinking. And if he hadn't understood her then—"Oh, your contact *lenses*"—he felt sure she would have bent over, peeled back an eyelid, and dropped one of the moist, all but invisible things into the palm of her hand as an offering of explanation and proof.

Back at the beach house, Jack worked as hard on the script all day as if he were trying to finish it in a week. He had begun to feel, in the last month or so, that it wasn't bad; it was turning out all right; it would make a pretty good movie. Late in the afternoon he called Carl Oppenheimer to discuss the handling of a tricky scene; it wasn't really a necessary call, but he wanted to hear a voice other than the voices of Jill Jarvis's house.

"How come you never come over, Jack?" Oppenheimer demanded. "Ellie'd love to see you, and so would I."

"Well, I've been pretty busy, is all, Carl."

"Got a girl?"

"Well, sort of. I mean yeah, yeah, I do, but she's—"

"Bring her over!"

"Well, that's nice, Carl, and I will. I'll call you again soon. It's just that right now I think we're sort of taking a vacation from each other. It's very—it's pretty complicated."

"Oh, Jesus, writers," Oppenheimer said in exasperation. "I don't know what the hell's the matter with you guys. Why can't you just get laid like everybody else?"

"Well—" Sally began when she called him a few days later, and he knew he would now be on the phone for an hour. "When Woody and Kicker got back that morning, Jill went out and met them on the terrace. She sent Kicker inside to wash up, and she said to Woody 'Look. I want you to disappear for a week. Please don't ask questions; just go. I'll explain this later.' Can you imagine a woman saying that to a man she's been living with for three years?"

"No."

"Neither could I, but that's what she said. I mean that's what she *told* me she said. And she said to me 'I'm not going to let anything interfere with what I have now.' She said 'Cliff and I are special, Sally. We're the real thing. We've established a relationship, and we're . . .' "

It occurred to Jack that if he held the phone well away from his head Sally's voice would dwindle and flatten out and be lost in tinny gibberish, like the voice of an idiot midget. Disembodied, bereft of coherence and so of all envy and self-pity and self-righteousness as well, it would then become a small but steady irritant serving no purpose but to chafe his nerves and prevent him from getting his day's work done. He tried holding the phone that way for five or ten seconds, flinching in the pain of his secret betrayal, and he abandoned the experiment just in time to hear her say ". . . and so listen, Jack. If we both agree not to drink too much, and if we're very careful with each other in every way, do you think you might—you know—do you think you might come back? Because I mean the point is—the point is I love you, and I need you."

She had said any number of loving things these past few months, but never that she "needed" him. And the effect of it now, just when he'd determined never to go to Beverly Hills again, was to make him change his mind.

". . . Oh, God," she said in the doorway of her room, half an hour later. "Oh, God, I'm glad you're here." And she melted into his arms. "I won't be awful to you anymore, Jack," she said. "I promise, promise. Because there *is* so little time left, and the least we can do is be nice to each other, right?"

"Right."

And with her door locked against any possibility of blundering intrusion, they spent the whole afternoon being as nice to each other as either of them had ever learned to be. Only after the long bank of Sally's western windows had gone from gold to crimson to dark blue did they rouse themselves at last to take showers, and to put on their clothes.

Then, before very long, Sally went back to the inexhaustible topic of Jill's behavior. She paced the carpet on her slim, stockinged feet as she talked, and Jack thought she had never looked prettier. But he let most of her talk go past his hearing, nodding or shaking his head at whatever intervals seemed appropriate, usually after she had whirled to stare at him in mute appeal for endorsement of her dismay. He began paying attention only when she got around to what she called the worst part.

". . . Because I mean really, Jack, the worst part of all this is what it's doing to Kick. Jill thinks he doesn't know what's going on, but she's crazy. He does. He mopes around the house all day looking pale and wretched and as if he's about to—I don't know. And he won't even let me talk to him. He won't let me comfort him or be friends with him or anything. And for the past two nights you know what he's done? He's taken off alone on his bike and spent the night with Woody, down in the studio. I don't think Jill even noticed he was gone, either time."

"Yeah, well, that's—that's too bad."

"Oh, and he hates Cliff. Absolutely hates him. Whenever Cliff says anything to him he freezes up—and I don't blame him. Because you know something else, Jack? You were right about Cliff from the start and I was wrong, that's all. He's nothing but a big, dumb—he's a dullard."

On Jill's instructions, Nippy had fed the boy at least an hour before the adults' dinner was served. She had also equipped the big dining-room table with two matching silver candle holders, each bearing three new candles, and she'd turned out the lights so that everything was bathed in a flickering glow of romance.

"Isn't this nice?" Jill inquired. "I always forget about candles. I think we ought to have candles every night." And the way she was dressed suggested other forgotten things well worth remembering, perhaps her own swift and careless girlhood as a privileged daughter of the South. She wore a simple, expensive-looking black dress with a neckline low enough to show the beginnings of her small, firm breasts, and a single strand of pearls that she twisted nervously at her throat with her free hand while toying with her food.

257

Cliff Myers was flushed and jovial with Old Grand-dad. He told one smiling, self-aggrandizing anecdote after another about his engineering firm, with Jill pronouncing each story "wonderful" in turn; then he said "No, but listen, another thing, Jill. This you gotta hear. First of all, I find I get some of my best thinking done when I'm driving the freeway to work. Don't know why that's true, but I've learned to trust it. So. Know what I thought up this morning?" He efficiently sliced open his baked potato and lowered his face to savor the rising heat of it, making his audience wait. He heavily buttered and salted it, forked up a slice of lamb chop, and looked happily reflective as he chewed; then, talking around the meat, he said "How's this for openers?" And he swallowed. "We've got this very high-grade industrial glue in the lab. You wouldn't believe it. Paint that stuff on any metal surface, touch it, and I swear to God you can't get your hand loose. Try soap and water, try any kinda detergent, try alcohol, or you name it. Can't get loose. So look." Almost half a chop went into his mouth, but he was scarcely able to chew because he had begun to laugh. "Look: supposing I get this little truck." He broke off, helpless with laughter, one hand spanning his forehead while he struggled for composure. Of his three listeners, only Jill was smiling.

"So okay," Cliff Myers said at last, and his mouth was apparently clear. "Supposing I get one of our company panel trucks. Supposing I dress up in one of our drivers' uniforms—they wear these kind of cream-colored coveralls with the insignia on the front pocket and the company name spelled out across the back? With these visor caps? And of course the truck's got the company name on it too, you follow me? 'Myers'? So I come driving up here with this aluminum tub fulla roses—three, four dozen American Beauties, the very best—and of course when I bring it out I'll be real careful to hold it by the dry part, so *my* mitts'll be free; then your little friend Woody'll come out there on the terrace to see what's up, and I'll say 'Mr. Starr?' And I'll shove that slick, glued-up tub into his hands and say 'Flowers, sir. Flowers for Mrs. Jarvis. Compliments of Cliff Myers.' And I'll get back into the truck and take off, or maybe I'll stay just long enough to kind of wink at him, and old Starr of Hollywood'll just *be* there. He'll just *be* there, you follow me? It'll take him maybe thirty seconds to figure out he's *stuck* to the son of a bitch, and maybe five or ten minutes more to realize he's been had, he's been faked out, somebody's pulled a fast one on him, and I swear to God, Jill, I'd bet money —I'd bet *money* the little bastard'll never bother you again."

Jill had looked enraptured through the latter part of his recital; now she squeezed his hand on the table with both of her own and said "Marvelous. Oh, that's marvelous, Cliff," and they laughed together, looking each other up and down with bright eyes.

"Jill," Sally said from across the table, after a while. "This is just a joke, isn't it."

"Well, of *course* it is," Jill said impatiently, as if reproving a slow child. "It's an absolutely inspired idea for a practical joke. The men in Cliff's firm play practical jokes on each other all the time—I think it's a delightful way to survive all the dull and boring parts of life, don't you?"

"Well, but I mean, you'd certainly never agree to going through with a thing like that, would you."

"Oh, I don't know," Jill said in a light, teasing voice. "Maybe; maybe not. But don't you think it's a delightfully wicked idea?"

"I think you're out of your mind," Sally told her.

"Oh, I think so too," she said with an attractive little wrinkling of her nose. "I think Cliff is too. Isn't that what it means to be in love?"

Later that night, when Jack and Sally were alone, she said "I don't even want to talk about it. I don't want to talk about it or think about it or anything, okay?"

And it certainly was. Any time Sally was unwilling to talk or think about Jill Jarvis was perfectly okay with Jack.

The following night he took her to a restaurant for dinner, and then out for an evening at the home of Carl Oppenheimer.

"Jesus," she said as they drove up the coast highway toward the better part of Malibu, "I'm really a little scared to meet him, you know?"

"Why?"

"Well, because of who he *is*. He's one of the few major—"

"Come on, Sally. There isn't anything 'major' about him. He's only a movie director and he's only thirty-two years old."

"Are you out of your mind? He's brilliant. He's one of the two or three top directors in the industry. Have you any idea how lucky you are to be working with him?"

"Well, okay, but then, does he have any idea how lucky he is to be working with me?"

"God," she said. "You've got an ego that nobody'd believe. Tell me something: If you're so great, how come your clothes are all falling apart? And how come you've got snails in your shower stall? Huh? And how come your bed smells like death?"

"Jack!" Carl Oppenheimer called from the bright doorway of his house, after they'd walked the long, heavily leaf-shadowed path from the place where they'd left the car. "And you're Sally," he said with an earnest frown. "*Really* nice to meet you."

She said it was certainly an honor to meet him too, and they went inside to where young Ellis stood smiling in welcome, wearing a floor-length dress. She looked lovely, and she rose on tiptoe to give Jack an eager little kiss of old acquaintance, which he hoped Sally would notice; then, as they moved chatting pleasantly into the big room overlooking the ocean, where the liquor was, she turned to Sally again and said "I love your hair. Is that the natural color, or do you—"

"No, it's natural," Sally told her. "I just get it streaked."

"Sit down, sit down!" Oppenheimer commanded, but he chose to remain standing himself, or rather walking, slowly treading the floor of this ample and excellent room with a heavy glass of bourbon tinkling in one hand while the other made large gestures to accompany his talk. He was telling of his frustrations over the past few weeks in trying to finish a movie that was well behind schedule, and of how "impossible" it was to work with its star—an actor so famous that the very mention of his name was a kind of conversational triumph.

". . . And then today," he said, "today everything on the set had to stop dead—cameras, sound, everything— while he took me off in a corner and sat me down to discuss what he called Dramatic Theory, and he asked me if I was familiar with the work of a playwright named George Bernard Shaw. You think anybody'd believe that? You think anybody in America'd believe how dumb the son of a bitch is? Christ's sake, this year he's discovered Shaw; three years from now he'll discover the Communist Party."

Oppenheimer seemed to tire of his monologue after a

while; he came heavily to rest in a deep sofa and put his arm around Ellis, who nestled close to him; then he asked Sally if she was an actress too.

"Oh, no," she said quickly, brushing invisible specks of cigarette ash off her lap, "but thanks anyway. I don't really do anything very—I'm only—I'm a secretary. I work for Edgar Todd, the agent."

"Well, hell, that's fine with me," Oppenheimer said expansively. "Some of my best friends are secretaries." And as if aware that this last line might not have been wholly successful, he hurried on to ask her how long she'd worked for Edgar, and how she liked her job, and where she lived.

"I live in Beverly," she told him. "I have an apartment in the home of a friend there; it's very nice."

"Yeah, well, that's—nice," he said. "I mean Beverly's very nice."

For the last hour or so of that evening in Oppenheimer's house, Jack found himself perched cozily with Ellis on two of the tall, leather-topped stools along the bar that occupied one side of the room. She told him at length of her childhood in Pennsylvania, of the summer stock company that had provided her first real "experience of theater," and of the wonderfully lucky sequence of events that had led to her meeting Carl. And Jack was so pleased with her youth and prettiness, and so flattered by her attention, that he only dimly realized he had heard the whole story before, during the time he'd stayed here.

Across the room, Carl and Sally were engaged in a steady and intense discussion. Jack couldn't hear much of it, in the several times he tried to listen, beyond the insistent, dead-serious rumble of Carl's voice, though once he heard Sally say "Oh, no, I loved it. Really. I loved it all the way through."

"Well, this's been great," Carl Oppenheimer said when it was time for them to leave. "Sally. Wonderful meeting you; good talking to you. Jack: we'll be in touch."

And then came the long, drink-fuddled ride back to town. For what seemed twenty minutes there was silence in the car, until Sally said "They've sort of—got everything, haven't they. I mean they're young, they're in love, and everybody knows he's a brilliant man so it doesn't really matter whether she's got any talent or not because she's a cute little sexpot anyway. What could ever go wrong in a house like that?"

"Oh, I don't know; I can think of a couple of things that might go wrong."

"You know what I really didn't like about him, though?" she said. "I didn't like the way he kept asking me what I thought of his movies. He'd mention one picture after another and ask me if I'd seen it, and then he'd say 'So what'd you think? Did you like it?' Or he'd say 'Didn't you think it kind of fell apart in the second half?' Or 'Didn't you feel so-and-so was a little miscast as the girl?' And I mean really, Jack. Isn't that a bit much?"

"Why?"

"Well, because who am *I*?" She rolled her window half open and snapped her cigarette away into the wind. "I mean Jesus, after all, who am *I*?"

"Whaddya mean, who are you?" he said. "I know who you are, and so does Oppenheimer, and so do you. You're Sally Baldwin."

"Yeah, yeah," she said quietly, facing the black window. "Yeah, yeah, yeah, yeah."

When they walked into the Beverly Hills house, Jack was startled to find Woody Starr instead of Cliff Myers sitting with Jill, until he remembered Sally's telling him that Cliff had agreed to stay away for a night or two so that Jill could sensibly and permanently disengage herself from Woody. And the way Woody looked now as he rose from the sofa to greet them—drawn, shamefaced, seeming to apologize for his very presence—made it clear that Jill had already broken the news.

"Well, hey, Sally," he said. "Hello, Jack. We're just having a—can I get you a drink?"

"No thanks," Sally told him. "Good to see you, though, Woody. How've you been?"

"Oh, can't complain. Not much business at the studio, but apart from that I've been—you know—staying out of trouble."

"Well, good," she said. "We'll see you, Woody." And she led Jack smiling through the clumps of leather furniture and out into the living room and up the grand staircase. Only when she had closed and locked her own door behind them did she allow herself to speak again. "God," she said. "Did you see his face?"

"Well, he didn't look very—"

"He looked dead," she said. "He looked like a man with all the life gone out of him."

"Well, okay, but look: this happens all the time. Women get tired of men; men get tired of women. You can't go around letting your heart get broken over all the losers."

"Ah, you're in a mellow philosophical mood tonight, aren't you," she said, leaning forward and reaching back to unfasten the hooks of her dress. "Very mature, very wise—it must've come over you when you were all cuddled up with Ellis What's-her-name at Oppenheimer's bar."

But within an hour, after she had cried out for love of

him and after they'd then fallen apart to lie waiting for sleep, her voice was very small and shy. "Jack? How much time is there now? Two more weeks? Less?"

"Oh, I dunno, baby. I may stay around a little longer, though, just for—"

"Just for what?" And all her bitterness came back. "For me? Oh, Jesus, no, don't do that. You think I want you doing *me* any favors?"

Early the next morning, when she brought their coffee up to the room, she could barely wait to put the tray on a table before telling him what she'd found downstairs in the den. Woody Starr was still there, lying asleep in his clothes on the sofa. He didn't even have a blanket or a pillow. Wasn't that the damnedest thing?

"Why?"

"Well, why didn't he leave last *night*, for God's sake?"

"Maybe he wants to say goodbye to the boy."

"Oh," she said. "Well, yes, I suppose you're right. It's probably that. It's probably because of Kick."

When they went downstairs and caught a glimpse of Woody and Kicker talking quietly together, they withdrew quickly into the kitchen to socialize with Nippy and to wait in hiding until it would be time for Kicker to leave for school. They didn't know, and Jill Jarvis wouldn't remember until later, that this was a school holiday.

"Oh, Jesus, Nip," Sally said, wilting onto a kitchen chair. "I really don't feel like going to work today."

"*Don't*, then," Nippy said. "Know something, Sally? I've never seen you take a day off the whole time I've been in this house. Listen, that old office can get along without you once in a while. Why don't you and Mr. Fields do something nice today? Go someplace nice for lunch, take in a good movie or something. Or take a drive; it's beautiful weather out. You could go down to

San Juan Capistrano or something nice like that. You know how they say in the song about when the swallows come back to Capistrano? Well, if I'm not mistaken, it's just about that time of year. You could go down there and watch the swallows coming back and all; wouldn't that be nice?"

"Ah, I don't know, Nippy," Sally said. "It'd be nice, but I think I'd better at least put in an appearance at the office or Edgar'll be eating his arm. And I'm practically fifteen minutes late as it is."

Leaving the kitchen at last, when Sally said it would be "safe" to face the den, they were relieved to find themselves alone. Jack noticed too, in passing, that the black velvet painting of the clown had been removed from the wall above the fireplace. But then, through the sunny panes of the French doors, they saw Woody and Kicker out on the pool terrace, standing close together and still talking.

"Oh, why can't he just *go*?" Sally said. "How long does it take *any*body to say goodbye?"

Woody Starr's luggage was heaped on the terrace beside him: an old Army duffel bag that he'd probably used in the Merchant Marine, a suitcase, and a couple of well-filled paper shopping bags, bright with department-store advertising and heavily reinforced with brown twine. He bent over to divide the load, and he and Kicker carried all the stuff down from the terrace and stowed it in his car. Then they came back up, Woody with his arm around the boy's shoulders, and walked up close to the house for their final parting.

Jack and Sally retreated well back into the den to avoid being seen watching, and they watched. They saw Woody Starr put both arms around the boy and gather him up into an abrupt, tight, clinging embrace. After that, Woody started to walk away and Kicker made for the house—but Kicker stopped and turned, and then they saw what had caught his eye: a small cream-colored delivery truck coming swiftly up the driveway with MYERS emblazoned in brown letters on its side.

"Oh, I can't bear this," Sally said, going limp and pressing her face into Jack's shirt. "I can't bear this."

The truck came to a stop a few yards beneath the place where Woody waited on the terrace and Cliff Myers got out, red-faced, with a self-conscious little smile, into the sunshine. He hurried around to the rear of the truck in his coveralls, which were several sizes too small for him, brought out his glistening metal tub with its massed and wobbling heads of a great many roses, carried it up to Woody Starr, and thrust it into his hands. He appeared to be talking as he did this—seemed, in fact, to have been talking steadily and perhaps mindlessly since his arrival, as though compelled to do so by an unexpected spasm of embarrassment—but once the tub of roses was in Woody's possession he was able to stop. He drew himself exaggeratedly straight, touched two fingers to the neat visor of his cap, and made his getaway to the truck in a stiff-legged run that was almost certainly faster and clumsier than he'd planned it to be.

Kicker had missed none of it. He went back across the terrace to join Woody, who had squatted to set the tub down, and now they were both huddled low over it in conference.

"It's okay, baby," Jack said into Sally's hair. "It's okay now. He's gone."

"I know," she said. "I saw the whole thing."

"Well, look: you think we could find something in the house for his hands? Think Nippy could find something?"

"Like what, though? Some kind of detergent, or solvent, or what?"

But it wasn't necessary to find anything in the house. After a minute or two Woody and Kicker moved away together with the bright roses riding between them, and with Jack Fields following at a stranger's distance. They went into the shadows of the big garage, where Kicker carefully poured gasoline from a five-gallon can down the surface of the tub and over Woody's hands until Woody was able to work them free. That was all it took. Then Kicker used the heel of his shoe to shove the tub raspingly across the floor of the garage and hard against the wall, where it would stay until long after the glue had dried to harmlessness and the roses were dead.

Alan B. ("Kicker") Jarvis was enrolled in what his mother described as the finest boys' boarding school in the West, and he left home to take up residence there almost at once.

Later in the same week Jill and Cliff went to Las Vegas to be married—she said she had always wanted to be married in one of the "adorable" little wedding chapels of that city. Their honeymoon plans, at the time they left Los Angeles, were still indefinite: they hadn't yet decided whether to spend a month in Palm Springs, a month in the Virgin Islands, or a month in France and Italy. "Or maybe," she confided to Sally, "maybe we'll say the hell with it, take three months and go to *all* those places."

Jack Fields's screenplay had been finished and accepted and quarreled over and finished and accepted again; then Carl Oppenheimer fervently shook hands with him. "I think we'll have a picture, Jack," he said. "I think we'll have a picture." And Ellis rose to give him a quick, sweet kiss.

He talked long and jovially on the phone with his daughters about the fine times they'd be having in New York very soon, and he spent a day buying gifts for them. With Sally's advisory help, he also bought two new suits of clothes at the Los Angeles Brooks Brothers in order to go home looking like a success. And at Sally's suggestion, secretly wincing at the cost of it, he bought quart bottles of brandy, bourbon, scotch, and vodka and arranged for them all to be gift-wrapped, packed in a gift box, and delivered to Jill's house with a brief, carefully worded note about her "hospitality."

When he'd closed out his occupancy of the beach place, he and Sally drove down to spend four days of a prolonged holiday weekend in an oceanside motel near San Diego that Sally recommended as being "wonderful." He would have liked to know when and with whom she had learned how wonderful it was, but with so little time left he knew better than to ask.

On the way back to Los Angeles they stopped at the Mission of San Juan Capistrano and walked slowly around and through it among many other cordially shuffling tourists, each with a handful of tourist brochures, but there were no swallows in sight.

"Looks like they've all taken off this year," Sally said, "instead of coming back."

That gave Jack what seemed a pretty funny idea, and when they were out at the car again he backed away from her into the roadside weeds with the nimble steps of an entertainer. He knew he looked all right in his new clothes and he'd always been able to sing a little, or at least to fake the sound of singing. "Hey listen, baby," he said. "How's this?" And he sang from a straight-standing crooner's posture, with both arms rising slightly from his sides, palms out, to convey sincerity.

When the swallows take off from Capistrano,
That's when I'll be taking off from you . . .

"Oh, that's sensational," Sally said before he could even go on to the next line. "That's really socko, Jack. You really do have a great sense of humor, you know that?"

On their last evening, seated in what Edgar Todd had solemnly promised them was the finest restaurant in Los Angeles, she looked disconsolate as she picked at her crabmeat Imperial. "This is kind of dumb, isn't it?" she said. "Spending all this money when you'll be on the plane in a couple of hours anyway?"

"Doesn't seem dumb to me; I thought it might be nice." He had thought too that it might be the kind of thing F. Scott Fitzgerald would have done at a time like this, but he kept that part of it to himself. He had tried for years to prevent anyone from knowing the full extent of his preoccupation with Fitzgerald, though a girl in New York had once uncovered it in a relentless series of teasing, bantering questions that left him with nothing to hide.

"Well, okay," Sally said. "We'll sit here and be elegant and witty and sad together and smoke about forty-five cigarettes apiece." But her sarcasm wasn't really convincing, because she'd met him at the office that afternoon wearing a new, expensive-looking blue dress that he could have sworn she'd bought in the hope of being taken to a place like this.

"Can't get over that dress of yours," he told her. "I think it's just about the best-looking dress I've ever seen."

"Thank you," she said. "And I'm glad I've got it. Might be useful in helping me trap the *next* counterfeit

F. Scott Fitzgerald who comes stumbling out to Movie-
land."

Driving her home to Beverly Hills, he risked two or
three glances at her face and was pleased to find it calm
and reflective.

"I guess I've had sort of an idle, aimless life, when you
think about it," she said after a while. "Work my way
through college and never use it, never do anything I
could be proud of or even enjoy; never even adopt a
child when I had the chance."

And a few more miles of illuminated city went by before she moved close to him and touched his arm with
both hands. "Jack?" she said shyly. "That wasn't just
kidding around, was it? About how we can write a whole
lot of letters to each other and talk on the phone sometimes?"

"Aw, Sally. Why would I want to kid around about
that?"

He took her up to where the shallow steps of the pool
terrace began and they got out of the car for their leave-
taking: they sat together on a lower step and kissed as
self-consciously as children.

"Well, okay," she said. "Goodbye. Know something
funny? We've really been saying goodbye all along, since
the very first time I went out with you. Because I mean
we've always known there wasn't much time, so it's been
a saying–goodbye kind of deal from the start, right?"

"I guess so. Anyway, listen: Take care, baby."

They got up quickly, in embarrassment, and he
watched her make her way up onto the terrace—a tall,
supple, oddly gray-haired girl in the best-looking dress
he had ever seen.

He had just started back for the car when he heard her
calling "Jack! Jack!"

And she came clattering down the steps again and into his arms. "Oh, wait," she said breathlessly. "Listen. I forgot to tell you something. You know the heavy sweater I've been knitting all summer for Kicker? Well, that was a lie—I'm pretty sure it's the only lie I ever told you. It was never for Kicker; it's for you. I took the measurements from the only ratty old sweater I could find in your place, and the whole plan was to get it finished before you left, only now it's too late. But I'll finish it, Jack, I swear. I'll work on it every day and I'll mail it to you, okay?"

He held her with what seemed all his strength, feeling her tremble, and said against her hair that he'd be very, very glad to have it.

"Oh, Jesus, I hope it'll fit," she said. "Wear it—wear it in health, okay?"

And she was hurrying back up toward the door, where she turned to wave, using her free hand to wipe quickly at one and then the other of her eyes.

He stood watching until after she'd gone inside, and until the tall windows of one room after another cast their sudden light into the darkness. Then more lights came on and more, room upon room, as Sally ventured deeper into the house she had always loved and probably always would—having it now, for the first time and at least for a little while, all to herself.

# THE HISTORY OF VINTAGE

The famous American publisher Alfred A. Knopf (1892–1984) founded Vintage Books in the United States in 1954 as a paperback home for the authors published by his company. Vintage was launched in the United Kingdom in 1990 and works independently from the American imprint although both are part of the international publishing group, Random House.

Vintage in the United Kingdom was initially created to publish paperback editions of books acquired by the prestigious hardback imprints in the Random House Group such as Jonathan Cape, Chatto & Windus, Hutchinson and later William Heinemann, Secker & Warburg and The Harvill Press. There are many Booker and Nobel Prize-winning authors on the Vintage list and the imprint publishes a huge variety of fiction and non-fiction. Over the years Vintage has expanded and the list now includes both great authors of the past – who are published under the Vintage Classics imprint – as well as many of the most influential authors of the present.

For a full list of the books Vintage publishes, please visit our website
www.vintage-books.co.uk

For book details and other information about the classic authors we publish, please visit the Vintage Classics website
www.vintage-classics.info

www.vintage-classics.info